Bright Ones

The War Scroll Series
Book 1

J.B. TUCKER

ISBN: 979-8-218-34931-8

First Edition

Cover art by MeLisa Stone
Copyediting by Lauri Schoenfeld

https://www.facebook.com/J.B.TuckerAuthor

To my Plot Twister Sisters who championed
me along this long and difficult path.

And to my family.
I live and breathe for you.

Bright Ones

In the beginning, there was darkness, an endless void blanketing space and time

Darklings floated through and over the darkness as an ocean, not knowing warmth from cold, light from dark.

A great light appeared through the void, a persistent flare shining into the deepest recesses of space.

Galaxies beyond comprehension glistened against the black backdrop.

Awakened, the Darklings turned toward a new existence. For eternity, they lived in the light and became the light—some more than others.

Then, on favorable lands, light begat life. Here was boundary; here was from. An end of old, a beginning of new—a place to be.

One by one, they gained mortality, for better…and for worse.

Bright Ones

Chapter 1

The high school gym was equivalent to a predator's hell pit for nerds like me. I pressed my sweaty palms together as I stared at the shiny wood floor. The black and gold cougar snarled back up at me with its razor-toothed mouth open wide, ready to devour me should I step *just right.*

Our school mascot, ladies and gentlemen. Go cougars.

With every tick of the caged clock on the wall, the crowded gym continued to fill with strangers speaking over each other in loud, sharp tones. Their combined energy filled the cavernous space, pressing in on me. My chest tightened from the pressure like an over-filled balloon, ready to explode. I took a deep breath just as a greasy-haired boy walked by my table, a stink cloud following his wake. Speaking of *pits.*

I coughed.

I still couldn't believe my mom had finally given me permission to enter that year's science fair. It was a miracle, really. First, there would be people from out of town in attendance. Second, said people would be forced to notice me. Something Mom avoided at all costs. Too risky.

My mother gave the phrase "helicopter mom" new meaning. She checked all the boxes for an over-protective parent with enthusiasm.

Texting me every hour.

Check.

Curfew at nine p.m. on the weekends.

Check.

Preventing me from following my dreams of becoming a biophotonic scientist.

Check.

She guarded me and my *abnormalities* like they were state secrets.

But, somehow, I'd convinced her to sign the permission slip, and there I was, getting ready to put my heart and soul on a cloth-covered table for the judges to judge.

Hell pit or not, it was worth all the months of begging and preparation. This was my best chance to earn a scholarship and get out of town. College wasn't cheap. There was tuition, housing, and books—all the reasons Mom needed to keep me home. My future freedom was riding on this science fair—

literally. The weight of it sat heavily on me like a pressing stone.

The crowd's combined voices echoed cavernously off the painted concrete walls as I waited. Tables and chairs had been set up in rows across the school gym floor, and a giant banner with the words "Tri-State Science Fair" hung in the center of the large, open space. My school, Rock Canyon High, was hosting the fair that year, which was the only reason Mom had finally agreed to let me enter. If it had been held in Denver (just a few towns over) or, heaven forbid, *another state,* my chances of convincing her to let me enter would have been negative zero-point-zero percent.

I took a deep breath and rearranged my presentation for the one-hundredth time before finally giving up. Biting my lip, I stood back and looked over the project that had occupied my every thought since my mom broke down and said *yes.* In the center of my table were two large professionally printed posters on easels with eye-catching graphics and pictures explaining my hypothesis and research. My groundbreaking— at least, I hoped it was—handheld device lay on the black tablecloth, front and center. It was like my body lay bare on that table for all to see—and to judge. Feeling suddenly naked, I pulled my long hair over my shoulders and folded my arms over my chest.

I watched the other students casually stroll across the gym, socializing with their friends or staring at their smartphones, appearing bored. I willed myself to care less, like them. But when had I ever truly been anything like *them?*

"Hey Kirie!" a familiar voice called from across the gym. Startled, I glanced up to see my best friend, Rylie, skipping toward me. My shoulder muscles relaxed a fraction.

"I thought I'd swing by and check out your project before heading to work," she said, draping her arm over my shoulder. Rylie waved a hand over my table like a perky magician with a wand. "Your presentation looks amazing, by the way!"

"You barely looked at it," I said with mock offense. Rylie never looked too closely at anything.

"Long enough to see that it makes all the other projects seem like preschool art projects."

"Thanks, Ry," I said, tucking my chin behind my curtain of long hair.

"Anything for my bestie! Well, I've gotta head out, but I'll stop by after work. Good luck!" She air-kissed my cheeks before skipping into the crowd, her glitter-studded purse swinging wildly behind her. I smiled a little and returned to staring at the ground, this time making sure to avoid eye contact with the painted predator at the center of the floor.

Feeling awkward standing there alone, I left the safety of my table to check out the other projects. I held my arms close to my sides as I maneuvered through the rows of tables and slow-moving spectators. One girl made a robot from Legos, and some guy created a solar-powered light bulb. Beyond that, though, most of their projects were fairly juvenile. I thought I even saw a guy walk in late with a clay volcano. Winning the first-place prize should be easy, I reassured myself.

I turned into the next row of booths and came face-to-face with a golden-haired giant. The boy was older than me, perhaps nineteen or twenty years old, and easily a foot taller than anyone else in the room. I stared up at him with wide eyes. He stood out amongst the crowd with his presence filling the room as much as his frame.

"Excuse me," he said in a deep voice. My face lit on fire when I realized I was in his way.

"Sorry," I squeaked, springing to the side to let him pass. Like a wide-mouthed bass, I gaped at the giant as he squeezed past me. His chest brushed against my shoulder, and a surge of pure energy rushed through me, awakening my internal spark. I sucked in a breath.

"Alright, everyone," Mrs. Calhoon, the Biology teacher, yelled out across the gym. I turned to see her standing in front of a line of cloth-covered tables, holding a microphone. "The fair starts in two minutes. All presenters must be at their booths in one."

It was as if a tornado swept through the gym, scattering people to the four corners of the room. I gazed back at the boy, who was already gone, presumably swallowed by the crowd. I closed my mouth and shook my head, internally scolding myself for being so awkward. Again.

As students rushed back to their tables, their excited energy crackled under the surface of my skin. A spark in my chest flickered in response, but I tamped it down, and hurried back to my booth, sliding into the cold metal chair behind my display. Beneath the tablecloth, my leg bounced up and down like a nervous jackrabbit as I waited for people to stop and ask questions about my project.

For the next few hours, I sat impatiently behind my project as visitors from all over the area wandered through the maze of booths. I received a few awkward compliments on my presentation and some interest in my device, but most walked by my table without a second glance. Part of me felt the familiar pang of rejection, but a bigger part was relieved I didn't have to make small talk with strangers.

During the lunch break, we weren't expected to answer questions, so I pulled my hair forward, creating a cocoon around myself, and nibbled on the PB&J my mom had packed for me. I pulled my phone out, expecting to see several missed calls and texts from her, but there wasn't a single one. A sense of unease swirled in my gut. I watched the doors, expecting Mom and Barry, my stepdad, to walk through. They promised to come by before I had to present to the judges who were due to make their rounds. I rechecked my phone—still nothing.

I didn't know why I was worried that she wouldn't come. Mom had never let me down before. Maybe it was because she seemed *off* that morning. I'd shown her my finished project the night before, and instead of making her happy or—I don't know—*proud* or something, it only seemed to upset her. She couldn't even look me in the eye during breakfast. So much for parental support. Nothing I ever did made her happy. It was like she thought the world would end or something if I appeared anything other than average. Deep down, I always assumed she hid me away because my abilities embarrassed her.

I peeked out from behind my curtain of hair and checked the clock on the black and gold brick wall again. What was taking them so long? I logged into the medical chat board app I kept in a hidden file on my phone and typed Parisxxxi8 a private message.

Brightgirl101: Hey. You there?

Parisxxxi8: Always. Have you presented yet?

Brightgirl101: Not yet. Soon, though.

Parisxxxi8: Nervous?

Brightgirl101: Very. What if something goes wrong?

Parisxxxi8: We've been preparing for months. Nothing will go wrong. You've got this.

Brightgirl101: What would I do without you?

Parisxxxi8: I shudder to think.

Brightgirl101: I'll let you know how it goes. Thanks for everything these past few months!

Parisxxxi8: At your service. *tips hat*

I smiled and slipped my phone into my bag. Paris, as I like to call him, had been helping me with my project since the beginning of summer. I "met" him on a medical chat board, and we instantly hit it off. We were both interested in the emerging field of biophotonics, and we'd both been research contributors in the scientific community. Mom didn't know, of course. I wasn't allowed to chat online, even for academic reasons. Too many perverts or something.

I knew online strangers were dangerous. Everyone knew that. But Paris was different. He'd been a lifeline for me. Whenever something went wrong with my device, Paris was there with brilliant advice and a listening ear. I didn't know much about him, other than the fact that he was British (I assumed) and a nice guy, but I felt this strange connection to him, like we'd known each other our whole lives. Stupid, I know.

After lunch, Rylie strolled through the gym doors with Kaylee and Cassidy in tow. The four of us were a group, but they were really more Rylie's friends than mine. I always felt like I was Ry's tagalong—her "plus one."

"Wow, Kirie! This looks great!" Kaylee said, staring at my table.

"Thanks," I said, wrapping a strand of hair around my index finger repeatedly.

Cassidy leaned down and examined my device with a puzzled look. She poked at the handpiece as if it were some strange creature. "What *is* it?"

"It's, umm, a Biophotonic X-ray machine," I explained. "It uses a powerful light instead of radiation to diagnose things like cancer."

"I seriously have the smartest friend in the world!" Rylie cried, clapping her hands like an exuberant seal. "You're totally going to win first prize."

"I hope so," I said, gazing down at my table with a modest smile. I was proud of my invention. I knew it was good.

The girls prattled on about the other entries for a while, but it was easy to see that Cassidy and Kaylee wanted to leave.

"Come on, girls, let's get some food," Cassidy finally said. There was an edge to her voice as she tugged impatiently on Kaylee's arm. "If I don't eat before volleyball practice, I may pass out."

"We need to feed Cassidy," Kaylee said with a serious expression. I nodded my head in understanding. Everyone knew what happened when Cassidy didn't eat. Hunger was to be avoided at all costs.

"Good luck, and text us when the judges decide, okay?" Rylie blew me a kiss.

I felt a twinge of loneliness as I watched them leave in a little cluster. It was as though I was on the other side of a large pane of glass looking in. Connecting with people wasn't my strong suit, mostly because no one had ever really gotten to know me beyond surface level. No one even tried.

I didn't know *why* I was excluded from my peer's inner circles. It wasn't like I was some kind of troll. I looked a lot like my mom, actually. Waist-length ebony hair, a heart-shaped face, and a petite frame. People often mistook us for sisters, but I thought she was beautiful, so I never minded. But that was where the similarities ended. Mom's eyes were hazel and mine were bright, clear blue, a trait (I'm told) I inherited from my birth father. He died before I was born and my mom had no pictures of him, so I just had to take her word for it. But our differences went deeper than eye color. Mom was brave and outgoing. I hated attention. Mom was normal and I…wasn't.

When I was young, I tried to put myself out there, but every time I did, the other kids shied away from me. They weren't really rude to my face, but I wasn't exactly invited to their birthday parties either. *It wasn't their fault*, I thought with a heavy sigh. They didn't know why I was so off-putting, either. It was like they could smell the "otherness" on me.

About halfway through the day, the judges arrived and began working their way through the booths. My biology teacher, Mrs. Calhoon, led the way, and fellow judges followed behind her like little ducklings wading through a shallow pond. I recognized a few of the other judges. Some were former teachers of mine, and a couple were from Barry's poker group. I straightened my maroon shirt and smoothed imaginary wrinkles from my gray slacks with shaky fingers as I waited for my turn.

I glanced around the gym again for my mom and stepdad but couldn't see them anywhere. Today, of all days, she decided to ignore me. For once, her crazy, obsessive attention might have come in handy. I pulled my phone out of my back pocket and dialed her number, straight to voicemail. My foot began to tap a frantic beat.

The judges were only a few tables away, so I checked my project one last time and noticed that the battery on the handpiece was blinking red. *Strange.* I'd charged the battery the night before. Too late to charge it now. Well, not the normal way, anyhow.

Making sure no one was watching, I picked the handpiece up and centered my thoughts on the empty battery cells within. The hairs on my arm stood on end as my palm began to grow warm, then hot. I imagined the cells filling with energy, and a few seconds later, the battery light blinked green. Fully charged and ready to go. I sighed in relief and reassured myself that nothing bad would happen. The first prize and that freedom-granting scholarship were as good as mine.

I'd been able to do this little trick–adding energy to things since I was young. I actually couldn't remember not being able to do it. The first time I showed it to my mom, I was 4 years old. I remember it clearly because I have a photographic memory, another abnormal trait to add to the long list. She totally flipped out, like I'd done something wrong or shameful, and told me never to do that again. Convinced everyone else would feel the same, I'd kept it to myself. Not even Rylie knew how big of a freak I was, and we'd been friends for years. I'd done my best to blend in with the kids my age. It was the only thing I ever failed at. On the bright side, though, I never had to worry about plugging in my phone.

Before long, the judges were one booth away. I listened politely to the boy's presentation, but I couldn't help myself from scanning the room every couple of seconds for my mom. In no time at all, they were moving on to me. A cold sweat beaded at the back of my neck as Mrs. Calhoon and the others walked toward me. They assembled in front of my presentation in a semi-circle, and I searched the gym one last time for my parents. I nearly fainted with relief when I caught sight of them moving through the crowd toward me.

"*Finally*," I whispered.

Walking up just behind the judges, they looked like the perfect couple, Barry in his slightly worn brown suit and Mom in a soft, pink cardigan. Instead of giving me the encouraging smile I expected, though, Mom wore a deep frown in its place. Her dark mood from that morning had turned black. A flash of anger swept over me. This was *my* day. The least she could do was pretend to be supportive.

"Kirie, why don't you tell us what you have here?" Mrs. Calhoon said, catching my attention.

I flushed red and turned toward the judges, pushing my hair back with shaky fingers. This was it.

"Umm, of course," I said. With feigned self-assurance, I picked up the used ultrasound wand that I had spent countless hours converting into something new and held it out for the judges to see. "For years, the medical field has used radiation to diagnose everything from a simple broken bone to stage-four cancer. Unfortunately, the radiation from these machines can be harmful to patients and may even *cause* cancer over time. A new, exciting field of science called biophotonics that focuses on using light to treat patients has opened up a new range of possibilities."

I carefully placed my device down and picked up a flashlight from the table. I held it to one side of my hand and showed the judges the other. My hand glowed orange.

"If you put a light up to your skin, it shines through, illuminating what is inside." I traded my flashlight for my device again. "My biophotonic x-ray machine does something very similar. When using a high-powered light, this machine digitally transfers images that can help to diagnose patients. This new technology is safe to use and, in time, may operate at a fraction of the cost of traditional X-ray machines. I project that biophotonics will one day replace harmful radiation-powered X-ray machines in hospitals and doctor's offices across the nation and one day throughout the world. Now, I'd like to demonstrate how it works."

In my hand, I rolled the handheld device over and turned the power switch to ON. Nothing happened. I flipped the power button on and off several more times with no success. Reaching my senses into the handpiece, I desperately searched for any trace of energy and found nothing but dead silence. Poisonous dread seeped through my veins.

"Is something wrong?" Mrs. Calhoon asked with raised brows.

"Um. I'm not sure. It doesn't seem to want to turn on." My voice cracked. I moved away from the crowd and pushed as much energy as I dared into the handpiece without creating noticeable light, but the battery cells were already full. Something else was wrong. Something my abilities couldn't easily fix. I examined the on/off switch and found scratch marks around it. I slid it back and forth and heard a jingling sound from within. The piece must've been broken from the inside.

Feeling unbalanced, I turned back around and set the broken device down. I pointed to my visuals with shaky hands. "Ummm, if you look at my posters, you can see that I used a special frequency to translate the images."

The rest of my presentation went by in a blur as I rambled on about my research and findings. The judges clapped politely at the end and moved on to the following table. And, just like that, my dreams fell around me like a house of cards. I didn't understand; I'd been so careful with the handpiece. I tried to think of a time I might have dropped it on the ground. Perhaps I had placed the box containing all my materials too firmly on the ground that morning. But no, I'd been careful. Extremely.

With hunched shoulders, I trudged over to my parents, who stood waiting for me in silence.

"I'm so sorry, honey!" my mom said, bringing me into a hug. I buried my face in her shoulder, and she rocked me back and forth slowly like I was her little girl again.

"I don't know what happened!" I said, pulling away. "It was working fine last night."

"These things just happen sometimes, sweetheart," Mom said, rubbing my back in little circles. "Maybe it's for the best. Now you can stay home and go to community college next year. Think of all the money you'll save by living at home."

"Mom!" It was an old argument; one I'd fought to put in the past. "You cannot be serious . . ."

Barry stepped in, cutting me off. "Sorry, kiddo. Sometimes life just doesn't go your way. There's always next time." He tapped my shoulder awkwardly. Leave it to my stepdad to say something shallow and cliché at a time like this.

"Thanks, Barry," I said, not even trying to hide the sarcasm in my voice.

He glanced down at his watch, oblivious as always. "Look, I wish we could stay until they announce the winners, but I've got to get back and finish the yard. The grass isn't going to cut itself!" Mom leveled him with a glare, and he finally had the decency to appear ashamed.

I sighed and folded my arms across my chest. "You two go. It's not like I'll win now anyway."

Mom gave me one last hug. "I'm so, so, sorry honey," she whispered. When she pulled back, I was surprised by the fresh tears in her eyes.

"It's OK, Mom. It's not your fault." The look on her face said she disagreed.

Barry grabbed her hand and led her away. I wrapped my hair around me like a security blanket again and sat silently at my table as the judges worked their way through the rest of the booths. Disappointment sat heavily on my stooped shoulders, pushing me to the ground as if the weight of my failure could bury me below the wooden floorboards.

A high-pitched whine screeched out across the gym,

followed by a thump, thump, thump. Mrs. Calhoon tapped on the head of a microphone. "Ladies and gentlemen, we'll be announcing today's winners in ten minutes. All presenters are invited to gather at the front of the gym for the award ceremony."

I ignored the passing students as I slowly folded up my posters and packed my materials into my box. I could hardly believe it; all my hard work had been reduced to a broken ON/OFF switch. I couldn't have imagined a worse outcome if I tried.

As I turned to walk away, my shoulder collided hard with someone passing by. The force of the impact knocked the box from my hands, spilling the contents everywhere. A sickening *crack* sent knives into my heart as my X-ray machine broke into tiny pieces on the hard, wooden floor.

Bile rose in the back of my throat, burning on the way up. I looked to see who I'd run into and came face to face with a pissed-off girl with shockingly bright red hair and unsettlingly dark eyes. Though the gym was well-lit, the darkness seemed to cling to her proud frame. She appeared to be about my age, but I was sure I'd never seen her at school. She must have been from one of the other participating high schools.

"Watch it, whore," she snarled at me, hate dripping off each word like venom.

I stepped back from the force of her hateful words, eyes

blinking in confusion. "I'm s-sorry," I stammered.

The girl moved forward as if she were going to hit me. I flinched and tried to step back again, but her unsettling stare somehow held me in place. The edges of her black, shark-like eyes tightened slightly, and a sudden feeling of great sadness slammed into my chest as though I'd been hit by a freight train. I sucked in a breath, stunned by its intensity. I let out a strangled gasp as despair like I'd never experienced attacked my body in punishing waves. Darkness edged around the corners of my vision and my legs began to shake. I tried again to move away from the girl, but my body wouldn't obey.

The girl leaned in and whispered in my ear, "I see you, little Bright Girl." The air around her was arctic cold, causing a chill to run up my arms. With a high-pitched laugh, she straightened and turned to walk toward the exit. I watched, frozen, as the doors swung shut behind her with a bang. The toxins inside me began to drain away like poison from an open wound with her absence. Still, I was left with a slight internal ache.

"Whoa . . ." I whispered, rubbing the center of my chest with the heel of my hand. What *was* that? I'd never felt anything so dark and hateful before. My teeth audibly chattered as I peered around the room, surprised that no one seemed to have noticed the altercation. Had they not seen the girl who wore darkness like a cloak? Could they not feel the chill she'd left behind?

I turned my attention back to the box lying on its side at my feet. My eyes clouded over with unshed tears as I looked down at the decimated project, clearly beyond repair. Determined not to cry in a gym full of strangers, I took several deep breaths. *In. Out. In. Out.* I knelt to gather what was left of my freedom and hoisted the box into my arms. My legs still shook as I hurried toward the exit.

Applause rang out across the gym behind me as I shouldered my way through the heavy wooden doors. Someone was just awarded the scholarship to State—and it wasn't me. Without a backward glance, I stumbled out of the building and through the parking lot to my car. With one hand, I unlocked my door and tossed my box onto the passenger seat. I sat numbly behind the wheel for several long minutes, unable to fully process what had just happened.

Out of the silence, a notification from my cellphone rang, making me jump. It was a text from Ry.

RYLIE: How did it go? TELL ME! TELL ME!

Her excitement sent fresh pain through my already tight chest. My fingers shook as I typed a reply.

ME: Not good. My project wouldn't turn on AND I dropped it on the floor. It's toast.

I kept the strange interaction with the scary girl to myself. Really? What was there to say? A mean girl threatened me, and made me feel sad? It was so much *more* than that. How could I describe to Rylie the intense darkness that had filled me in her presence when I didn't fully understand it myself?

RYLIE: *Seriously? That SUCKS! I'm so sorry.*

Tears stung my eyes again, blurring my phone. She had no idea. My thumbs moved instinctively over the screen.

ME: Yeah. Bad day.

RYLIE: Cheer up. Justin's parents r out of town, and he's having a party! Come. U will feel better!

ME: Justin who?

RYLIE: OMG! Justin from the football team. You know…the hot one!!!!!!

If I'd had any happiness left in me, I would have laughed out loud. There was *no way* mom would let me go to Football-Team-Justin's impromptu party. Too many teens, not enough parents. I would have to sneak out or lie to my mom about where I was going, which I never did. Ever. Plus, wasn't exactly part of the popular group.

ME: Sorry, my mom would freak.

RYLIE: Seriously??? When are you going to cut the umbilical cord Kir???

ME: Hey! I'm not that bad!

RYLIE: . . .

I sighed and slumped in my seat. No, I really *was* that bad. In all my seventeen years, I'd never done anything rebellious or stupid. The worst thing I'd ever done was steal a box of my mom's favorite chocolates she kept hidden in her closet when I was nine. I still felt bad about it, too. With Mom hovering over my shoulder all the time, I'd never had the time or space to even *think* of stepping out of line.

I loved my mom, but I was suffocating under her excessive love and care.

RYLIE: Kirieeeeee . . . Come onnnn!

My thumbs hovered over the screen. I looked at my ruined science project and a strange feeling came over me. Something I'd never felt before. Rebellion. What did I have to lose? My fingers shook as I typed.

ME: I'm in!

RYLIE: YAY! I win!!! Kay and Cass are coming. Pick us up @ my house @ 8!

Typical Rylie. Invite me to a party and then expect me to drive.

ME: Fine. See you tonight.

Screw those judges and their scholarship. And screw Mom's rules.

Donovan 1

Downtown Berlin, Germany

1 day earlier

The assassin stood next to the open window and breathed in the crisp, fall air. Sounds of a bustling city surrounded him, mingled with dead leaves rustling in the gentle breeze. As he watched the pedestrians pass by, the assassin wiped his hands with a white handkerchief, staining the fabric red.

Sighing happily, he turned away from the window and stepped carelessly over the crimson pool spreading at his feet. Shame, he thought. The original wide-plank floors would be ruined.

"*Riiiing.*"

The killer put his phone to his ear, and a lazy grin formed on his scarred face.

His next assignment.

He ended the call without response and gathered his black duffle bag from the floor.

The assassin loved his job. With perks like international travel, a black credit card, and an unlimited amount of Children of Light to kill, how could he not?

Standing at the threshold of the pricey downtown apartment, the killer looked back at his handy work one last time, and his chest swelled with pride.

"Damn, I'm good," he said in a low, British accent.

With a spring in his step, he walked out to the sidewalk where a nondescript black sedan parked along the busy downtown street. A young redhead in dark sunglasses waited behind the wheel, the shadows in the cab clinging to her like a lover. The assassin tossed his bag of tricks in the backseat and slid in beside the girl. The killer instantly felt the chill coming off her pale skin.

"Where to, boss?" she asked in a high-pitched voice that belied her lethal nature.

"The airport."

"Another assignment?" the girl asked with a sharp smile. She loved the hunt as much as he did. It was why he chose her as one of his apprentices. "Where we headed this time?"

"America," he said, sliding on sunglasses identical to the girl's. "I hear the Rockies are beautiful this time of year."

Chapter 2

Justin lived in an exclusive golf course community in an enormous house along the green. I'd heard his parents were hotshot surgeons at a downtown hospital who wanted to live outside the city so they could have "more land." And by "land," they meant an exclusive golf course in their backyard.

I swung by Rylie's house just after eight to pick up the girls. We both lived in an older neighborhood where the houses didn't need their own zip codes. When I pulled into her driveway, Kaylee, Rylie, and Cassidy came bouncing out with smiles on their made-up faces. They climbed in, filling my 2005 Mazda with a cloud of perfume and giggles. As I drove toward the party, I fought the bile rising to my throat. I couldn't believe I was actually doing this.

"So, how did you break out of the compound tonight?" Rylie asked from the passenger seat.

"I told my mom we were going to dinner and a movie," I

confessed.

"Wait!" Cassidy gasped from the backseat. "You mean you *lied to your mom*?"

Rylie reached over the center console and hugged my neck tightly, making me swerve wildly on the empty neighborhood road. "Kirie Sorenson, I am so proud of you! Our baby is finally growing up!"

I pushed her off and straightened the wheel. "It's your fault. You're practically forcing me to come."

"Well, someone had to step in. You're almost an adult, Kirie, and you're still attached to your mommy's skirt," Kaylee said from behind me.

That stung.

"Sooooo," I said, changing the subject, "who's going to be there tonight?"

"Everyone," the girls said in unison.

Oh great. I hated big crowds. A lot. "They aren't all going to be drunk, are they?"

"No, just most of them," Cassidy said brightly.

"Don't worry, as long as we stay together as a group, you'll be fine." Rylie patted my arm in reassurance. "But there are always at least a couple of grabby creepers that show up, so no sitting in dark corners by yourself," she warned.

"This is supposed to be fun?" I asked.

"Just seeing you surrounded by a room full of drunken

idiots will be all the fun I need," Cassidy said with an evil laugh.

"Thanks." I rolled my eyes.

"Anytime," she threw back at me.

When we turned onto Justin's street, my anxiety levels rose to new heights. The entire block was lined with cars. As it turned out, everyone really *did* show up.

As soon as I found a place to park—nearly half a mile away—the girls climbed out, and I reluctantly followed suit.

On the street, Rylie looked me over head to foot and laughed. "Kirie, seriously? We aren't going to church." I'd dressed in a chiffon shirt and a pencil skirt with three-inch black heels. My hair was down, of course.

My face heated. "Hey! I've never been to a party before. I didn't know I was supposed to wear summer clothes in October." I pointed to Kaylee's short shorts and wedge sandals. Kaylee simply shrugged and glanced up the hill toward Justin's house.

"It's OK," Rylie sighed. "We can fix it."

Rylie circled me like a shark on the hunt and pulled my shirt tightly from behind, tying it in a knot. She moved my skirt down low on my hips, leaving a large section of my abdomen showing. Goosebumps broke out over my exposed skin in the cool night air. She pulled my heavy hair across my right shoulder and braided it, tying it off with a hairband from her wrist. Without the protection of my hair, I felt utterly naked.

"Well, it'll have to do," Rylie said, staring at her handiwork. "Come on, let's go. We're probably the last ones to show up."

I followed at the back of the group as we made the long uphill trek to Justin's house. We crossed the wet grass in the front yard to the grand door, slightly opened. Music pumped through the opening in ebbs and flows, and my heart rate sped up to meet its frenzied pace. Without knocking, Rylie entered the house as if she owned the place. Her sheer confidence never ceased to amaze me, and, not for the first time, I wished I was more like her.

The opulent foyer inside was filled with about a dozen teens holding red cups and talking loudly over the blaring music. Rylie boldly pushed through the crowd into a large, open room with high ceilings and oversized couches. It, too, was overrun by teens, all holding some kind of drink in their hands. Some of them I recognized from school, but most were complete strangers to me.

The spark inside me flared at their combined energy, and I had an overwhelming urge to soak it in, let it fill me. Instead, I tamped the spark down, my body shaking slightly from the effort.

"Come on, let's go get something to drink," Rylie said, elbowing me in the side. She laughed at my panicked expression. "Don't worry, they'll have soda."

I followed closely as the girls moved into the crowded

kitchen. The beautiful marble countertops were littered with glass bottles and plastic cups. A large, metal keg dominated the center island. Rylie steered us around the crowd to a cooler sitting on the floor.

Inside, beer and soda cans were floating in a bed of half-melted ice. Following the girls' examples, I reached in and grabbed a Coke. The condensation was cold against my sweaty hands.

With sodas in hand, Rylie, Kaylee, and Cassidy headed toward the living room and began mingling, saying hi to those they recognized. I hung back awkwardly and waited. Not knowing what to do with my arms and legs, I stood still, sure that I looked every bit as much a dork as I felt.

Behind me, a tipsy girl bumped into my right shoulder, causing me to spill my Coke all down the front of my skirt. I quickly brushed the droplets off as the drunk girl stumbled away without an apology. When I looked up, I saw Rylie motioning for me to follow them downstairs. I put my Coke down on the nearest flat surface and ran after them, glad to leave the crowded room behind me.

We walked single file down a set of wide, curved stairs that led to a large open room with two pool tables, several antique arcade games, and a big-screen TV mounted along the far wall.

Cassidy, the only one in our small group who played video games, immediately made a B-line to the arcade. Rylie and

Kaylee wasted no time making their way over to the pool tables, where the majority of the football team stood around, bragging about their complete awesomeness. Several of them held pool cues in one hand and a drink in the other, but none of them seemed to have any interest in actually playing pool.

With her trademark sass, Rylie sauntered up to Justin, grabbed the pool cue from his hand, and boldly challenged the group of boys to a game. Of course, the naturally competitive males rose to the challenge. I tucked myself into the corner of an oversized loveseat and quietly watched her hustle the football team out of their money. I almost felt bad for them.

Just as they were setting the eight ball, a boy I recognized from school sat clumsily in the open space beside me. I leaned away, surprised by his sudden nearness.

"Hey, don't I know you?" he slurred. His rancid breath washed over me, causing my eyes to water. His mouth was a pit of marijuana smoke and hamburger.

"I don't know. Do you?" I asked, scooting over as far as the space allowed.

Of course, I knew exactly who he was. We had been in many of the same classes for years. He was that alternative kid who always showed up late to class and slept at his desk in the back. His locker was just a few down from mine where he regularly made out with his freshman girlfriend between classes. He wasn't unattractive per se, but he could've been a lot cuter if he put some effort into showering and haircuts.

"Yeah, you're that smart girl who's always raising her hand in class." He scooted closer to me, trapping me against the side of the couch. I leaned my torso over the armrest, straining the muscles in my back.

"Oh, um . . ."

"Hey! How come I didn't notice how *hhhhot* you are . . ."

I cringed at the rancid air that blew over me. His glassy eyes dipped to my exposed torso for a prolonged moment before suggestively following the lines of my body. I wondered if his cute little girlfriend knew her boyfriend was a scumbag.

He proceeded to lean his body over mine until the entire front of him was draped over my side. I tried to push him off, but he was surprisingly heavy for such a short guy. I turned my head away as he moved in closer, attempting to kiss my face with his wide-open mouth.

Suddenly, a hand reached in, gripped him by the back of his shirt and pulled him off of me just in time. I breathed in a gulp of fresh air.

"Dude! Gross!" Justin slurred angrily, holding the odorific guy up by his neck. Like a sack of flour, Justin tossed him to the floor where he lay, confused. "What the hell is your problem, Anderson? She clearly doesn't want what you're selling." Alcohol-infused spit flew out of Justin's mouth with every word. I stared up at him, stunned by his sudden anger in my defense. I didn't know we were that close of friends.

Justin gestured to his fellow football players, who stalked forward with puffed-up chests like a band of gorillas, and the room went silent as though someone had pulled out an electrical cord. The gang converged on the terrified boy, and I sank lower into the loveseat, trying to disappear as every eye stared in our direction.

"I think it's time you leave, man." Justin snapped his fingers and the guys proceeded to drag the half-baked boy up the stairs by the armpits, presumably to be tossed out the front door. Within moments, Justin and his friends stomped back downstairs with self-satisfied expressions.

My avengers made a victory tour around the room, and everyone cheered loudly for the local heroes. None of them looked my way or asked if I was OK. Every girls' face in the room was one of pure adoration. I sank back into the chair. Grateful as I was, their little show had nothing to do with me. Within minutes, the party resumed in full force as if nothing happened.

Rylie, having finally clued in on what was going on, came rushing over to see if I was all right. It took several minutes of reassurance to convince her to go back to her game, and soon, I was invisible once more.

Adrenaline slowly seeped out of my body like poison from a wound, and the reality of the situation began to sink in. I was nearly sexually assaulted in a room full of people! I gazed down at my rumpled clothes and brushed furiously at them, trying to wipe the memory of the boy's sweaty hands off me. With shaky fingers, I reached behind me and untied my shirt, tucking it safely back into my skirt. I undid my hair, and ran my fingers through the waves, pulling it back in front of my face. The whole night was beginning to feel like a big mistake.

It was easy to sneak away without notice. I quietly tiptoed upstairs into the kitchen to a pair of French doors that led to the backyard. Stepping out onto a large patio, I made my way through the oversized outdoor furniture that was being occupied by couples displaying an embarrassing amount of PDA. Looking straight ahead, I carefully maneuvered around them toward the golf course lawn.

My heels sunk into the grass as I stepped out onto the perfectly manicured green at the edge of Justin's property. With my face to the sky, I stood underneath the bright, full moon and let its rays soak into my skin. I shook my heavy hair out, and it fell behind me like a cascade of moonlit water. Peace washed over me as the pulsing music and loud voices faded into the background, the tension in my shoulders loosened, and anxiety slowly seeped from my pores.

Crowds and creepers aside, I was still glad I'd decided to come. I couldn't stay hidden from the world forever. After all, college was sure to have parties, too, and I needed to learn how to live outside the cradle sooner or later. Next time, I would carry mace. Lesson learned.

Soon, dark clouds slowly rolled over the darkening moon, creating shadows all around me. I hugged my arms around my chest and shivered at the sudden cold. Off to my left, a slight movement caught my eye. I stepped forward and narrowed my eyes, searching for what had moved. For several long minutes, I stared into the shadows, waiting, but the darkness remained still . . . almost *too* still.

I looked around, making sure none of the partiers were near, and let my energy fill the palm of my hand. A small light grew in the center of it, lighting up the night. I stretched my arm out in front of me, palm forward, and searched the empty golf course beyond. When my light hit a tall pine tree, the darkness seemed to move, quickly fleeing my light like a sewer rat.

Unexplainable dread slowly crept up my spine. Keeping my light trained on the ground before me, I slowly turned my back to the darkening golf course and began walking toward the house. Chills raced up and down my back. I'd never felt so exposed. Just as I reached the edge of Justin's property, I held my glowing palm to my chest and threw one last glance behind me. My breath caught in my throat.

Standing beneath the same tall pine tree was the dark form of a man. The man-shaped shadow stood perfectly still, facing in my direction as though he was staring at me. Unable to move or look away, I peered back into the darkness. The light in my hand went out like a flame doused in cold water. My vision blurred, and, bit by bit, I began to lose feeling in my arms and legs. Just as the numbness reached my core, a voice called out into the night.

"Kirie? Kirie! Are you out there?"

At the sound of my name, I jerked back, sucking in freezing air through my clenched teeth. I huffed out white clouds of frozen breath as I forced my nearly numb body away from the green and clumsily ran back to the house.

The once-crowded patio was deserted as I weaved through the overturned furniture, throw pillows, and piles of trash littering the ground. I nearly cried out in relief when I saw Rylie standing at the back door like a beacon against the dark night.

"Where the heck were you?" She yelled. "You scared the crap out of me!"

"Rylie!" I panted. "Do you see that guy out there? On the golf course." I turned and pointed to the tree, but no one was there.

"What guy?" she said, looking out into the darkness.

"There was someone there . . ."

"You're freaking me out, Kirie! What are you doing out here all alone? We need to stick together, remember?"

"Sorry, I just needed to get away for a minute. I was

suffocating in there," I said, trying to rub feeling back into my arms.

"Well, tell someone next time. I thought that perv came back for you or something. Sheesh!" Rylie folded her arms tightly over her chest and gave me her best glare.

"Sorry, Ry. Really," I said apologetically.

"Whatever. Just come inside already. It's like freaking winter out here all of a sudden. Brrr!" Rylie grabbed my hand and pulled me inside.

Crumpled plastic cups and empty pizza boxes covered every flat surface of the dimly lit kitchen, and the energy inside had mellowed since I'd left. The music was turned down, and the boisterous yelling and crashing sounds had been replaced by soft laughter and whispers. A group of girls stood around the island gossiping about some unfortunate girl while the guys sat at the round table in the breakfast nook playing poker and smoking cigars someone must have stolen from Justin's dad's office. I took my phone out of my back pocket to check the time. 11:45 PM.

"Shoot, we have to go," I said to Rylie.

Rylie nodded once. "Right, let's round up the girls." Linking arms with me, she steered me toward the basement. "Last time I checked, Kaylee was making out with some guy, and Cassidy was playing pinball."

It took forever to pull Kaylee off the couch where she was

draped atop our local hero, Justin, and several more minutes to pull Cassidy from her game. When we reached my car, it was well past midnight—my curfew. I was totally screwed.

The car ride home was short and quiet. Rylie, Kaylee, and Cassidy stared at their phones as I drove back to Rylie's house. Thick clouds still covered the moon, and, for some reason, the streetlights had failed to turn on, leaving the streets pitch black. I held on tightly to the steering wheel, my knuckles turning white as I struggled to see the road, my headlights seeming inadequate against the overwhelming darkness.

After dropping the girls off, I drove back home in a funk. The night—that *whole day*, really—had been a complete disaster, and to top it off, I was going to get in trouble for being out past curfew. I considered just telling my mom where I'd gone, but the thought made me nauseous.

As I parked my car in the garage and walked toward the side entrance, I had a strange, irrational feeling that I was being watched. Afraid to turn my back toward the night, I sidestepped the rest of the way into the house, quickly shutting the garage door on my way in.

Hoping my parents had gone to bed, I tiptoed through the kitchen—no such luck. Mom and Barry were still cuddling on the living room couch, watching *Casablanca*.

"Hey, honey. You're home pretty late," Mom said, glancing over her shoulder.

"I know. I'm sorry. We went to ice cream after the movie, and I lost track of time." The false words tasted like ash in my mouth.

She twisted around in her seat. "OK. Just shoot me a text next time. I was beginning to think you got in a wreck or something," she said with a worried expression.

Nope, just getting felt up by a creeper at an alcohol-infused party, I thought.

"I'm just going to run upstairs and go to bed," I said, walking over to the couch to kiss her on the cheek. It felt like another lie. "Enjoy your movie and try not to fall asleep on the couch again."

"Love you, honey. See you in the morning."

"Love you, too, Mom. Goodnight, Barry."

"Goodnight, Kiddo." Barry waved to me without looking away from the screen.

In my bathroom, I washed my face and brushed my teeth. The pale girl staring back at me in the vanity mirror looked beaten down, defeated. Just before bed, I turned my laptop on, hoping that "Paris" would be online.

Brightgirl101: You up?

Parisxxxi8: Always. How did it go?

Brightgirl101: Not good. Something went wrong with the power switch.

Parisxxxi8: How? You tested it, didn't you?

Brightgirl101: A hundred times.

Parisxxxi8: Upload a picture. I'll help you find the problem.

Brightgirl101: No use. I dropped it on the floor. It's trash now.

Parisxxxi8: Bugger . . . I'm sorry.

Brightgirl101: Me too. I'm headed to bed. Night.

Parisxxxi8: Sorry for your loss, love.

Brightgirl101: Thanks . . . for everything.

Parisxxxi8: At your service. *tips hat*

I shut my laptop and sighed. I walked across the room to close my blinds. The entire day had left me depleted. Feeling the weight of the night outside my window, I decided to keep my bedside lamp on.

Chapter 3

RASH!

I bolted upright in bed. What was that? I strained to listen but was greeted with nothing but silence. With wide eyes, I searched my room, but my bedside lamp had gone out sometime during the night, rendering it pitch black. The chilled air and something else I couldn't quite name caused the hairs on my arms to stand on end. Something was . . . wrong. I sat perfectly still and listened harder.

The silence was *complete,* like the deafening quiet that only happens when the power's out and all the electrics are dead. Opening my inner senses, I reached for the residual electricity that normally infused the air and came up empty. With trembling fingers, I fumbled for my lamp. My left hand bumped into its base, and I quickly used both hands to find the switch. I turned the knob several times before giving up.

Lifting my palm, I tried to conjure light as I'd done

hundreds of times before when no one was watching. Nothing happened. My stomach sank. I'd never experienced a lack of energy so acutely in myself or in my surroundings.

THUMP!

The floor vibrated with the sudden sound. I jumped so violently, my legs tangled in the sheets, and I nearly fell off the edge of the bed. My heart pounded loudly in my ears as the panic inside me began to grow. Again, I fumbled for my bedside table, this time looking for my cellphone. With trembling fingers, I turned on the flashlight function and illuminated the space in front of me.

Nothing was out of place in my room, yet the space felt foreign and threatening. The darkness blanketing the room was thick like tar and fought against my phone's light. The shadows in corners moved in fluid motions as if the darkness itself was breathing—as if it were . . . alive. I blinked hard, trying to clear my vision, but the moving shadows remained.

My breathing came out in white puffs. I pulled my knees into my chest at the head of my bed and pointed my phone outward, sweeping the light back and forth across my room. Though there was nothing physical to see, the room was full of some form of dark energy I'd never encountered before. All light beyond my phone was absent.

Something cold and clammy caressed the back of my neck. I yelped, nearly dropping the phone from my sweat-slick palms. With my free hand, I frantically swatted the back of my neck, searching for what had touched me.

"It's not real. It's not real. It's not real," I chanted silently to myself. Feeling as though I was losing my mind, I squeezed my eyes shut and willed myself to calm down.

Like a ghost, a quiet whimpering drifted up the stairwell. I tilted my head and strained to identify the strange sound. At first, it resembled the mewing of an injured cat, but as the sound grew louder, the more human it became.

My body broke out in a cold sweat. I knew I should get up and find the source of the noise, yet I held tightly to the bed sheets. Like many children, I'd grown up believing monsters lived under my bed at night, ready to grab my ankles the moment I touched the floor. Unlike most children, however, I'd never grown out of that childish fear. More than ever, I dreaded leaving the safety of my bed.

Another wail drifted down the hallway. Someone was hurt. Despite my terror, I *had* to help. Making as little noise as possible, I gripped my phone tighter and slid over the edge of my bed. When my toes hit the floor, I bolted toward my bedroom door and swung back around to illuminate the underside of my bed. Nothing had followed me, of course. My muscles loosened a fraction, and I cracked the door open slightly, turning my ear to the hallway. I reasoned that Barry or my mom probably tripped or stubbed their toe on their way up to bed—no big deal.

Suddenly, a woman's gut-wrenching scream smashed the silence. It was not the sound one made when stubbing a toe. Something was very, very wrong. I sprung away from the door and flattened myself against the wall, terrified. I covered my mouth to hold in my scream.

Had someone broken in? Dread trickled like acid through my veins, and the metallic taste of fear filled my mouth. Was someone *else* in the house? The instinct to lock the door and hide beneath my covers was nearly overpowering. Only the fear of my mother being hurt was enough to push toward the door again.

I switched my phone light off and silently eased out into the hallway. The eerie silence that followed the scream was more terrifying than the scream itself. Pushing my trembling body forward, I felt my way along the wall toward the staircase. The shadows in the hallway were thick, and I had a strange sense that something followed me. Biting my bottom lip to the point of pain, I resisted glancing back, fighting the urge to flee with every step.

When I reached the top of the staircase, I felt around for the banister and clung tightly to it. Holding my breath, I quietly tiptoed down the steps one by one. Soft whimpering floated up the staircase again, and I paused to listen, heart in my throat.

"Please, what do you want?" my mom begged.

In an instant, fear shifted into panic. With shaky hands, I quickly turned my phone's flashlight on again and leaned over the banister, illuminating the room below.

Barry was lying face down on the wood floor in a pool of blood, unmoving. His right arm was bent behind him at an unnatural angle. Just beyond Barry's body, a large, middle-aged man wearing black from head-to-toe held my mom captive from behind. It was difficult to see his features amidst the shadows surrounding him. He had one arm wrapped around her torso, and the other held a knife to her throat.

The light from my cellphone caused both the intruder and my mom to look up. I jumped and dropped the phone over the banister. It landed face-up, illuminating the living room below. My mother's beautiful face was distorted by terror. Just behind her, the intruder's face was twisted into a Cheshire cat smile. His unblinking stare held me captive.

"Mommy . . ." I cried feebly.

I wanted to go to her, help her somehow but my eyes were locked with the monster's gaze as if by force. My limbs turned to ice as the man continued staring unblinkingly back at me. It was as though he was sucking all the light and air from the room. The longer I looked into his soulless, black eyes, the more frozen I felt.

A sense of hopelessness filled my chest. I was drowning in a dark, deep pool. My vision narrowed and my breathing slowed. I slumped forward, suddenly too dizzy to stand.

"Kirie, run!" Mom cried out. The sound of her voice broke me from my trance. I shook my head and stumbled back.

The man let out a menacing laugh that chilled the room.

"Yes, Kirie. *Run.* I do love a good chase," he taunted in a heavy British accent.

Using the banister as support, I began slowly walking down the stairs on shaky legs. I moved carefully, trying not to alarm the man, thinking that maybe I could reason with him. Perhaps I could *think* our way out of this alive . . .

"Please, let's talk this through. Whatever you came here for, it's yours," I said, hands up in surrender. "Just let my mom go, and you can have whatever you want."

"Deal!" he said with an evil grin.

In one swift movement, he slid the knife across my mother's throat and released his hold on her. She fell forward onto her knees, hands to her throat. Her eyes widened, and ugly gurgling noises came from her neck as she struggled to breathe. Bright red streams ran rivers down the front of her silk pajama top.

I stood frozen in horror, bile rising in my throat.

I watched her struggle for what felt like an eternity. Mom dropped her hands to her sides and gazed up at me one last time. Instead of panic, her eyes were full of sadness, acceptance, and love. She traced my face with her eyes as if trying to memorize it. I did the same. Then she slumped sideways to the ground, where she lay still and lifeless.

The light in my mother's expressive hazel eyes was gone, absent. The finality of it was soul-shattering.

"Mommy!" I sobbed.

The killer carelessly stepped over her lifeless body and began stomping toward the staircase where I stood, frozen and useless. In his right hand, he held the long, blood-covered knife. Adrenaline shot through my veins, and I turned, stumbling back up the stairs. But as I reached the top step, a strong, rough hand wrapped around my ankle and pulled my feet out from underneath me.

I landed face-first, hitting my cheekbone on the edge of the stairs above. The man dragged me down the staircase, carpet burning my exposed skin. I clawed at the stairs, but my fingers found no purchase. Just before he managed to pull me to the first floor, I jerked my foot out of his stronghold and flipped onto my back with surprising speed.

Just as fast, the man was on top of me, pinning me awkwardly to the staircase with his heavy body. His pungent odor enveloped me, a sickening mixture of cigarette smoke and blood. The stairs dug into my backbone, bending it at a painful angle. I struggled to draw breath.

"Well, well, well," he sneered. "Look who's coming into their power. Unfortunately, you're a bit too late, bird."

"I have no idea what you're talking about," I cried. I strained beneath him, trying to break free of his weight.

"The best part is that we sussed it out before they did," he said, ignoring me. "Even with all that *light*, those arse holes can be so bloody blind," he laughed.

His nonsensical words made my head spin. "Who? I don't know what you mean. Please, why are you doing this?" I sobbed.

"Because your light makes me sick!" Spittle flew from his mouth, and I turned my head away from the foul wetness.

Like the flip of a switch, his features smoothed out, and with his free hand, he stroked my hair almost lovingly. I cringed. "Your mum and dad were fun enough, but there's nothing quite like extinguishing a *Daughter of Light*."

I'd been wrong trying to reason with him earlier. You can't reason with an insane person. The murderer lifted the knife, and panic took over my body like I'd never felt before. With strength I didn't know I had, I muscled my arms out from underneath him and began hitting and scratching his face and arms.

He threw my hands away and backhanded me across the cheek. My head snapped backward, and black spots filled my vision. My arms fell lifelessly onto the staircase as confusion and fear took over. Cold metal pressed against my exposed neck, and all I could think was I wasn't ready to die.

A burst of heat shot out from the center of my chest in waves as if electricity were flowing out of me. The pictures on the walls all around us began to tremble and shake.

"Cool trick. I'm impressed," he said sarcastically, pushing the knife harder into my throat. Little drips of blood began running down my neck.

An angel figurine that my mother kept on the entryway table inexplicably barreled through the air and slammed into the back of the killer's head. A look of astonishment crossed his scarred face just before his eyes rolled back in his head. He slumped forward, squeezing the remaining breath from my lungs. The knife slipped from his hand and fell through the banister onto the floor below with a *clank*.

Without hesitation, I pulled myself out from underneath his large body and ran back up the stairs. I frantically felt my way down the dark hallway toward the first door on the left. I turned my parents' doorknob and threw myself into their room, locking the door behind me.

9-1-1, I needed to call 9-1-1.

But my phone was downstairs. Heart in my throat, I put my hands out and searched the darkness for my mother's bedside table where she left her phone to charge each night. As I approached the bed, my shins collided with the corner of the king-sized footboard. Fresh pain shot up my already battered legs, and I covered my mouth to muffle my cry.

Tears clogged my throat as I felt for the sharp corners of her mahogany bedside table, tapping every flat surface for her cellphone. Like the fingers of death, cold streams of air brushed along my skin. My heart beat faster. I sensed my time to call for help was running out.

When I finally found the edge of the bedside table and touched the phone's smooth metal face, something hit the door. The walls shook from the massive force. I screamed and knocked the phone to the floor. I fell onto my hands and knees and searched blindly for it. The man-shaped monster continued his assault on the door as I brushed my hands back and forth along the rough surface of the carpet. I nearly cried with relief when I found it. With the phone tucked into my chest, I slid underneath the bed on my back.

My whole body shook as I dialed 9-1-1. It rang once, twice, three times. I stared up at the bed's wooden frame just inches from my face, illuminated by the phone's screen.

"9-1-1, what's your emergency?" a male dispatcher asked in an apathetic tone.

I pressed the phone into my cheek and cupped my free hand around the receiver. "Please help me," I whispered. Tears ran freely down my temples and into my hair. "There's a man in my house. H-he killed my parents." I pressed my lips together and sobbed silently.

"What's the address of your emergency?" the man asked

more urgently. I quickly rattled off my home address.

BANG!

The outer door burst open, slamming into the wall. The light from the phone vanished, and I was enveloped in a cocoon of darkness. Footsteps walked across the carpet directly toward the bed. I held my breath and prayed he wouldn't see me.

The man's shushing footsteps sounded close when he halted. Holding my breath, I remained perfectly still and counted my heartbeats. One beat. Two beats. Three. Perhaps he wouldn't see me. Perhaps he would leave. Four beats. Five beats. Six. I held onto the childish hope that if I didn't move an inch, the monster couldn't see me.

Two arms reached under the bed, and rough hands grabbed me by the hair. The phone slipped from my grip as he dragged me out from under the bed. Screaming at the top of my lungs, I hit and kicked out at him with all my strength, but he was undeterred.

"I haven't had this much fun in years," he laughed as he held me up by my hair.

I clawed at his hands, trying desperately to get free of him. My scalp felt on fire as clumps of my hair came loose in his fist.

He was too strong.

Instinctively, I lifted my knee and nailed him in the crotch.

He bent over in pain, releasing his hold on my hair just enough for me to pull free.

I stumbled toward the open door, knowing this was my last chance to get away. Just before I reached the doorway, he tackled me from behind. My chin connected with the floor as I fell. I flipped onto my back before the attacker was fully on me. I reached up to hit him again, but he grabbed both of my arms, pinned them to my sides, and straddled my body. I dug my heels into the ground and tried to buck him off, but his dense weight held me firmly to the ground.

"Now, now, luv. Don't leave just yet. The fun's just starting," he cooed.

All the fight left me then, and I began to sob. Laughing as if it were a game, the maniacal killer switched his hold so that my arms were pinned beneath his knees. Sitting on my chest, he wrapped his hands around my throat and squeezed. The pain in my neck was intense. Warm blood ran from my split chin, coating the man's hands as he happily choked me.

Maybe it's better this way, I thought as I struggled in vain to breathe.

My beautiful mother, so full of life . . . gone.

My stepfather . . . gone. I was alone in the world.

In a moment of clarity, I understood I was dying. Strangely, that realization wasn't as upsetting as it should've been. Instead of fear and panic, a sense of peace and acceptance encompassed me. I was going to be with Mom.

As I began to lose consciousness, flashing lights appeared on the ceiling above me. In my delirium, I thought perhaps the lights were there to guide me to the other side. I slowly floated into oblivion, hoping to step into my mother's embrace on the other side.

The last thing I heard was loud noises in the distance and a sudden release of pressure. I peacefully welcomed death as the darkness filled my mind and I slowly floated away.

Tyger tyger burning bight

In the forests of the night;

What immortal hand or eye,

Could frame thy fearful symmetry?

The Tyger

By William Blake

Chapter 4

BEEP.

BEEP.

BEEP.

BEEP.

ill someone please make it stop?' The insistent beeping drilled into my head like a construction worker with a jackhammer.

UGH . . . the pounding in my temples pulsed with the tempo of the damn beeping.

I tried to reach out and swat the noise away, but my body felt as though it was stuck in molasses. There was a painful tightness in my throat that refused to be ignored. I tried to pry my eyes open but was only able to lift them into slits. Not that it helped much; everything was a bleary blob of light.

Something moved across my vision. I struggled to focus, but it was as if my eyes weighed a thousand pounds. I let them fall shut again. There was a movement to my left, a rustling sound. Again, I pried my eyes open just a fraction, and a bright, blinding light pierced my retinas like spears. A small moan escaped from my throat, sending sharp pains up my neck.

"Shhhh." The sound came somewhere just outside my limited sight.

As my vision adjusted to the light, I saw a pair of piercing green eyes staring down at me. They were verdant and bright like a boundless forest, full of life. Beyond the eyes was a halo of light. It warmed my skin as though I were standing under the noon-day sun.

I'm dead, and this must be heaven. The realization didn't cause me sadness, though. How could it be when death was so beautiful and warm?

I wanted to reach out to the angelic being, but my arms wouldn't obey. My eyes, heavy from fatigue, drooped closed, and pain came rushing to the forefront as I sank back into the darkness once more.

I was wrong. Heaven wouldn't be this painful. This must be hell. That would explain the beeping that never stops.

A warm, rough hand enveloped my cold and clammy fingers, and a sense of calm blossomed in my chest like a flower reaching for the sun.

"You're strong," the angel quietly said in a deep, clear voice. "Not many have survived what you did."

His slight British accent triggered some far-off memory. I tried to grab ahold of it, but it drifted back into the dark recesses of my mind like smoke dissipating into the night air. A new set of footsteps entered the room.

"Hey, Luca," a deep male voice said, not as angelic as the first. "Stop gawking. Her throat, man."

"Bugger off, Arin. I've got it," the boy said in irritation.

Light suddenly shone through my closed eyelids, and warmth enveloped my body. The angel's rough palms carefully cradled my neck, and an intense heat spread through my sore muscles and tissue. A moan formed in the back of my throat as the pain and tightness began to drain away. All too soon, however, the light faded, and his hands left my throat. The sudden cold was a shock to my battered system.

"I'll see you again soon." Soft, full lips brushed against my forehead, leaving a trail of goosebumps across my cooling skin.

Unconsciousness began to tug at my mind once more, pulling me back into its cold embrace.

"Kirie," The angel whispered as I drifted back into oblivion.

I drifted in and out of dreams of light and angels with emerald-green eyes for eternity. I felt happy and safe, and I never wanted to wake up. However, all too soon I became aware of my physical body again.

It happened in stages. First, the pain returned to my face and neck. Then, my lower half. As each part of me woke up, so did the pain. Each new agony warred for my attention. The worst part, though, was the large object blocking my mouth and throat. I probed it with my tongue, but the thing wouldn't move. It was stuck in my mouth.

I tried to scream out, but I couldn't form words around the obstruction. My chest tightened in panic. *I'm choking!*

I attempted to move my arms to remove whatever was blocking my airway, but they wouldn't lift more than a couple of inches from my sides. *I'm going to suffocate!*

The rhythm of the damned beeping quickened, and my heart felt as though it were pumping out of my chest. *Please, someone, help me!* My attempted cries came out as strangled moans.

"Hold on there, honey," a kind voice said above me. "You're ok. Just try to stay still for me."

A cold hand touched my left arm in what I assumed was meant to be a reassuring gesture. *I'm okay? Can't she see that I can't breathe?*

From somewhere near my head, a lower-pitched beep rang.

"Please inform Dr. Owen that his patient in room 104 is waking up," the woman said.

"I'll let him know right away," an electronic voice answered.

The woman began humming softly again as she moved

around the room, but I ignored her as I willed my heart rate to slow to its normal rhythm. *If I was suffocating,* I reasoned, *I would be dead by now.*

I struggled again to open my eyes; at first, all I saw was light, painful and bright. After several long minutes, my eyes adjusted to the room around me, and bits and pieces of information began to fall into place. I was propped up in a white bed wrapped in an off-white blanket, thin and coarse to the touch. An IV line had been inserted in my left elbow, and a blood pressure cuff was wrapped around my upper arm.

It was a standard, white-walled hospital room. Clearly, I'd had an accident or something. That would explain the pain that covered my entire body like a shroud. I looked around for the source of the insistent humming and saw a large, dark-skinned woman bustling around the small space, checking the blinking lights and beeping sounds coming from the tower to my left. She must have felt my gaze because she turned to me and smiled.

"Ah! There are those pretty blue eyes," she said in a Southern sing-song voice.

I tried to respond to her before remembering the blockage in my throat. I gazed down at my nose, my eyes crossing as I stared in horror at the large plastic tube sticking out of my mouth. I raised my heavy arm to remove it, but the nurse took my hand in hers and gave it a reassuring squeeze.

"Don't be alarmed, honey. We had to intubate you. You're getting plenty of oxygen, I promise. The doctor is on his way to see if we can take that tube out for you. Hold tight, okay?" She gave my hand another squeeze before busying herself around the room again.

Feeling frustrated and helpless, I stared at the white tiled ceiling and pretended that I didn't want to rip all the cords from the walls. I distracted myself by trying to remember what happened to me. The last thing I remembered was taking Rylie and the girls home from the party. Maybe I fell asleep at the wheel on my way home. Maybe someone slipped something into the Coke I was drinking. I should've never gone to that stupid party.

The door opened, and a thin man with a long face and salt-and-pepper hair entered the room. He was wearing a white lab coat and a stethoscope around his neck.

"Well, look who's awake. It's good to finally meet you," he kindly said as he pulled a chair beside my bed. "I'm Dr. Owen, and I'm the attending physician. I'm going to take a look at that throat of yours, okay?" Warm hands gently probed my throat, and I realized much of the pain from before had eased. "We try not to leave an intubation tube in for longer than 24 hours, and we're getting close to that time mark now. I'm going to check and make sure it's safe to take it out. okay?"

I nodded my head slightly. "Your neck is looking

dramatically better. You're healing rather fast, actually," he said, leaning back in his chair. "I think we can go ahead and remove that tube for you."

The doctor turned to the nurse and instructed her on helping him with the extraction. After the tube was removed and I was able to breathe on my own, I relaxed a fraction. I opened my mouth to ask what had happened, but the doctor put a hand up to silence me.

"You shouldn't try to speak for a while. Your throat has sustained significant damage, and we need all those muscles to heal without putting any added strain on them, okay? Though it does appear you're healing rather rapidly, we don't want to cause any new damage. Nod your head once if you understand." I bobbed my head up and down but stopped when the room began to spin.

"Great! Now that you're stable, the best thing to do is rest. We don't want you doing too much too soon." Dr. Owen gave me a reassuring smile and pat on my hand. He left the room with the promise that he would be back to check on me soon.

I was growing frustrated with my foggy memories. Why was I there? What happened to my throat? As I tried to reason it all out, something in the corner of my mind rattled like a tiny monster locked in a box, dangerous and begging to be set free. I glanced around the room. Something was missing, though I didn't know what. My eyes landed on the visitor's chair in the corner where the innocent piece of furniture bothered me—a lot.

Then it hit me. The chair was *empty*. My eyes searched the room.

Where's my mom?

She *never* left my side for long. For better or for worse, she was always annoyingly present. I squeezed my eyes shut and tried to reason through my growing panic. Maybe she went for coffee. Or, perhaps, she had to use the bathroom. I turned my stiff head to the nurse and tapped my hand on the bed to get her attention. She gazed at me with a questioning look, and I mouthed the word 'mom.' Her smile melted into a sad pout. It was the obvious pity on her face that did it. The thing my mind didn't want to remember, couldn't process, came bursting out of that locked box.

Suffocating darkness . . . screaming . . . blood . . . bodies.

My mother's face, so familiar and dear to me, in a mask of fear and horror just before he slit her throat.

Running through the dark, terrified and unable to save myself or my family.

Those black, soulless eyes stared down at me as he squeezed the life out of me.

Or didn't because there I was, left behind.

Strange gasping noises came from somewhere inside the room, increasing in intensity. It took me several moments to realize they were coming from me. Like the breaking of a dam, panic flooded my body and crashed down on me like a wave that no amount of reason could ever calm. Tears bleared my vision as I tried to scream and cry, and a burning pain stabbed at my throat.

"I need some help in here. Page Dr. Owen, STAT," the nurse said into the intercom by my bed.

Cold hands ran up and down my arms, and I tried to throw them off. "Shhh, it's okay, honey. You're safe now. No one's going to hurt you anymore. You need to calm down, or you are going to hurt yourself."

There was a flurry of movement in the room as several nurses rushed in. I didn't know what they were doing, nor did I care. This world held no meaning or value to me anymore.

"We need to sedate her. She's going into shock." At the sound of the doctor's voice, I began to feel a new emotion: anger.

How could he have looked me in the eyes and smiled like everything was alright? How could that woman have told me I was safe when everything in my world was dead and gone? How could they have *lied* to me like that?

I didn't want to be there in this hospital with those liars. I wanted to be with my mother, wherever she was. We hadn't been apart for more than a few days at any point in my life, and I didn't know how to live without her.

How could she leave me behind like that? I felt like an abandoned kitten on the side of some old farm road.

There was a tug on the IV in my left arm, and a cold liquid filled my veins. My eyes began drooping, and the chaotic scene around me faded into blackness.

To hell with all of them . . . their smiles, their lies. I hated them for saving me when all I wanted was death. My last thought before the darkness claimed me again was of the killer's black, empty eyes.

Chapter 5

The next few days were a blur. Physically, my body continued to heal, but my spirit . . .broken. The double homicide of a local lawyer and his wife with the attempted murder of their daughter was noteworthy enough to make national news, adding a layer of stress. I was momentarily famous in the most horrible way. Pretty soon, everyone I had ever met in town wanted to come and see how I was. My hospital room was overflowing with flowers, cards, and get-well bears. The happy floral smell sickened me.

Once everyone realized I was unresponsive and unable to speak, the visits became fewer and farther between until only Rylie, Kaylee, and Cassidy were left.

My friends took turns coming over after school to stay with me until visiting hours were over. I still had doctor's orders not to use my voice, so the girls brought magazines and books to read to me. Sometimes, they just turned on the TV and sat with me without talking for hours.

There were also security guards standing outside the door to my room due to the nature of my attack and the fact that the murderer was still at large. Despite all the warm bodies surrounding me, however, I'd never felt so alone.

Still, their presence kept the monsters at bay. That was, until nightfall when the girls headed home, and my hospital room was empty. I tried to stay awake but would inevitably fall into a restless sleep. That was where my parents' murderer waited for me. He held me captive with his black stare, and I watched in frozen terror as my mother's bloody death played on repeat. I woke each time clutching my heaving chest, grief and guilt strangling me from the inside.

It should have been me lying dead on the floor, not them. Their deaths were so senseless. He'd been there for *me*.

Each morning, the nightmares burned off with the rising sun, and the room filled up with the living once again. Among my visitors were Detective Wadman and Detective Peterson who came each day to check on my progress. Detective Wadman was in his late 40s with a receding hairline and a protruding mid-line. His partner, Detective Peterson, was his opposite in every way. A short, perky blond in her early thirties.

From the beginning, Detective Peterson did most of the talking while her partner sulked in the corner. She complimented my eyes and hair and talked about girly things like she expected us to bond or become each other's BFFs because we're both girls. But I couldn't work up any positive feelings toward her. She was only here because my parents were dead. Murdered.

My doctor instructed the detectives not to encourage me to talk, so they brought a whiteboard for me to write down what I remembered from that night. I could tell they were trying to be patient with me, but they obviously wanted answers. I guess I did too.

The first day, I couldn't work up the energy to write anything down. I knew this frustrated them, especially Detective Wadman, but I couldn't move my hands or think beyond basic thoughts. The second day they came by, I could write one word down.

Dark

Both detectives looked at me like this bit of information was insignificant, seeing that the attack happened the night of Justin's party. But they didn't understand. The darkness was *everywhere,* suffocating all light. The man who killed my mother and Barry *was* dark. Not in his skin tone or coloring, but in his overall aura. He was darkness personified.

It was difficult to convey all of this to them on a small, rectangular whiteboard. I grunted and forcefully underlined the word "DARK" over and over with the black dry-erase marker, trying to get them to pay attention to it, but they continued to stare at me with confusion and a bit of pity, so I gave up.

I could finally give them more information about the perpetrator's appearance on Wednesday, (four days after the attack). It took forever on the small whiteboard, but I wrote down his description: Short dark hair, middle-aged, tall, British, black eyes. The detectives seemed satisfied with my answers and backed off from questioning me for the rest of the day. I knew that wouldn't last forever, and I dreaded recounting the night in full.

There was a lot of discussion about where to send me once I left the hospital since my house was empty and I had no family members to take me in. Also, there was the issue of my age. I would turn eighteen in April, so I was almost too old to be put into foster care, which was fine with me. My mother had been raised by the system, and I got the impression she had it rough.

Several families in the community I had known for years offered to have me stay with them. Ultimately, it was decided that I would live with Rylie until I graduated since I was close to her family, and they had an extra room in their basement.

By Friday—after a full six days in the hospital—Dr. Owen made the decision that I was well enough to be discharged. When the paramedics first brought me in, my windpipe had been crushed. Now, my throat looked nearly normal, and the bruises had faded to mere smudge marks. Even the cuts on my chin forehead had closed up.

They cleared me to speak for the first time since the attack. Still, I was hesitant to do damage to my voice, and truthfully, I was more scared of telling my story out loud.

"It's really astounding how quickly you've healed, young lady. I'm sure I haven't seen anything quite like it," Dr. Owen said as he signed my discharge papers in a flurry of illegible letters.

Each time someone commented on my miraculous recovery, which was often, it reminded all me all over again of a dream I had about deep green eyes, warm hands, and bright light.

"Thank you for all your help," I rasped. My voice sounded so different to my ears; another thing about me that might never be the same.

"My pleasure! Take care of yourself, now." He patted my hand in a fatherly way and left the room.

I still felt residual anger toward him and my nurses. Logically, I knew none of this was their fault, but I continued to resent them for their hope and cheerfulness during the worst moments of my life. They should've had the decency to appear sad.

A nurse led me from the hospital room where Detectives

Wadman and Peterson and a pair of police officers waited to escort me out of the hospital and to my home to get my things. Though I knew it was a necessary trip, the thought of returning to that house made bile rise in my throat.

No one spoke as we rode the elevator to the first floor and walked through the main lobby. My body nearly vibrated with nerves. I hadn't been outside since the attack, and I wasn't ready to step into a world where my parents were dead, and their killer was waiting around to finish the job.

I stopped in front of the double automatic sliding glass doors that led to the parking lot. The detectives must've realized I needed a minute and politely waited from a distance. It was a blue-sky day, and the sun filtered in through the glass, bright and full of natural energy. The spark inside me awoke in response. It was the first time I'd sensed that part of me since that horror-filled night and I worried it had died along with my family. I placed a hand to my chest and my eyes swam with unshed tears.

"Are you ready, Kirie?" Detective Peterson asked.

I took a deep breath and nodded. *I could do this.* I stepped forward and the glass doors slid open with a *whoosh*. I was immediately hit with a cacophony of sound. Reporters carrying microphones and cameras surrounded me on all sides. I pulled my hair in front of my face and tucked my chin down.

"Kirie, can you describe your attacker?"

FLASH

"Kirie, look over here!"

FLASH

"Kirie, tell us! How does it feel to be the only surviving member of your family?"

FLASH

"Seriously? Get a life, Carl," Detective Peterson yelled at the young reporter in a suit and bowtie. "Don't let him get to you, Kirie. Just keep your head down."

The detectives put their arms protectively around my shoulders and ushered me through the crowd toward a Crown Victoria parked near the entrance. One of the uniformed officers opened the back seat for me and helped me slide in. Their older base model was exactly what one would expect of a detective's car—dingy cloth seats that smelled of stale coffee and sweat.

I placed the plastic bag the nurse gave me with all my pain medications and anti-anxiety pills on my lap and held tightly to it. I knew the news covered what happened, but I wasn't prepared for pushy reporters. The day was quickly unraveling, and my anxiety levels were rising.

I wished they'd given me Valium before I left, I thought with true regret.

During the entire short trip to my house, Detective Peterson threw concerned glances at me in the rear-view mirror. I guessed I must've looked as scared as I felt. The two policemen were in a squad car behind us, following the entire way.

As we drove through the streets of my sleepy neighborhood, I closed my eyes tightly and tried to clear my mind. *I could do this. I could do this.* It wasn't until the car stopped that I realized we'd arrived. I opened my eyes and stared up at the home I'd grown up in. My breath quickened.

I wasn't ready for this.

I'd never be ready for this.

Lightheaded, I bent over and hung my head between my knees, trying to steady my heaving breath.

"Ahem. I think I'll go walk through the house with Officer Rockford. I'll just see you two inside," Detective Wadman said, obviously uncomfortable with my mild meltdown in the back seat.

"Good idea," Detective Peterson said before turning back to me. "I'll just wait outside my door until you're ready to go in. There's no rush, ok?" I nodded my head, and she climbed out of the car.

When it was quiet inside the cab, I took a few more calming breaths and prepared myself to make the quick trip through the house. I mentally cataloged the items that I would need and separated them into categories based on each item's location in my room and bathroom. I estimated how many bags I would need in order to hold all those items and where those bags were put away. It helped to look at the situation as a problem to be solved rather than an event to be avoided.

Get in. Get out. Done.

I could do this.

I slowly opened the car door and stepped out onto the driveway. Detective Wadman nodded approvingly and led me to the open front door. The two-story house looked smaller and older than I remembered as if I was coming home after a long time away. Disoriented, I nearly tripped on my way up the cement front steps.

The strong smell of chemicals hit me the moment I entered my home. I covered my nose and quickly walked through the front entryway, staring straight ahead. I climbed the stairs and went to the end of the hallway where my room was located. I moved directly to the back of my closet, retrieved my overnight bags and suitcases and began piling my clothes and shoes into them.

Next, I moved into my room where I packed my schoolbooks, art supplies, and laptop. The thought of returning to school anytime soon nauseated me, but I didn't want to have to come back for anything . . .ever.

I ran across the hall to my bathroom and quickly threw my make-up and hair products into an overnight bag. It was bound to be a mess in there by the time we got to Rylie's, but I couldn't stop myself from rushing through my motions. I felt as though I was very close to losing control and tried desperately to get through this task without falling apart.

One of the officers poked his head into the bathroom and asked if there was anything else I needed to grab before they locked up. I shook my head and followed him out and down the hallway toward the stairs. When we passed my parents' bedroom, I stopped.

"Could you give me a second, please?" I asked the officer.

"Sure. I'll just wait out here." He leaned against the wall and politely looked away.

I slowly turned the handle to their door and pushed it open. Their room looked mostly the same, except for the plastic cup and notepad that must've been knocked from the bedside table during the scuffle. I took a fortifying breath and stepped into the room. Mom was everywhere–in the lingering scent of her floral perfume, the paisley bedspread she'd picked out, the mascara still sitting on her bathroom vanity. Barry was there, too, a companion ghost.

I walked into their closet and let my hand lightly brush along Mom's hanging clothes, remembering what it felt like to hug her when she was wearing them. I gazed at her stiletto shoes and remembered how she looked when she wore them on dates with Barry. Surrounded by their things, I could almost imagine they were still alive.

In a matter of minutes, I would leave the only home I'd ever known and never return. My heart squeezed painfully at the thought. All our things would be sold or thrown away and I'd have nothing left to remind me of Mom. I wanted–no, needed–to keep something beyond my memories of her to prove she once existed.

I slipped an oatmeal-colored cardigan from its hanger and slid my arms inside the sleeves. Mom's scent–fresh-cut flowers–enveloped me like a hug. I wrapped it tightly around my torso. I trailed my fingers over the polished lid of the jewelry box she kept on one of the shelves. Inside was a pair of diamond stud earrings she wore for special occasions. I always thought they made her hazel eyes sparkle. My fingers trembled as I put them in my ears.

I abandoned the rest and went back into the bedroom. On my way out, I picked up the cup and notepad and placed them back on the bedside table, wanting the room to look the way she left it. Without much thought, I opened the top drawer. It was full of the typical stuff you might find in a bedside table drawer: lotion, magazines, and earplugs for when Barry snored (which was often).

I gently closed the top drawer and opened the bottom one. There wasn't much in there besides a tablet and notepad. I moved them around, and a white envelope a little further to the back appeared under the other items. My name was written on the front. My brows furrowed.

What is it?

I picked it up.

"All done in here?" the officer asked from the doorway.

I jumped.

"Um, yeah. I think I have what I need," I said, slipping the letter into my back pocket.

I followed the officer down the first few stairs, where the others gathered around the front door. Without thinking, I glanced over the banister into the living room below and froze.

The wood floor where my mom and Barry's bodies were had been removed, leaving the subfloor exposed. Not a speck of blood remained. Still, I would never be able to get the image of them lying lifeless from my mind. No amount of bleach or cleaning agent could ever erase what happened in this room.

The look of horror on my precious mother's face flashed through my mind again. The tenuous control I held over my emotions earlier was completely lost as tears and great sobs ripped from my body. Strong hands wrapped around my arms and guided me down the rest of the stairs.

Unable to see through my tears, I allowed them to lead me out of the house. I stumbled into the backseat of the detective's car, curled into a ball, and let the pain take over. Detective Wadman quickly drove down the street and out of my neighborhood. I knew with certainty that I would never be strong enough to return to that house again.

Chapter 6

The sun warmed the beige canopy above my head, and the energy seeped into my skin, filling my waning energy stores. Yet it did little to warm the ice that had settled around my heart.

It was a quiet, peaceful day. A cloudless October blue sky smiled on a vibrant-colored blanket of reds, oranges, and yellows from the surrounding oak trees. My mom loved fall. I did, too—once. Now, to me, the fallen leaves that lay over the browning lawn only represented death.

I pulled my mom's cardigan tight around my chest and closed my eyes, trying to unsee the twin caskets in front of me. Rylie reached over and touched my arm. I jumped.

"You okay?" she whispered. Her warm hand raised goosebumps on my chilled skin.

The plastic chair squeaked beneath me as I shifted uncomfortably. I opened my mouth to speak, but nothing came out. I'd said little in the past few days. My throat was still raw, and I was always at a loss for words. What was there to say really? I felt out of place. Everything around me appeared the same as if nothing had changed except me. I felt as though I was trapped in an old, yellowed photograph of times gone by.

Rylie tapped my arm again, and she nodded toward the parking lot to our right. "Looks like your detective friends made an appearance."

Wadman and Peterson stood at the edge of the crowd, arms folded and feet apart. They looked like a pair of bad actors in a low-budget movie with their aviator sunglasses and cheap suits. Detective Peterson gave me a slight nod when I glanced in her direction. I didn't know if having them there was a comfort or simply a reminder that my parents' killer was still unaccounted for. I nodded in return before turning back to the coffins lying out in front of me.

They were surrounded by fake grass and draped in vibrantly colored flowers as if covering the dead with representations of life and beauty could make them less dead.

Low murmurings moved around me as the seats beneath the large canopy began to fill with my people. I assumed they were my parents' friends and neighbors, but their faces were all a blur to me. Rylie and her parents sat like guards to my left and right. Her little brothers sat at the end of the row, swinging their small feet back, rocking their plastic chairs back and forth wildly in the soft grass. Rylie's mom stopped them with a harsh look.

A warm presence washed over me like a sunrise over a frozen ridge and I searched for the source. I'd always been able to sense a person's energy. Each one had a unique frequency; some dimmer, some brighter. Yet this energy was much stronger than anything I'd ever felt before. My tense muscles loosened slightly under the warmth, and my lungs took in an easy breath for the first time in over a week.

I turned slightly in my seat. From the corner of my eye, I saw a boy in the chair directly behind me. Light encompassed him like a halo and bright energy pulsed off him in gentle ebbs and flows. It bathed my exposed skin, soothing my battered soul. I looked around to see if anyone saw the light coming from the boy, but no one seemed to notice. How could they not see? I sat forward and placed a hand over my chest. My heart was beating a strong and measured rhythm.

Slowly, I moved slightly to the side and studied the boy again. Beyond the light, he wore dark sunglasses and a black tailored suit. Though I didn't know much about men's fashion, I could tell the suit was expensive, too expensive for a small-town funeral. His long, lean legs stretched out in front of him, nearly touching the back of the seat in front of him. The light clung to him like a second skin, and for a moment, I felt a powerful stab of longing to be that light. I swung forward again, startled by the intense emotion. My heart pounded heavily in my chest as grief, adrenalin, and confusion all warred within me.

Someone tapped on a microphone. I blinked until my eyes cleared and the strange commotion inside me from the boy's presence dispelled. The pastor from my church stood behind a microphone stand at the front of the tent. He said a few words about Barry and my mom, but his words soon melted together until they were meaningless.

Several minutes later, he was replaced by neighbors, friends, and associates who stood, one by one, in front of the closed caskets and shared their memories of my parents. Many commented on Mom's beauty and Barry's charitable contributions, but mostly, they talked about their love for each other. A few of Mom's closest friends spoke of her love for me and that I was the center of her world.

I think the open forum intended to help people to heal through sharing, but it didn't help me to hear their memories; it only made me realize how much I had truly lost. As they prepared to lower the coffins into the ground, the choir from our church sang, "Nearer My God to Thee." I held my breath and fought the pressure building behind my eyes as the mournful music surrounded me. I'd fought tears throughout the long service, knowing that once they started, I wouldn't be able to get them to stop, and I was determined not to lose the fight. Rylie held my hand tightly.

When the song ended, four men walked over to the coffins and began lowering them into the ground.

And I was undone.

Large tears clouded my vision, and my shoulders shook with racketing sobs. Heads turned toward me; brows knit on concerned faces.

Those men . . . they were putting my mommy into the ground where I couldn't see her or hold her again. They were going to cover her body with dirt and put her in a place where light would never find her. I was overcome by an intense urge to crawl into the grave and lay on top of her coffin so she wouldn't be alone in the dark.

The tops of the twin coffins sank like a sunset as the men continued to lower them into their final resting place. An unexpected fury at these unnamed men lit up inside me. I wanted to scream at them, beat at their chests, and make them stop. My frozen center began to thaw, and my skin grew hot. Something heavy gathered in my chest as my sobs intensified. The pressure quickly built, crushing my insides under its immense weight, and heat pulsed through my veins with the tempo of a heartbeat.

Rylie whispered my name and reached out to touch me, only to flinch back in her seat as her mom made little shushing noises from my right. Mrs. Anderson rubbed a hand down my arm. I shook her off, worried she'd break the heat bubble building inside of me.

From off to my left, a hand wrapped around my arm. It was warm and steady. I turned and came face to face with the boy behind me. Light reflected off his mirrored sunglasses. He leaned over my shoulder until his lips nearly touched my ear.

"Shhh," he whispered. I tried to shrink away, but he only tightened his grip on my arm.

"Relax," He breathed, his baritone voice even and hypnotic. "You need to calm down."

As he spoke, the hand on my arm heated, the warmth steadily growing in intensity until it nearly burned my skin. In an instant, the crushing pressure in my chest shattered like glass into a million tiny pieces, and broken energy scattered out through my limbs, leaving a trail of pins and needles in its wake. All at once, my sobs quieted, and I sagged back into my chair like a marionette whose strings had been cut.

The boy dropped his hand and leaned back in his seat. I was bathed in ice once more. Our pastor stood and prayed for my parents, but I was unmoved by his hopeful reassurances of palaces in the sky. My mind was on the boy behind me. I could feel his eyes on me, like sunshine on my back.

One by one, people stood and formed sad clusters on the lawn. I turned to find the boy again, but he was already halfway to the parking lot. He had an other-worldly grace that set him apart from everyone else.

I felt a cold hand on my wrist. Rylie leaned in, "Are you okay?" she whispered. I nodded my head once in response, not daring to use my voice. "Who was that guy behind you?"

As I shook my head, something dark moved to the right in the parking lot. I wiped the tears from my eyes and squinted to see what had caught my eye. Behind the hood of an SUV stood a tall, middle-aged man wearing dark sunglasses and a haughty smirk.

Instinctively, I knew who he was. I knew without seeing that behind those glasses were a pair of black, soulless eyes.

He was staring directly at me.

Cold fear trickled through my veins. I turned and whispered to Rylie, "He's here."

"Who is?" she whispered back.

I turned and pointed in the direction of the SUV. No one was there.

"I thought I saw him over by that car," I said helplessly.

"Saw, who, Kirie? The guy sitting behind you?" she asked. Worry etched deep in her brow.

I walked parallel to the parking lot to see if I could get a better view of the other side of the SUV, my black heels sinking into the soft grass. My distress must have alerted the detectives because Wadman and Peterson immediately pushed their way through the crowd in my direction.

"What is it, Kirie?" Wadman asked, leaning over me.

"He was *here*," I whispered in a hoarse voice. Something dark began spreading through my veins like poison.

Wadman and Peterson shared a look. "Who was here?" Peterson asked.

"The killer," I breathed, almost afraid to hear my own words.

Peterson turned and whispered something to Wadman, who immediately began barking orders into his cellphone.

"Let's get you out of here," Peterson said, angling her body toward me as though she were acting like a shield. "I assume you came with the Andersons?" she asked. I nodded and she steered me back over to Rylie's parents who were waiting at the far end of the parking lot.

"Mr. and Mrs. Anderson, will you please take Kirie over to the country club now?"

"Absolutely! We were on our way there next." Mrs. Anderson said, wrapping a protective arm around my shoulders.

We climbed into the minivan. Rylie and I sat in the back bench seat and her twin brothers sat in the captain chairs in the middle, fighting over who got the PlayStation when they got home. Their high-pitched voices grated on my nerves. As the van pulled out of the cemetery parking lot, a police cruiser drove behind us.

My thoughts were a riot in my head. *He came to their funeral!* Panic was slowly building up in me as I thought of those dark eyes staring at me from behind his sunglasses. There was something predatory about how he'd watched me, like a cheetah stalking its prey.

"Kirie, you look like you are going to throw up," Rylie whispered, leaning into me.

I threw another glance at the police cruiser following close behind. The officer was alone in the car's darkened interior. I shook my head. "I just want this day to be over."

"I know. It's almost done," she said softly, patting my hand. "We won't stay long, I promise."

I nodded my head and let her warmth and energy seep into my skin and soothe me.

The wake was held at the same small-town country club my family had been members of for over ten years. The caterers had set up a colorful buffet of fresh fruit, antipasti trays, and a variety of meats. In the room's corners, speakers softly played my mom's favorite music, Gershwin. Round tables covered with floral centerpieces set atop white tablecloths had been set in intervals around the dining room. It looked more like a wedding reception than a wake. My stomach soured, and I focused on the floor in front of me.

As we entered the dining room, I broke away from Rylie's family who had stopped to talk to some friends and got in the food line behind an elderly couple. The woman wore a formless blue and purple floral dress and black orthotic shoes. The man dressed like a farmer in his suspenders and brown boots. They must've been acquaintances of my parents, though I didn't recognize them.

"I heard Claire's throat was cut," the old lady loudly whispered at one of her husband's hearing aids. "And Barry's neck was broken."

The old man nodded, his jowls jiggling like Jello beneath his chin. "That's why I tell you to lock the doors every night, Myrtle. You have to lock your doors, or this kind of thing happens," he blurted out, unaware he was yelling.

I moved my head away from them and bit hard on my tongue. The metallic tang of blood filled my mouth.

When it was my turn at the buffet, I placed food liberally on my plate full and found a seat in the back corner. I pulled my heavy hair over my shoulders and slumped in my chair, hoping everyone would see the invisible "back off" sign written on my forehead.

No such luck. A steady stream of neighbors and friends found me. I did my best to be kind and gracious, but every time someone tried offering their condolences, I comforted them instead as they broke down in tears. I just wanted them to go away. My grief was heavy enough to carry without having to shoulder theirs as well.

I needed to get out of there. I looked around for my ride, hoping to convince Mr. and Mrs. Anderson that it was time to go, but they were locked in a somber conversation with their friends, and Rylie was talking to Kaylee and Cassidy near the dessert table.

Everyone in the room kept throwing worried glances in my direction like I may have a mental breakdown at any moment. Their pity was suffocating. I briefly considered walking the five miles to Rylie's house, but I was wearing heels, and there was a murderer nearby, so I reluctantly tossed that plan aside.

I was about to carry out Plan C, which consisted of sprinting to the bathroom to hide in a stall, the boy from the grave-side service walked in. Again, I was struck by his overwhelming presence. He was not only practically vibrating with energy, but he was also insanely attractive. Just as I'd guessed, he was well over six feet tall. He had a square jaw and a lean, toned build. His hair and skin tone were a warm golden brown like he'd spent most of his days in the sun.

He was easily the most beautiful boy I had ever seen.

And he wasn't alone.

His companion was a curvy blond with long legs and caramel-colored skin. The girl was also full of excess energy, far more than anyone else in the room, with one exception. Her energy was to the boy's as a spotlight is to the sun. Still, she exuded confidence and allure, making me feel small and ugly.

The boy whispered something to the goddess who held onto his arm while his eyes scanned the room. When his gaze landed on me, my heart stopped. A small gasp escaped my lips as our eyes met, and my body went numb all over as he boldly returned my stare. His eyes . . . they were the *exact* color of diamond-cut emeralds. My whole body began to shake. I couldn't understand it. Those were the eyes from that night in the hospital room—the angel eyes.

He was the boy made of light, the one who'd healed my neck. He was really there.

And he had a girlfriend.

The girl beside him cleared her throat loud enough for me to hear from across the room and elbowed the boy in the side, disdain written plainly on her face. I tore my eyes away from his and blushed all the way to my hairline, making my embarrassment glaringly obvious. I quickly tucked my chin behind my hair and pretended to be invisible.

Doubts began to surface. Maybe this wasn't the boy from the hospital. Maybe it had really been a dream, and the fact that he had the *same* unique eye color was just a strange coincidence. It made more sense than him being real.

I counted to twenty under my breath and peeked from the curtain of my hair to see the boy walking toward me. His girlfriend waited by the buffet table, her arms folding over her full chest. I instantly peered down at my plate and began smashing the food with my fork into an unrecognizable mess.

"Hello, Kirie," he said.

I peeked out from behind my hair and stared up at him mutely. Every nerve in my body sang as his energy flowed over me. I had never met anyone so beautiful and full of *life*. And he knew my *name*.

"I just wanted to tell you how sorry I am for your loss," he said, speaking with a polished British accent that seemed too perfect to be real.

I sat up straighter. "Um, th-thank you. Do I know you?" I stammered, frantically checking my teeth for food with my tongue and fidgeting with the hem of my skirt.

"I went to Rock Canyon High School with you two years ago. I know we weren't close, but I heard about what happened on the news and thought I would stop by and offer my condolences," he explained.

I almost laughed at that. Clearly, he was lying. I would've remembered him. In fact, he would've been the highlight of my high school years, along with at least half the student body and maybe even some of the staff. Someone like him didn't go unnoticed. There was no way I was calling his bluff, though.

"I'm sorry, I forgot your name," I began. My legs bounced up and down beneath the table with nervous energy.

"That's ok. We weren't exactly friends. I'm Luca." He held

out his right hand for me to shake.

I stared at his perfectly formed hand for an embarrassingly long moment before realizing his intent. I quickly reached up and grabbed it. A shock of energy zinged through my body, causing me to jump a little. When I let go, my hand tingled where we'd touched. We stared at one another silently for an awkward moment.

I cleared my throat and said, "Um, thank you for your help before."

"Help?" His dark brows lifted in question.

"Back at the funeral. I kind of lost it there for a minute." I looked down at the mush-covered fork still in my hand and quietly said, "You calmed me down somehow."

"I'm sure I don't know what you mean," he said in his ridiculously prim accent.

I glanced up at him again, and he met my gaze with an earnest look as if urging me to believe him. But I didn't believe him, and I didn't understand why he was lying again. My shoulders suddenly slumped forward as exhaustion washed over me. Burying my parents had taken a toll on my mind and body, and I wasn't emotionally stable enough to play games with mystery male models. Plan C was calling to me stronger than ever.

He must have sensed that I was done with our conversation because he whispered, "Again, I am sorry for your *incredible* loss."

"Th-thank you," I said to the tablecloth.

He nodded before returning to his goddess-like girlfriend. Together, they walked from the dining room, his hand on the small of her back. My insides turned over painfully at the sight of them together—so perfectly beautiful and confident, like they belonged together. The moment they disappeared through the doors, the room seemed darker.

I sat further into my chair, deflated. Not much in my life made sense anymore, but one thing I knew for sure was that Luca was the 'angel' in my hospital room that night. He'd given me light and comfort when I needed it the most. Twice. And I was pretty sure he did something to heal my throat as well.

There was something different about him. Luca. His energy was unlike anything I had ever felt or seen before. It called to whatever was inside me. Who was he, and why did he keep showing up? Why lie about what he'd done at the funeral? A crazy thought broke through my grief and confusion. What if he was like *me?* I dismissed the idea right away. No one was like me.

From across the room, Rylie caught my eye and mouthed, "Are you ready to go?" I nodded my head 'yes,' and Rylie gathered up her family so we could leave.

As we left the clubhouse, we passed by a police officer standing by the entrance. I looked up at him and immediately stopped in my tracks. He was a twenty-something-year-old man with average features and build, but something about his eyes startled me. They were so dark, nearly black. A cold breath swept over me, making me shiver.

"Is everything alright, Miss?" he asked in a friendly tone.

"Y-yes. I'm fine, thank you," I said, breaking eye contact. The hairs on the back of my neck stood on end as I followed the Andersons to the parking lot.

As we headed back to the Anderson's home, I could see a police car following us from the back window. I recognized the dark-eyed officer in the driver's seat. He must've been assigned to watch over me in case the murderer showed back up, I reasoned. The thought was unsettling.

When we reached Rylie's house, the twins bolted out of the van, pulling their suit jackets and ties off before they even made it into the front door. The police cruiser parked just down the street, the lone officer at the wheel.

I thanked the Andersons for their kindness and headed to my room in the basement. I changed into flannel pants and a T-shirt and crawled under the covers. The day's emotions left me raw and exhausted, and I fell asleep quickly. That night, instead of darkness, I dreamt of pools of emeralds.

Donovan 2

The assassin watched the girl from behind a row of cars as a group of tone-deaf children sang a nauseatingly annoying song in front of the twin coffins.

Clearly, he'd made a mistake killing the parents first. It had been all too easy to justify their deaths. He didn't want them coming to help her when she began screaming, now did he?

In hindsight, he should've done them after completing the assignment. Now, he had two useless bodies in coffins and one living, breathing Daughter of Light. He fisted his hands in frustration and anger. No one had ever escaped him before. The humiliation was unbearable.

The assassin's unnaturally sharp eyes zeroed in on her neck where the bruising should have been. Someone had paid her a visit; that much was clear.

Those Society bastards always showed up *afterward* to clean up his mess. The fact that she was still alive and in their care made his blood boil.

The girl suddenly raised her head in his direction and stared right at him. He gave her a half smile, relishing the look of terror on her face. At least he could take pleasure in the fact that he'd significantly dimmed her light.

It wasn't enough, though. Not by half.

The assassin shrouded himself again and walked back to his car, feeling more confident than he had in days. It was only a matter of timing and preparation.

Chapter 7

You know, Kirie, you don't have to go back today. You can wait a bit longer if you need to," Rylie said at the breakfast table on Monday morning.

"If I stay locked up in the basement any longer, I may go crazier than I already feel. I need something else to think about." I gingerly lifted some eggs to my mouth. My appetite was slowly returning, but food still made me nauseous.

It had been two weeks since the funeral, and I'd spent most of that time either in the downstairs bedroom hiding from phantom black-eyed monsters and staring at the unopened letter I'd found in Mom's bedside table, or at the police station providing testimony about that night . . . again. The authorities were actively searching for the murderer and kept asking for yet *another* statement. They had no leads, and I needed a change in scenery.

"Well, if you're sure. The girls and I have already agreed to intercept anybody that might try to harass you. The news hasn't mentioned your story for a few days, so hopefully, everyone's moving on," Rylie said.

"Thanks, Ry. I don't know what I would do without you," I said, swallowing down a bite of eggs before it got stuck in my tightening throat. I washed it down with orange juice.

The twins ran wildly through the house, hitting each other with their plastic lightsabers while Rylie and I made our lunches and grabbed our backpacks. I checked my bag to ensure Mom's letter was inside for the fiftieth time before zipping it up and slinging it over my shoulder. I reached up and twisted one of the diamond earrings in my ears. Like the letter, I always had them on me.

Mr. Anderson had brought my car to their house the week before so I could drive us to school without bothering Mrs. Anderson for a ride.

She has enough to worry about.

A soccer ball sailing over my head and into the wall behind me, distracting me from my thoughts.

"Kaden! No soccer in the house!" she yelled from the other room.

"That wasn't me. Brody did it," Kaden lied.

"Did NOT!" his brother protested, hands on hips.

Mrs. Anderson rounded the corner looking harried and disheveled with a pair of pajama pants clenched in her fist. One of the boys must have stripped again. She stopped and huffed out a breath when she saw that Rylie and I were about to leave. "Kirie, are you sure you're going to be okay today? No one would blame you if you waited a few more weeks."

"Mom, she's fine," Rylie whined. "The girls and I are going to watch her back. Stop worrying so much. She isn't even *your* kid!"

"I can't help it. I've known Kirie since she was little." She turned to me and held both of my hands in hers, "Call me if you need anything, and I'll be there in ten minutes, okay?"

"I appreciate it, Mrs. Anderson," I said. Her show of motherly affection made me miss my mom so much at that moment; my chest ached, and unshed tears clouded my eyes.

"Oh, call me Melissa, honey." She dropped my hands and walked us to the door. "Have a great day, girls." Mrs. Anderson waved at us from the front porch until we drove out of sight.

As I drove to school, I saw my ever-present police detail in my rearview mirror. The dark-eyed officer had been my shadow ever since the wake. If his presence was meant to help me feel safer, it wasn't working. He was creepy. I focused on the road ahead and pretended he wasn't there, as I did every day.

The student parking lot was nearly full, so we parked behind the gym next to the slackers and early morning smokers. Rylie and I grabbed our bags from the back seat and began our long trek to the front doors. It was early November, and the air was cold and biting. Rylie wore a long, tan coat, ready for the season. I shivered in Mom's thin cardigan which was inadequate for the weather. I hugged my arms tightly around my chest and quickened my pace.

"Sorry, I should've reminded you to wear a coat," Ryle said, noticing my discomfort.

"It's okay. We're almost inside now anyway," I shrugged.

In front of the main doors, Kaylee and Cassidy were waiting for us. Their faces were stern, and they bounced on their toes like they were about to enter a boxing ring. They flanked Rylie and me like a pair of bodyguards when we approached.

"Are you ready for this?" Cassidy asked as we stood in front of the main entrance.

"Well, I'm already here. I might as well go inside," I said with fake confidence that I didn't feel.

"We won't let anyone mess with you. Promise," Kaylee said and linked arms with me.

Together, we walked through the tall glass doors into the main hallway. Rylie and I arrived a bit late which meant the halls were already filled with kids hurrying to their first-period classes. As we pushed through the crowd, clusters of students stopped and stared at us. Well . . . at me.

"What are *you* looking at?" Kaylee yelled at a freshman boy who stood at his locker with his mouth hanging open.

"Nothing! S-sorry." He stammered and ran off in the

opposite direction.

"Honestly, freshmen get smaller and dumber every year. Don't let these idiots bother you, Kirie," Kaylee said loud enough for a group of girls nearby to hear. They quickly peered down at the ground and pretended they weren't just gawking at us. Kaylee could be a little scary at times, which was one of the things I liked most about her.

When we reached my first-period classroom, Rylie, Kaylee, and Cassidy hugged me and offered to walk me to my next class. I assured them it wasn't necessary, and we agreed to meet again at lunch. I waved goodbye to them, took a deep breath, and entered my A.P. History class. The late bell rang out just as I sat in my front-row seat.

"Good morning, everyone!" A man in a sweater vest and bow tie I didn't recognize called out. I glanced around the room for my usual teacher, Mr. Maloy, but he was nowhere to be seen. Substitute, I reasoned. "Please quiet down and put your cellphones *away*." The man gave a boy in the back row a meaningful look.

The teacher was in his late 60s with gray hair, a domed belly, and half-moon glasses that he looked over more than through. He appeared more like a nerdy professor than a high school teacher.

"Welcome to class everyone. My name is Dr. Johnson. Mr. Maloy has taken ill, and I'm his replacement for the foreseeable future. Let me introduce myself. I have a doctorate in philosophy from Cambridge University and have traveled the world extensively over the past thirty years teaching youth. When I got the call to teach world history here at Rock Canyon High, I jumped at the opportunity."

I stared up at the man, transfixed. There was something *extra* about his presence that I couldn't quite put a name to. The light in the room seemed to cling to him, making him stand out against the drab surroundings. It reminded me of the power radiating off Luca and his girlfriend, though Dr. Johnson's energy wasn't quite as powerful. I chewed on my bottom lip and narrowed my eyes. What were the chances that this was just some crazy coincidence?

"Alright, let's get into it," he said, clapping his hands once. "Raise your hand if you have heard of the Dead Sea Scrolls."

It was Monday morning. Basically, most of my fellow students were either half asleep or mindlessly surfing on their smartphones under their desks. "Old Kirie" would've raised her hand and said something equally nerdy and profound. She would've ignored the snickers from the back row. I was no longer that girl. New Kirie stared at her desk and waited for someone else to answer.

"Anyone?" Dr. Johnson asked, gazing around the room with a hopeful expression. I studied the wood grains on my desk as if the secrets of the universe might be written there.

"Ok. I guess I'll have to call names at random." He trailed his finger down a sheet of paper on his desk and called out, "Kirie." *Damn.* "What do you know about the Dead Sea Scrolls?"

The girls in the back began twittering like satanic canaries. I pulled the sleeves of Mom's cardigan over my cold fingers and looked up. "The Dead Sea Scrolls were found in a cave near the Dead Sea by a goat herder in 1947. They're believed to contain early copies of the Bible written by a Jewish group that lived between 200 B.C.E and 68 C.E. Due to age, many of the scrolls had disintegrated, but some were partially preserved." I ignored the snort from the back row. I understood their derision. What *normal* teenager knew that kind of stuff? I pulled my hair forward to shield myself from their stares.

"Well put, Kirie. Thank you. Today, we're going to learn about one portion of those scrolls called the 'War Scroll." Several boys in the back perked up at the mention of the word "war." "Seven scrolls were originally found in what's now considered Cave One. One of these scrolls contained what some believe is a prophecy of the Apocalypse." Several hands shot up in the air.

"Yes?" Dr. Johnson said, calling on one of the whispering girls in the back.

"Do you mean like the movie 'Armageddon?'" she said

sweetly. I tried not to roll my eyes.

"Not at all." Dr. Johnson replied bluntly. Jessica's posture deflated, and I smiled a little. "Most of the movies and books these days view the end of days as being brought on by some major natural disaster that destroys the earth. However, the War Scroll describes an end to darkness and evil. In fact, the War Scroll is also known as *The War of the Sons of Light*."

My heart skipped a beat, and the air grew heavy, making it hard to breathe. Suddenly, the classroom around me faded into darkness until all I could see was a pair of black eyes staring down at me. The killer's thin lips curved into an evil grin and his words filled my mind.

"Killing always brings me so much joy . . . but there's nothing quite like extinguishing a Daughter of Light.*"*

I began to shake as hopelessness filled my chest, breaking out in a cold sweat as the light began to drain from my body.

"Kirie?" Dr. Johnson touched my shoulder, and light and sound came rushing back in. Dr. Johnson stood over my desk with an expression of concern. I stared up at him with wide eyes. "Are you all right? You look as though you've seen a ghost."

Every eye in the room was on me. I sank low in my seat. My cheeks were twin flames.

"I'm f-fine," I said, clearing my throat. "I just forgot to eat breakfast and got a little lightheaded."

"Would you like to go to the nurse's office?" he asked kindly, looking over his ridiculous half-moon glasses.

"I think I'll be okay, thanks."

"Well, if you are sure . . ." He said with raised eyebrows.

I nodded and he moved back to the center of the room to continue his lecture. I kept my eyes on my desk to avoid the other students' stares. The girls in the back whispering and giggling again. I really hated high school.

"As I was saying, the War of the Sons of Light was a prophecy of sorts detailing the eventual defeat of what they referred to as the Sons of Darkness."

Dr. Johnson turned on the projector and pulled a white screen down in front of the chalkboard at the head of the room. A picture of an ancient-looking paper with curled edges and full of holes appeared on the wall. It was obviously ancient.

As Dr. Johnson talked, the words "Sons of Light" played over and over in my head. The murderer had called me a "Daughter of Light" that night. At the time, I had assumed they were just the ramblings of a deranged psycho-murderer. Now, I wasn't so sure.

"According to the scroll," Dr. Johnson continued, "the war between the Sons of Light and the Sons of Darkness would be broken up into several stages or battles, spanning thousands of years. During the final stage of the war, angels and individuals with special abilities would aid both sides, but in the end, divine intervention would result in the demolishment of the Sons of Darkness.”

“So, you’re saying a war will be fought by a group of supermen, sort of like The Avengers?” A scrawny boy with bad acne blurted out.

“Well, if you must equate ancient prophecy to modern pop culture, then, yes, it’s sort of like The Avengers, in a way. Although, the scroll doesn’t describe what powers these beings might possess,” Dr. Johnson explained.

“That’s awesome!” The boy said in total awe. Ten to one said he had Spiderman sheets on his bed at home.

“Yes, completely awesome, for sure,” Dr. Johnson indulged. “Your assignment this week is to study ‘The War Scroll’ and write a summary and review. This assignment’s due next Monday morning, bright and early.”

The bell rang out, startling me. I stood on jelly legs. My body was still unsteady from my episode earlier, and I swayed a little on my feet.

“Kirie, are you sure you’re well?” Dr. Johnson asked as he walked me toward the door.

I paused in the doorway. “I think so. There was just something about your lecture that caught me off guard.” I shook my head and stared down at my feet. “Sorry, I know that doesn’t make any sense.”

“On the contrary! I think it makes perfect sense, given

current events. If you need to talk or bounce any ideas off me for this assignment, I'm free anytime," he said with an expression that seemed to hold more than surface meaning.

"Thanks. I'll keep that in mind." I waved weakly and headed down the hall to my next class with a strange feeling in my chest.

The rest of the day, I was preoccupied with thoughts of light, darkness, and end-of-day wars. I didn't even notice the stares and whispers that followed behind me or the black eyes watching me from the shadows.

Chapter 8

The words **"Sons** of Light" were on replay in my head like a bad song for the rest of the week. I knew it had to be a coincidence. There was no way this ancient prophecy, if you could even call it that, could have anything to do with my parents' deaths. After all, how could a modern-day murderer be connected to an ancient prophecy that had been hidden in a cave for thousands of years?

And yet, something about the way he called me a "Daughter of Light" unsettled me. Ugh. It was just too weird. I'd lost sleep all week thinking over the possibilities and improbabilities of it all.

On the bright side, I'd made it through the school week with only a handful of flashbacks and bathroom stall panic attacks. Given my fragile emotional state, I counted that as a win. By Friday, nearly everyone had lost interest in my real-life horror story, a modern-day miracle made possible by social media and smartphones.

Art was my last class of the week, and our term projects were due. I'd nearly finished the painting I had been working on since before my parents' deaths, adding more greys and blacks to my original work.

The lower half of the canvas was full of shadows and twisted grey objects. I hid two black eyes behind an overturned chair near the bottom of the canvas, a representation, I supposed, of the soulless eyes that seemed to follow my every move. The dark picture faded to a bright summer sky in various shades of white and yellow. There, amid the billowy clouds floating across the canvas, were a pair of brilliant green emeralds.

Luca had been on my mind that week almost as much as the "War Scroll." There were so many things I'd wanted to ask him since the funeral. Why had he visited me in the hospital the night of the attack? How had he calmed me down during the funeral? Did he know what I was? The unending, unanswered questions fought for space in my mind, like people elbowing one another for space in a crowded room.

"Your painting is really inspiring, Kirie."

I jumped and put a hand over my now racing heart. I spun in my seat to see my art teacher standing with her head cocked to one side, appraising my painting. Mrs. Balderman was a heavy-set, middle-aged woman who embraced her natural side, and by that, I mean she'd never shaved her legs, worn makeup, or styled her salt and pepper-colored hair. The look fit her free spirit perfectly.

"Thank you," I replied with a shrug.

"I love the contrast between light and shadows. What was your inspiration?"

I turned back around to my canvas, not knowing how to respond. Art teachers were always doing this, looking for deeper meaning in everything. In this particular case, I supposed the significance did run deep. I wasn't going to tell her that, though.

"I guess I just wanted to study the contrast between light and dark," I said, swallowing the lump forming in my throat. "The meaning is left to interpretation." My answer seemed to satisfy her because she nodded and moved on to the next student, her peasant skirt swaying behind her like the swish of a cat's tail. I quietly breathed a sigh of relief.

Since our projects were due that day, we were allowed to relax and wander around the room to see what other students had created. All around me, students were either sharing the latest gossip with their friends or texting on their smartphones. The old Kirie might have stood up and mingled a bit, but post-trauma Kirie sat alone.

I pulled my cellphone out of my back pocket and briefly considered messaging Parisxxxi8. Though we'd only ever talked about science, our conversations had been the highlight of each day. With a heavy sigh, I slipped my phone back into my pocket. I hadn't had the energy to contact Paris since the attack. My interest in biophotonics seemed to have died with my parents and my dream of inventing a safe X-ray machine suddenly seemed small and selfish.

Instead, I turned my thoughts to the "War Scroll" and its possible connection to my attacker. I needed more information so I could reason it all out. I needed time in the library to do more research.

After the final bell, I walked through the crowded hallways toward my locker. Rylie was already standing at hers, haphazardly stuffing her books onto the high shelves and grabbing her coat. In the past week, she and I made a routine of meeting at our lockers at the end of school so we could drive home together.

She turned to me and smiled. "Hey, Kirie! Ready to go?"

"Actually, I was thinking of staying after school to do some research in the library for my history paper. Could you grab a ride with one of the girls?" I felt guilty ditching her at the last minute, but my need to find answers could no longer be ignored.

"You want to study at school on a Friday night?" she asked with a confused look.

"You know me, Ry," I said with a shrug. "Is it really that weird?"

Rylie shook her head and laughed. "No, it's not. You can be such a dork sometimes." She threw her arms around me, squeezing hard. "But I love you anyway."

"Love you, too," I whispered in return.

Rylie stepped back and hitched her bag over her shoulder. "I'll tell my mom you're going to be home late. She'll freak out if you don't come home right after school. I swear, that woman worries more about you than she does her only daughter!" she said in faux disgust.

"I don't mind," I said, nearly reminding her that she still *had* a mother, unlike me. That wouldn't be fair, though.

"Well, I better catch up with Kaylee and Cassidy before they leave. I'll see you back at the house tonight?"

"I won't stay out that late. The library closes at 9:30," I replied.

"'Kay, bye!" She blew me a kiss and skipped down the hallway toward the exit.

I carefully put my textbooks in my locker and made my way to the library. The crowded hallways were beginning to empty as students either headed home or to the locker rooms to prepare for basketball and volleyball practices.

Unsurprisingly, I was the only one moving in the direction of the library, a lone fish moving upstream. How many students were there, really, who wanted to spend their Friday afternoon in the school library? The answer was clear when I entered the silent library: just one. On the bright side, I didn't have to wait in line to use a computer.

I found a spot in one of the computer cubbies near the corner and hung my things over the back of my seat. I reached into my bag and pulled out Mom's cardigan and slid it over my shoulders. Next, I set the unopened letter my mother had written to me on the desk beside me. Feeling steadier with her things surrounding me, I rolled up my sleeves and got to work.

First, I searched for books and websites with information on the Dead Sea Scrolls as a whole. Once I better understood their origin and history, I narrowed my focus to the War Scroll itself. The first section of the scroll detailed the correct way to wage war. The scroll's author described in painstaking detail everything from the type of formations the soldiers should use to the banners they should display. None of it was particularly helpful or interesting. I moved on.

Part of the challenge in researching this scroll was weeding through varying interpretations of it. Some scholars thought The War Scroll was a war general's instruction book on battle, while others believed it was an end-of-days prophecy.

Those theorists claimed the scroll prophesied a centuries-long war between the "Sons of Light" and the "Sons of Darkness." The war would be divided into seven smaller battles. The light and darkness would win three battles each. That was where the scholars believed the "end-of-days" nonsense came in. During that seventh and final battle, each side would receive aid from angels and those with supernatural powers. In the end, the light would win, saved by divine intervention, of course. Turned out, the superhero-obsessed boy from my class was right, after all. It *was* like The Avengers.

I pushed back from the computer and put my hands in my hair. This whole thing was completely insane. Angels and darkness? The end of the world? Ridiculous.

But was it? I stared down at my palm and let the energy warm my skin. Warm light filled the small cubicle. Didn't I glow? Wasn't *that* ridiculous too? Maybe, but it was also true.

I shook my head in disgust. I was far from being some prophesied superhero who battled darkness. The idea that there was some real-life connection between an ancient scroll and my parents' murders was nothing more than a desperate attempt to make sense out of a senseless act of violence. My shoulders sagged forward. This was a stupid waste of time.

I let out a long sigh and sat upright again in my chair. Stupid or not, I still had a paper to write.

Memory, hither come

And tune your merry tones;

And, while upon the wind,

Your music floats,

I'll pore upon the stream,

Where sighting lovers dream,

And fish for fancies as they pass

Within the watery glass.

I'll drink of the clear stream,

And hear the linnet's song;

And there I'll lie and dream

The day along:

And, when night comes, I'll go

To places fit for woe,

Walking along the darken'd valley,

With silent Melancholy.

"Song: Memory, Hither Come"

By William Blake

Chapter 9

y the time I left the library, the hallways were eerily silent save a soft whirring of the Zamboni-like floor buffers driven by sleepy custodians. I hitched my bag over my shoulder and hurried toward the front exit, the slapping of my soles on the linoleum floor echoing down the long, cavernous hallways.

It had grown dark outside, and the fall air had a sharp sting. I shivered as I made my way through the empty student parking lot. My ever-present police escort sat blanketed in shadow at the back of the lot beneath a mature oak tree. The engine was off, but I could see the faint outline of the officer sitting behind the wheel. His dark form was as still as a mannequin, as if he'd fallen asleep waiting for me. I would've felt guilty for making him wait so long if it weren't for the fact that he creeped me out so thoroughly.

I kept one eye on the squad car as I fished around my bag for my key ring. I came up with handfuls of pencils, erasers, and hair ties but no key. The lights in the lot were dim, making it hard to see inside the shadowed corners of my bag. With a frustrated sigh, I tossed it onto the hood of my car. Looking back at the officer once more, I created a small halo of light around my palm and illuminated the inside of my bag. Instantly, the silver key glinted at me, wedged beneath the edge of one of my textbooks.

I quickly extinguished my light and unlocked the door, casting wary glances around the dark lot. It was all too easy to imagine dark things hiding behind the trees and bushes. As I locked myself in the car, I shook my head at "Sleeping Officer." Fat good he'd do me if the murderer decided to show up again. I'd probably be dead before he woke up from his nap.

I started the engine and drove toward Rylie's house, taking some satisfaction as I left my police escort behind. With a heavy foot and white-knuckled grip on the wheel, I drove along the empty two-lane highway that wound through the nature reserve separating Rylie's neighborhood from the high school. During the day, it was just an innocent windy road through barren hills, but at night, it was a dark and desolate wasteland, filled only with chirping cicadas and coyote howls that echoed across the moonlit hills.

Needing something to calm my frayed nerves, I turned the radio dial and found a classical station. Bach filled the car. The familiar chords loosened my tight muscles and my hands relaxed on the steering wheel. Soon, Bach was replaced by George Gershwin, Mom's favorite composer. My home was often filled with the jazzy sounds of his 1920s compositions. Memories of her floated to the surface.

"Kirie, come help me make this salad. You've been working on that paper for hours now." The trilling cords of "The Man I Love" played softly from the radio. She swayed in a circle with her arms outstretched as if she were dancing with some invisible partner. "It's not good for your eyes to stare at your laptop that long," she sang over one shoulder.

I rolled my eyes. "I know, I know. I'm almost done, I promise," I lied. I'd been tweaking my thesis for hours, but I still wasn't happy with it.

Mom stopped dancing and put a fist to her hip. "Kirie! Don't make me pull the mom card here. I haven't talked to you all day, and I'm starting to get jealous of a stupid computer," she said, giving me her best glare. I almost laughed. It was hard to take her seriously when she got upset. She looked like an angry kitten.

I put my hands up in surrender. "Ok, you win. I'm putting it away." I closed the laptop and joined her in the kitchen.

"That's my girl," she said, wrapping a slender arm around my shoulders. "You know, it won't matter a bit which college you get into if you can't feed yourself when you get there. Come on; I'll teach you how to

make the perfect Waldorf salad." She turned me toward the kitchen and showed me "the correct" way to peel and chop an apple.

A pair of headlights appeared in my rearview mirror, returning me to the present. As the car drew closer, I could see the outline of the row of lights across the top. My police stalker must have woken up from his nap. I sighed, and the ghosts filling the cab dispelled.

I shifted in my seat and tightened my grip on the wheel. Not for the first time, I reminded myself that the officer was there to keep me safe. The squad car followed at a safe distance as we weaved through the windy roads. Suddenly, the headlights on the cruiser turned off. Without warning, the officer accelerated, the sound of his revving engine aggressive and threatening. I waited for him to pull into the other lane, pass me, or something. Instead, he aimed directly for my bumper.

I swore and pressed the gas pedal to the floor in a desperate attempt to put some space between our two bumpers, but it was too late. My body was thrown forward as the squad car slammed into me from behind. The impact caused my car to veer into the oncoming lane, and I instinctively yanked the wheel to the right to compensate.

In one swift movement, time and gravity reversed. My backpack floated past my head as the ground became the sky. My windshield careened toward the gravel, and I squeezed my eyes shut just before the hood crashed into it. Instantly, I was suspended again only to be thrown back against my seatbelt.

My stomach was thrust up into my throat and then down to my feet over and over again. My screams were drowned out by the screeching of metal and crunching of gravel as my car rolled across the land like tumbleweed. The car slid along the dirt and halted on its hood. My world stopped spinning.

The car popped and hissed as it settled, and the chaos from moments before wove into a dark silence. A soft wind blew through the broken windows like a sigh. Somewhere in the distance, the cry of a hawk pierced the stillness.

All at once, time rushed forward. I cried out in pain and fear as the realization of what just happened flooded over me. I'd been in a car accident. No, not an accident. Officer Stalker hit me! He *hit me!* The man who'd been my shadow for weeks had run me off the road, and he was likely still out there for all I knew.

The seatbelt held true, tethering me to my seat. I dangled toward the ground like a broken marionette as hot tears rolled down my face, creeping into my hairline. I put a trembling hand to my mouth to keep myself from puking. Nothing seemed broken, but my head and shoulders ached fiercely. I reached up and touched my throbbing forehead, and my fingers came away warm and sticky.

I breathed in deeply. In. Out. In. Out.

"It's okay. I'm okay," I whispered in the dark.

With shaky hands, I took another deep breath and pushed the release button on my seatbelt. At first, it didn't budge. The pressure from my body weight strengthened its hold on me. I pressed harder until my thumb began to throb, and it finally released. I landed shoulder-first onto the car's crumpled hood. Groaning, I sat up in the small space and lit the cab with a shaky palm. I searched around for my backpack and found it smashed between the passenger seat and the car's hood. I grunted as I worked to get it free. I pulled out my phone and mom's letter, slipped them into my back pocket, and tossed the bag aside.

The windshield was gone, smashed into a million tiny pieces of shattered glass that glittered like black diamonds in the glow of my light. It was beautiful in a way only destruction can be. I crawled out of the compacted opening on wobbly hands and knees like a baby colt. The shards pierced my hands and knees. Fresh blood budded on my hands, making them slippery against the coarse dirt.

Free of the wreckage, I took a deep breath, the cold air burning my lungs, and turned in a circle, searching for the police cruiser. The night had grown darker, and I could see no more than a few feet in front of me, even with my light. I raised my palm, and the wreckage came into view. Steam and smoke rose with a quiet hiss from the crunched tin can that was once my car.

The weight of its loss hit me firmly in the chest, squeezing the cold air from my paralyzed lungs. Barry had given me that car, and although it was nothing special, it was yet another lost link to my parents. Fresh grief washed over me like a tidal wave, and it felt as if I'd lost them all over again. I released my light and backed away from the car, cradling my bloody hands to my chest.

A coyote's howl echoed across the barren plain, a warning that there were predators nearby.

I pulled my cellphone from my back pocket. The phone blinked on as blood flowed over my left eye, blinding me. I reached up, swiped it away with the sleeve of my sweater, and dialed 9-1-1. Calling emergency services was quickly becoming a habit.

It rang once, and then the line went dead. I stared down at the blank screen, pushing the power button repeatedly in vain. A strong sense of Deja vu crept up my spine. I sent a bit of charge from my blood-slick hand into the device, but it was as if the energy cells were unable to accept the power. Just like the night of my parents' deaths.

Dread slithered through me. I wiped my palm along my jeans to clear away the blood and raised an illuminated palm in sweeping arcs. Near the road, the shape of a car came into view. My light touched the tires first, then it reflected off the word *Police*. I raised my trembling hand higher, and the face of the officer came into clear focus. He sat motionless behind the wheel. His dark eyes absorbed my light, reflecting nothing back. Visible tendrils of darkness swirled around his unnaturally still frame. He seemed completely unsurprised by my glowing hand.

I gasped.

I had been so stupid. Detectives Peterson and Wadman never mentioned a police escort. No one had. I'd just assumed he was assigned to me. The officer had the same black eyes as my attacker, the same darkness. They were *the same*. I'd been right to fear him.

It was all so stupidly clear now that he'd been planning this from the beginning. This stretch of road was empty for miles. There was no one to hear my screams and nowhere to go. It was the perfect place to make someone disappear.

I stepped back slowly, afraid to turn my back on him. I had two choices: run down the road and hope someone would drive by and pick me up, or run and hide. Common sense told me if I ran down the road, the officer would simply run me over with his cruiser and then bury me in the hills.

Really, there was only *one* option. I knew from driving this road every day that a dried-up riverbed was nearby, far away from the road and inaccessible by car. I lowered my hand, let the darkness fall over me like a cloak, and turned to run.

Pure adrenaline shot through my veins, forcing me forward

with more speed than I knew I was capable of. Behind me, a car door opened and slammed shut. Quick footsteps ground into the gravel at my back. My heart began to pump harder. I was being chased!

"Crap, crap, crap," I chanted under my breath. I pushed myself harder, picking up speed.

I didn't realize I'd made it to the edge of the riverbed until my feet began to slip down the steep decline. My arms flailed out in search of something to hold onto, and just before I fell face-first into the ravine, my hands grasped the rough surface of a tree branch. I held on tightly and steadied myself.

Carefully, I swung my legs over the edge and slid down the loose gravel to the bottom of the ravine. Pain seared through my cut palms as twigs and gravel drug into my wounds. I bit my lips hard to keep myself from crying out, and a coppery taste filled my mouth and coated my teeth.

As soon as my feet hit the bottom, I ran again. I stumbled over the uneven ground time and time again, but my panic thrust me forward. All around me, the darkness came to life. Indefinable shapes swirled in the dark recesses of the ravine. I itched to use my light to banish the living shadows but didn't dare reveal my location. With gritted teeth, I pushed past the dancing shapes.

The heavy pounding behind me grew louder, and I knew the officer would be on me in mere moments. I turned my head back to look, and my body collided with a large bush, throwing me onto my back. The footsteps were just feet behind me. I rolled beneath the bare branches of the bush. The fibers of Mom's cardigan snagged on the branches as I curled into the fetal position.

Squeezing my eyes shut, I listened for his approach, but my racing heart pounded in my ears like a bass drum, drowning out every other sound. Surely, he couldn't see me hidden there in such pure darkness. He'd race right by.

Several seconds passed with no sound. The night was silent as if it, too, were holding its breath. A minute passed, then two. The adrenaline that had been coursing through my body began to seep from me, as did the numbness it had brought with it. I raised my aching hands to my chest and gently cradled them close to my body. My head wound throbbed with the heavy beat of my heart. Twigs and branches dug into my back, adding to my discomfort as the seconds passed, each ticking away like a timebomb. It took all my concentration not to wiggle into a more comfortable position.

Suddenly, the fall air turned to ice. Violent shivers seized my aching muscles, sending sharp pains through my shoulders.

As if on the wind, came the sound of whistling. It was a lazy tune better suited for bright Sunday afternoons. Heavy footsteps strolled casually along the bottom of the riverbed toward my hiding place, the whistling growing louder with each step. My shaking increased as new terror gripped me with razor-sharp teeth, and I held my hands to my mouth to stop myself from screaming out.

Please don't find me. Please don't find me.

I feared he could see me. Like my parents' murderer, this man seemed to be made for the night.

A deep voice chuckled in the darkness. "Kirie, Kirie, Kirie. Look at you, hiding in a bush like a little rabbit."

A hand reached into the bush and gripped a fistful of my hair. The scream I'd been holding burst out of me. He dragged me out into the open, tearing Mom's still-tangled cardigan from my body. I kicked and hit the man with all my strength, but it was like fighting a brick wall. He turned me around until my back was pressed to his uniformed chest. The officer wrapped his large biceps around my torso, pinning my arms to my sides tightly as if in a lover's embrace.

"Now, now, Kirie," He whispered in my ear. His lips brushed against my earlobe. I cringed back. "Relax. I promise to make it quick."

"P-please," I sobbed.

"Shhh. It will only hurt for a moment." He laid his chin on my head and rocked me back and forth gently as if to an imaginary tune.

Shink. The sound of a switchblade sliding free from its

sheath pierced the air, and every cell in my body froze. Tears rolled down my cheeks as inky tendrils of despair seeped into my veins. I was going to die the same way my parents did, and I was powerless to stop it this time.

"That's a good girl," He crooned. He turned me around so that we were chest to chest. With one hand fisted in my hair, he pulled my head back, exposing my neck. He held the knife's edge to my throat. The cold metal bit into my skin.

"Such a waste," He sighed dramatically. He pressed the knife deeper, its edge breaking skin. "A beautiful girl like you should be enjoyed first." He ran his other hand down my spine and pressed me closer to him. I strained my neck backward to avoid pressing further into the blade's edge. "But orders are orders."

Anger flared in me at his suggestive words, and a fire lit within my chest. My skin grew hot, casting a halo of light around our entwined bodies. I stared boldly back at him and let the pressure build inside my center until I thought it would break me. With one last scathing look, I let the fire go.

The night sky lit up as if it were suddenly day. The light wasn't just coming from my hands this time, but all over my body. The officer cried out and pushed me away from him, and the knife fell from his hands, clattering to the dirt. I landed hard on my back, and my light dimmed slightly. I held on to the remaining energy coursing through my skin, desperate to not let the darkness back in.

"You little bitch!" he roared. I rolled onto my hands and knees, searching wildly for the knife. My fingers met metal and I held on tight. The officer sprang from the ground and rushed at me as I turned around, arm raised. He collided with me hard, and the knife slid smoothly into his chest.

Time stopped.

We stared at each other in mutual shock. My eyes traveled down to the knife's handle that was now sticking out of the middle of his chest. Warm liquid flowed over my hand, making the knife's hilt slick. With a startled cry, I dropped my hand and stumbled back. The officer looked down at his chest one more time and then back at me.

"Aw, shit."

His face drained of all color, and he dropped onto the ground. He released one final, rattling breath and lay motionless in the dirt. A red stain quickly spread around his body like a macabre bullseye.

I stared at the lifeless body at my feet. I didn't need to check for a pulse to know that he was gone. By now, I was well acquainted with death.

My mind went blank, and my legs were numb. I fell forward onto my knees and let the darkness swallow me whole.

Chapter 10

hough my body lay rooted to the ground, my mind wandered amongst the heavens, untethered. Time and space lost their bind on me as multi-colored constellations filled my vision and a blanket of twinkling stars spread across an expansive sky. Somewhere in my subconscious mind, I knew something important had happened, that it should mean something to me, but I was unbound from earthly cares.

I floated in a numb haze before I slowly became aware of my body again. Gravel dug into my back and the cold night air clung to my sweat, freezing my muscles and bones.

Previously veiled, the full moon now shone down on me like a spotlight. I turned my head, the gravel grinding into my scalp, and saw the still form of a man lying in the dirt mere feet away. The moon's rays reflected off a glassy pool of black liquid surrounding his unmoving body.

Fear tightened around my chest. The pressure increased and

the air around me grew thinner. I tried to inhale deeply, but my paralyzed lungs would not obey.

I pushed myself to sitting, gasping like a fish out of water as the world around me spun. My arms and legs began to lose feeling and my vision narrowed to a point. Violent shivers assaulted my body, and the muscles in my shoulders and back cramped and spasmed as I fought to breathe.

I cried out for my mom, needing her more than ever. Her face filled my mind, not dead and cold like the last time I'd seen her, but happy and alive. She smiled at me, and her image sparked a tiny flame in my chest. I grasped that minute ember and wrapped myself around it, letting it grow. It spread through my torso into my arms and legs, slowly easing the pressure on my chest.

As my body warmed and the shock began to wear off, the gravity of my situation settled over me, heavy and painful. I'd killed a man. *Killed him.* And not just any man. A police officer. I'd never even gotten in a fight before, let alone hurt someone.

I had to get out of there. I had to hide from what I'd done.

I rolled onto my knees and slipped my phone from my back pocket. It blinked on as soon as my hands brushed along its cold, smooth surface. The officer was dead, and my phone was not.

I pressed the side button. "Call Rylie," I whispered.

The automated female voice shattered the silence. "Calling

Rylie Anderson."

The phone rang once.

"Hi, Kirie!" Rylie chirped. "You almost home? I was thinking we could watch a movie and stay up late. Or we could watch The Office again if you want."

"Rylie!" I whispered. "I need your help." Hot, sticky tears rolled down my face.

"Where are you? It sounds like you're outside. What are you doing coming home from the library so late? I *knew* you would lose track of time. It's a good thing I told my mom you were going to be late because she'd totally be freaking out right now!" she said all in one breath.

"RYLIE!" I yelled, slapping a hand over my mouth. My eyes darted around for hidden listeners, but the night remained still. I lowered my hand and cupped it around the phone. "I was a-attacked. I need your help."

"What?" She shrieked. I held the phone away from my ear. "Kirie, you need to call the police *right now!*"

"I don't think the police are going to be very helpful in this situation." My eyes traveled to the motionless police officer lying still in a dark pool of blood. "I can't explain right now. I need you to come pick me up."

"Kirie, I really think you need to call the police. Tell me where you are, and I'll . . ." She paused mid-sentence. Her voice dropped. "That's weird. The power just went out."

Fresh dread settled over me like a cold, wet blanket. Their power was *out*. Just like the night my parents died. Just like my phone when the officer was alive and near. Warning bells were screaming in my ears.

Crash.

"Ouch!" Rylie yelped.

My stomach forced its way into my throat. Had the killer gotten to the Andersons, too? "Rylie! Are you okay?"

"Yeah, I'm fine. I just ran into something. Oww, that hurt!" she whined pitifully.

I took a steadying breath. "Rylie, listen to me. Call 9-1-1 and lock the doors. I think someone might have cut the power."

"What are you talking about? What's going on? You're really starting to scare me, Kir."

Riiing

A cellphone rang out in the dark, and I nearly dropped my phone. I spun around and saw a light shining from the dead officer's front pocket.

Riiing

My mind raced. Perhaps the person calling had ordered the officer to kill me. But who and why? I had to find out.

"Rylie, call the police and lock your doors, okay?"

"But . . ."

I disconnected the call and slid my phone back into my rear pocket. I knelt beside the body and hesitated, my hand just above the officer's glowing cellphone. The thought of touching any part of his body again made me physically ill.

Riiing

"Just do it, Kirie!" I commanded myself.

Reaching into his pocket with my fingertips, I wiggled the smartphone free. The illuminated screen read "blocked." I swiped my thumb over it and put the phone to my ear.

"Is it done?" A deep voice growled.

My blood ran cold. I knew that voice. The rough British accent was as distinct and terrifying as my nightmares of him. I gripped the phone tighter in my stinging hand and held my breath.

"Cole!" he growled. "You'd better not have mucked this up. Is. it. done?"

I quickly bunched my shirt and rubbed it across the screen, creating static. Then I disconnected the call and dropped the phone as if it'd sprouted fangs. My heart beat wildly. Cellphones were easy to track; Mom had taught me that. I bent down and picked up a melon-sized rock. Positioning it high above the phone, I brought it down onto its glass surface with a satisfying *crunch*. I swept the broken pieces under a nearby bush, praying my parents' murderer hadn't tracked its location yet.

My eyes strayed to the body lying in the dirt nearby, and a strong sense of guilt washed over me. It had been an accident.

Even if it hadn't been, he'd been trying to kill me. It was either him or me. Still, I'd taken a life. It was a thing too big, too horrible to comprehend.

Accident or not, it looked bad for me. I was at the scene of a crime with the victim's blood all over my body and clothes. I could tell them that it was self-defense, but I was the only witness, and he was a *cop*. Or not. Who knew? Either way, there was a real chance that I could be charged with *murder*. I had to get out of there.

I pulled myself back up the ravine, using shrubs and bushes as leverage. Every muscle in my body burned, and my mangled hands screamed in pain as I fought my way to the top.

I hoisted myself over the uneven ledge and lay on my side, sucking in labored breaths, before bringing myself to my feet again. Even in the bright moonlight, I tripped over rocks and bushes. When the road came into view, the carnage of metal and glass looked uglier than I'd thought. It was a wonder that no one had driven by and seen it yet.

Headlights appeared up the road. My first instinct was to run out and flag them down, but the body lying in the ravine behind me and the voice at the end of that call gave me pause. Maybe they were random passersby. And maybe I didn't destroy the phone fast enough. I dropped into a crouch. The car slowed and pulled off the side of the road where my wrecked car lay.

The two front doors opened and slammed shut. The sound echoed through the night air like gunshots. I sunk lower to the ground and prayed the night would be a friend for once and hide me from sight. The tall and lean driver left the car running with its headlights pointed in my direction, blinding me.

"Crap!" I whispered to the dirt.

"She's not in here," a deep voice called out. All hope that they were random motorists died. I kept my head low, too afraid to look up. *This was bad.*

"Let's spread out and search for her. Use your light. It's bloody dark out here." Twin-searching beams swept across the landscape, and I sunk lower to the ground.

Broken glass crunched under their feet as they began moving in my direction. "Dude, looks like your buddy Cole's been here," the other boy said with a wary tone.

Warning bells rang loudly in my ears. They knew the officer's *name.*

The first boy growled a curse. "I should've known Donovan was playing another one of his bloody tricks. We should've never left our posts."

Every cell in my body begged to run as their flashlights swept dangerously close to the place where I lay. It was only a matter of seconds before they saw me.

"Over here!" the tall boy yelled, shining a light directly at me. Adrenalin shot through my veins, and I bolted to my feet.

In a blind panic, I ran back toward the ravine, chasing my own shadow cast by the powerful lights behind me.

I risked a glance over my left shoulder to see how close they were and tripped over a rock in the uneven earth. My right shoulder hit the ground first, sending sharp pains up my back and neck. Before I could gather myself, there was a weight on me, holding me down.

"Don't touch me!" I shrieked, lashing out like a cornered animal. Strong hands grabbed my wrists and pinned them to the ground at my sides.

"Kirie, stop! I'm not going to hurt you."

I froze and peered up at the familiar, beautiful face staring back at me.

Luca?

His bright green eyes glowed in the darkness. Pure, bright light poured from his exposed skin, creating an ambient glow that instantly warmed my frozen body. Behind him stood a tall boy with a beam radiating from his open palm.

They *glowed*. Like me.

All at once, the fight left me. A torrent of tears ran down my cheeks as I openly sobbed.

I'm not alone.

I'm not alone.

I'm not alone.

"Aw, crap," the large one groaned. "What'd you do, Luca?"

Luca's thick brows collided, and he looked me up and down. "Tell me where you hurt." He patted my arms and legs, searching for injuries.

I pointed at the tall boy's glowing hand. "H-how?" I stammered between sobs.

Luca craned his neck, and the boys shared a look. "We can talk about that later. First, we need to get you somewhere safe before Cole returns to finish the job."

I sucked in a trembling breath. "That won't be a p-problem."

"No?" Luca asked with raised brows. "Why not?"

Unable to look him in the eye, I gazed up at the sky and whispered, "Because I killed him."

Arin let out a barking laugh, making me jump. "Yeah. Okay, Tiny." I stared at him, open-mouthed. Did he think I was kidding?

"Stop being a dick, Arin," Luca snapped back. He turned back to me and softened his tone. "Where's Cole now, Kirie?"

I pointed in the direction of the ravine. Luca nodded to his friend. "Check it out, Arin."

He brought me into his arms, and I was bathed in his scent. He smelled like sandalwood and something bright. Luca held me tight against his chest, and his heat surrounded me like a warm blanket. My shivers subsided. "I'm sorry," he whispered in my ear. My brows drew together. What did *he* have to be sorry for?

Arin was gone mere moments before a gust of wind and crunching gravel signaled his return. *How did he move so fast?* Luca pulled away slightly and the cold rushed back in. I balled my hands into fists to keep from pulling him back to me.

"Dude. She was telling the truth," Arin said between breaths. "Knife to the chest." He studied me with narrowed eyes as if I were a strange bug. I shrank back into Luca's arms, weary of Arin's giant frame and disapproving frown.

"Was he alone?" Luca asked.

"No other bodies," Arin replied.

"Fine. Call it in." Luca's sigh held a hint of disappointment. I craned my neck to look at him. Would he have preferred *more* dead bodies?

Arin pulled a sleek black phone from his back pocket and turned back toward the ravine, his fingers moving quickly across the glowing screen.

A sharp, cold wind blew over us, and my body began to shake again. Luca stared into the darkness, worry written on his striking features.

"I didn't mean to kill him," I said through chattering teeth. "H-he was trying to hurt me, and I-I tried to stop him. It was an accident." For reasons I couldn't name, I wanted this boy to know I wasn't a monster.

Luca sighed again and pulled me back into his firm chest.

His skin grew brighter, and warmth spread through me once more. My jaw relaxed a fraction. "Don't apologize for doing what had to be done, Kirie. Cole wasn't a good man. He deserved to die." His cold words were in direct contrast to his physical warmth.

I hadn't heard Arin return when he said, "The cleanup crew will be here soon. We need to move, Luca. Donovan is still out there."

My mind spun. Clean up crew? Who *were* these guys? And who was Donovan? With each passing minute, my list of questions grew.

Luca stood, pulling me to my feet. I swayed a little and he put a steadying arm around my shoulders. I wanted to burrow into his side, breathe in his heady scent, and hide from the horror show that was my life.

"Steady now," he whispered. "Let's get you somewhere safe, shall we?"

The thought of leaving with Luca and Arin was both thrilling and terrifying. Never in my life had I met anyone who could use energy the way I did. Not being alone in my abilities was more than I'd ever dared hope for. But that didn't mean I was safe with them. For all I knew, these boys could be complete psychos. Either way, I couldn't simply go back to the Andersons' home after what I'd done.

I gasped. "Oh my gosh!" I jerked away from Luca, suddenly

feeling wretchedly selfish. Rylie! I'd completely forgotten about her. She could still be in trouble. I had to go to her.

"We need to go back to my friend's house. I think she and her family are in trouble."

They shared a look. "We should stick to the plan," Arin said, shaking his head. I narrowed my eyes at him. He was quickly getting on my nerves.

Luca turned to me with an apologetic look. "Sorry, Kirie. We need to get you to safety."

Fresh tears filled my eyes as I gazed up at him. "Please. She's all I have left."

Luca ran his hands through his hair, leaving the ends sticking up at weird angles. He looked between Arin and me, seemingly weighing the options. Finally, Luca nodded once. "Fine. But I'm driving."

Arin let out a huff of breath. "Sure. Why not?"

Some say the world will end in fire,

Some say ice.

From what I've tasted of desire

I hold with those who favor fire.

"Fire and Ice"

By Robert Frost

Chapter 11

I rested my forehead against the cold glass of the backseat window and watched house after cookie-cutter house fly by. Streetlights along the residential road blinked across my face like the inside of an old slideshow reel, and the words, "I'm not alone" played over and over in my mind.

All my life, I'd lived with the certainty that I was an anomaly, a freak, a fact confirmed by my mom's insistence that we keep my light hidden from the world. We never even discussed what might be wrong with me, like she was too ashamed of my strangeness to put it into actual words.

But now? Now, everything I knew to be true was crumbling like a house of cards. I was not the only one like me.

A million questions piled on the tip of my tongue. Who were these boys? Were they really like me? How did they know Cole? And who or what was the 'cleaning crew' Arin mentioned?

I shifted uncomfortably on the leather back seat and drew

an arm across my tear-stained face. The movement sent pain through my left temple. I held back a groan. Absolutely *everything* hurt. I needed a hot shower and a warm bed, preferably soon.

Ugh. Guilt settled over me again. I'd just killed a man and I was thinking about a hot shower. Something was definitely wrong with me.

As Luca pulled into Rylie's neighborhood, I realized I hadn't told him where she lived. The closer we got to Rylie's street, the more uneasy I became, though I couldn't say why. I sat up in my seat and searched the night. The streets were hazy, and the air smelled faintly of smoke. I gazed out at the sky. It was lit with an eerie orange glow.

When we turned onto Rylie's street, my anxiety level rose to heightened levels. Though it was well after midnight, the sidewalks leading up to the Anderson's home were filled with neighbors in robes and slippers, each frowning and shaking their heads.

Several fire trucks and police cruisers also lined the street, blocking our way forward. Luca pulled the car to the side of the road several houses down from Rylie's. Before he could shift into park, I was out of the car, jogging toward the crowds of people and emergency vehicles that barred my view of the house.

"Kirie, wait!" Luca yelled after me.

"Let her go," I heard Arin say. "We need to check the perimeter."

Without sparing them a backward glance, I ran toward Rylie's house, fresh adrenaline pushing me forward. I wove through fully outfitted firefighters, fire trucks, and police cruisers until the house came into view. The scene in front of me made me drop to my knees.

The Anderson's home was completely engulfed in flames. My hands covered my mouth in disbelief as I watched my friend's home burn to the ground. The intense heat felt as though it could melt my exposed skin. Firefighters worked furiously to extinguish the fire, but it was obvious it was a losing battle.

Someone tapped me on the shoulder. "Miss? Miss, are you alright?" I turned around and saw a woman in her mid-twenties wearing a paramedic uniform and blue latex gloves. She stared down at me with a strange expression on her face.

"What?" I asked, confused.

"You look like you could use medical attention. Why don't you follow me and let my crew check you out." She motioned to an ambulance not far to my left. I covered my blood-encrusted forehead with my palm and shook my head.

"I need to find my friend. I need to make sure she made it out okay."

"Do you know the family that lives here?" she asked,

gesturing toward the flames.

"I live here with my friend," I said. "Please, do you know if they all made it out?"

She nodded. "They're being treated for smoke inhalation down the street." She pointed several houses down to where an ambulance with flashing lights was parked. "Your friends are pretty lucky; they made it out of the house just in time."

I quickly stood and pivoted in the direction she indicated, nearly falling over. I put my arms out to steady myself and then began to hobble down the street like a drunken co-ed.

"I really think you should let me examine you," the paramedic called after me. I threw her a half-wave and continued on.

My body must have run out of adrenaline because my feet felt like they were made of cement blocks, and each step was a struggle. The distance to the ambulance seemed to grow with each punishing step. Every cell in my body cried for rest, but I continued to push forward. I had to see with my own eyes that Rylie and her family were safe.

Light spilled out of the ambulance's back door and several people gathered around it. I could see the top of Rylie's dad's head at the center of the group. He was breathing deeply through the oxygen mask that covered his face.

I stumbled my way through the small crowd of paramedics and police officers to where Rylie and her twin brothers were sitting on the back bumper, flanked by their parents. Like Mr. Anderson, they all wore oxygen masks over their soot-covered faces.

"Rylie! Are you okay?" I stumbled forward, hugging her tightly. She pulled my arms away and threw off her mask.

"Oh, my gosh, Kirie! What the heck?" She yelled at me. "You never called me back, and I was completely sure you were off being murdered on some back road!"

"Oh, thank goodness!" Mrs. Anderson broke in, respirator dangling from her neck. "Rylie said you ran into car troubles and couldn't get home. I meant to come get you, but the power went out, and then the fire started, and . . . sweetheart, you look awful. What on earth happened to you?"

The weight of the night caught up with me, and my body slowly leaned sideways. "I think I need to sit down."

Rylie quickly stood and guided me to her seat at the back of the ambulance. "What happened to you? You look worse than we do!" Her hands shook on my shoulders, and I felt bad for being there, adding to their stress. Somehow, I knew the house fire was my fault. I imagined my parents' murderer skulking outside the Anderson's home holding a lighter while Cole was hunting me in the dark ravine. The killer likely knew I wasn't home and started the fire anyway. No one, it seemed, was safe around me.

"I'm okay," I lied, patting her hand in what I hoped was a

reassuring gesture. "Someone accidentally clipped my back bumper, and I rolled my car. I got a little cut up trying to get out." I tucked my hands into my chest, hiding the worst from sight.

Mrs. Anderson gasped. "Oh, my goodness. That's horrible!" Fresh tears puddled in her eyes.

"It's okay," I said again. "A couple of guys saw my overturned car and stopped to help. I'm just a bit banged up, that's all." I managed a small smile, and Rylie and Mrs. Anderson relaxed a little.

Mr. Anderson pulled his mask from his face and put a hand over his wife's shoulder. "Well, it sounds like we've all had a bad night," he said, turning to face the inferno, the flames tinting his skin an eerie orange. "I'm pretty sure the house is a total loss. I'm just so glad we're all okay."

Without warning, Mr. Anderson slumped forward, and he began to cry, his shoulders visibly shaking. Immediately, the twins threw their oxygen masks to the ground and wrapped their arms around his middle. Rylie and her mom followed suit, and soon they were a mass of sobbing bodies, holding each other together as they fell apart. Sitting outside their huddle, I felt more alone than ever. My family *didn't* make it. They were gone, and there was no getting them back.

It all became clear. I didn't belong in this normal world. The realization left me feeling weightless, as if the thing that held me to the ground, the thing that tethered me to this earth, had been severed. It was terrifying. It was freeing.

Kaden broke from the hug first. "Dad? Where are we going to sleep tonight?" The normally fierce little man now looked so small and scared.

Mr. Anderson peered down at his son with a sad smile. "I'm not sure, buddy. We'll probably have to live in a hotel until we can get a new house."

"We're going to live in a hotel?" Brody asked, soot-covered and wide-eyed.

"Looks like we may have to," Mrs. Anderson said, heartbreak plain on her face. "We no longer have a house."

I knew how they felt. I, too, had lost everything within a few awful moments. I racked my tired brain for a way to help them the way they helped me. I sucked in a tiny gasp. They might not have a house, but *I* did.

"Mr. Anderson," I called, and the group swiveled as one toward me. "You all could stay at my house for a while. It isn't on the market yet, and all the furniture's still there. It would be more comfortable than staying in a hotel. That is, if you don't mind being there." I would never be able to enter that home again, but that didn't mean they couldn't.

"It's not a bad idea, honey," Mrs. Anderson said, staring up at her husband. "The kids wouldn't have to leave their neighborhood, and they'd be close to school."

Mr. Anderson sighed heavily. His ash-covered shoulders hunched over, giving him the look of a defeated man. "Are you sure, Kirie? I wouldn't want to delay your plans to sell your home."

"It's not a problem. It's just sitting there empty," I said. "Plus, Rylie already knows the code to get into the garage, so you won't have a problem getting in tonight. It would make me feel so much better if you used it."

"Well, we sure do appreciate it, Kirie. A lot." Mr. Anderson reached out to his family again and gathered them around him.

Rylie poked her head out from under her father's arm. "But, Kir, won't it bother you to stay there?"

"She can stay with Alena," Luca broke in. He and Arin emerged from the smoke like a pair of male models walking some avant-garde runway. They joined our pathetic little group, stopping beside Mr. and Mrs. Anderson.

For the first time since they'd appeared on the side of the road, I got a clear look at Arin's face. Square-cut jaw, blonde hair curled over bright eyes, broad shoulders. Recognition had me stepping back. I'd seen him before. I scanned his features, and the memory of our first meeting came flooding back. Arin was the boy I'd bumped into at the science fair. Our interaction had only lasted a few seconds, but his larger-than-life presence made him hard to forget.

"Alena?" I asked, trying to hide the thundercloud of

emotions inside me from the Andersons.

"Yeah, from school, remember?" Luca said. He caught and held my attention, his jewel-green eyes full of meaning. "She was just saying the other day that she was searching for a roommate."

I opened my mouth to call him on his lie, but the words stuck in my throat. As I stared back at Luca, two clear paths stretched out before me. Stay and pretend to be normal or move on. Since my parents' deaths, I'd been living in an in-between world where my former life no longer existed, but I was still unable to move forward. Going with Luca and Arin was risky. I knew nothing about these boys beyond the fact that they might be like me, but staying with the Andersons would be a kind of purgatory, a holding place full of grief.

No. I *had* to move on. Besides, it was past time I found answers about who and what I was. Luca and Arin might just be the key to unlocking it all.

I sat up straight and said, "Oh yeah. I remember Alena. From my sophomore year, right?"

Mrs. Anderson glanced between Luca and Arin through slitted eyes. "I don't think we have had the chance to meet," she said slowly. "Are you two friends of the girls?"

"Please excuse my poor manners," Luca apologized smoothly. He stepped forward and offered his hand and a smile. He was all British charm. Mrs. Anderson, a little dazed, shook his hand. "My name is Luca Durant, and this is my friend, Arin Bullock."

Arin bowed in subtle mockery of Luca's formal British tone. "Nice to meet you."

"Likewise. How do you know our girls?" Mrs. Anderson asked.

Luca shrugged. "We went to school with Kirie and Rylie a few years back. We were seniors when they were sophomores, but our groups still hung out from time to time."

"We did?" Rylie asked, turning to stare at me with knitted brows. I gave her a pleading look, hoping no one else would notice. She nodded slightly, apparently catching my meaning. "I mean, we *totally* did." Rylie walked over and sat next to me on the bumper. She grabbed ahold of my hand and squeezed. I winced. "You have some explaining to do," she whispered. I nodded in response.

"So, did this Alena girl go to Rock Canyon, too?" Mrs. Anderson asked.

"Yes," I answered this time. "She and I were friends before she graduated with Luca and Arin. I haven't seen her much since, but we still try to keep in touch."

"Lena has a spare bedroom in her apartment and is looking for a roommate. This could be the perfect solution for both of you," Arin cheerfully said.

Luca's and Arin's ability to create a believable story on the spot was impressive *and* disturbing. Obviously, they couldn't be trusted completely. Still, their little charade was my best chance of escaping my old life, so I continued to play along.

"Are you sure you're ready to live in an apartment without a responsible adult, Kirie?" Mrs. Anderson asked, clearly torn.

Rylie huffed in exasperation. "Mom! She's almost eighteen years old. Her birthday's, like, months away. She's completely old enough to move out on her own. Stop worrying about her so much. Sheesh!"

Mrs. Anderson put her hands up in surrender, obviously too tired to fight. "You're right. You're right. I'm being overprotective, and I have no right to be." Mrs. Anderson turned to me. "Kirie, if you feel comfortable living with this Alena girl, I think it's a great idea. Heaven knows *we* have nothing to offer you anymore."

With that, she threw her hands over her face and began to sob. Her husband brought her into him and whispered comforting words while rocking her back and forth. The moment felt incredibly intimate, and instinctively, we all looked away.

"Thanks, Rylie," I said, giving her a side hug.

"You are in trouble, Kir!" she stage-whispered to me. "You've been holding out on me. Where the heck have you been hiding these two hotties? Friends share!"

"I have no excuse," I whispered back with a shrug.

"Seriously, they *never* went to Rock Canyon. I would know. I would've stalked them *every day*." Rylie turned and looked Luca and Arin over from head to toe, not worrying about how obvious she was being.

"Seriously," I snorted softly. I watched as Arin and Luca quietly talked with their heads together. I narrowed my eyes. They were probably plotting their next lie. I silently vowed to keep both eyes open around these boys.

All around me, paramedics gathered their equipment and loaded it back into the ambulance. A uniformed man approached Mr. and Mrs. Anderson, breaking them out of their quiet conversation.

"Mr. Anderson, you and your family have been cleared to go. Do you have a place to stay tonight?"

"We do," Rylie's dad answered, nodding.

"Great! If you or anyone in your family has worsening symptoms, contact your on-call doctor or go to the ER immediately. Otherwise, you should be good to go."

Mr. Anderson shook hands with the entire team of first responders before herding the twins away. Unfortunately, that was also my cue to move. I stood on shaky legs and dragged my heavy feet over to where Luca and Arin were waiting. I fully intended to get answers from them, but first, sleep.

"I'm just going to say goodbye and then I will be ready to go."

"We'll wait for you here," Luca said, stuffing his hand in his pockets.

While I walked over to where Rylie and her family were loading into their minivan, I threw a wary glance back at Luca and Arin. I briefly reconsidered hitching a ride with Rylie to the nearest hotel, but after looking again at the Andersons' sad, sooty faces, I decided I didn't really have a choice. I just couldn't ask any more of them.

Rylie stood just outside the van's back door, waiting to say goodbye.

"I'm going to head off with Luca and Arin," I said. "I'm really glad you're safe." Unshed tears clouded my eyes.

"Aw, I love you, Kirie! I'm going to miss living with you." She gave me a quick hug and then pulled back. "Thankfully, I still had my cell on me when the fire broke out, so I can call you tomorrow morning to make sure those mystery hotties haven't kidnapped you. Come to think of it, I wouldn't mind coming along if they did," she giggled.

"Very funny. I'll be alright, I promise." *I hoped . . .*

I stepped back and let Rylie get into the back of the minivan with her little brothers.

"Kirie, let me know if your arrangement doesn't work out. I want to make sure you have a place to stay," Mrs. Anderson yelled through the open door.

"Will do. Bye!"

I waved to them until their minivan disappeared down the road. Once they were out of sight, I returned to where Luca and Arin were waiting.

"Ready to head out?" Luca asked.

I gazed around at the street I'd grown up on, at the faces of the pajama-clad neighbors I'd never really gotten to know. All these years I was pretending to be normal to fit in with these people, and I still felt like I was on the outside. This life was never really mine. "Yeah," I said. "I'm ready."

The walk back to the car was punishing. The distance seemed like miles rather than yards. The boys led the way, their eyes searching the shadows as if they expected something to jump out of Mrs. Jackson's bushes at any moment. I supposed someone just might.

The further we walked, the further the distance between us grew. On my best day, my short legs would've been unable to keep pace with their long strides. After several more feet, I had to stop to catch my breath. Never in my life had I been so tired. Arin and Luca turned in unison when they realized I was no longer following them.

"I got this one, brother," Arin said. He jogged back to where I stood, swept my legs out from under me, and carried me cradle-style.

"Hey!" I yelled. Arin chuckled in response.

The crowd of neighbors and first responders had thinned

out, but the few who remained threw curious glances our way. I felt my face blush in embarrassment. I let out a sigh of relief when we got back to the car, and Arin set me on my feet again.

"Thank you," I said.

"Anytime, babe! You weigh about as much as a pillow," he laughed. I ground my teeth in frustration at his apparent never-ending humor.

Luca unlocked the car doors and we all climbed in. Moving into my seat, I was surprised that my backpack sat on the floorboard in the backseat.

The boys must have grabbed it from the wreckage.

I pulled it onto my lap and held it tightly. The Andersons weren't the only ones who had lost everything that night. First, my car was totaled, and then all my clothes and belongings went up in flames. My backpack and its contents: my wallet, phone, the letter from my mom, and a few textbooks were all I had left in the world. It would have to be enough.

As Luca started the car's engine, I assessed my options. Obviously, staying with a girl who may or may not exist wasn't an option. Neither was staying with a couple of boys I didn't know. I wasn't naive enough to think they'd found me on the side of the road by accident. They had a habit of following me around and showing up after everything went to hell, but did that make them bad guys? Maybe. Maybe not. But if I'd learned anything that night, it was that looks could be deceiving.

I had enough money from my parents' life insurance to care for myself for the foreseeable future. I didn't *need* to rely on anyone anymore. First thing tomorrow, I promised myself I'd find a place to stay until graduation. Then, I'd go to whichever university accepted me. But for that moment, I just needed a safe place to sleep.

I leaned forward in my seat and cleared my throat. Luca and Arin turned their heads toward me in tandem as if they were connected by a string, suggesting a closeness I hadn't noticed before. "Look, I appreciate your help tonight, but I don't know if staying with your friend, Alena, is a good idea. I think it's best if I stay at a hotel for the night."

Arin snorted. "You do, huh?" he said with a jack-in-the-box smile that put me on edge.

"Yes. I do," I said, narrowing my tired eyes at him. "Do you guys think you could drop me off at a hotel near Denver?" The more miles between me and Cole's dead body, the better.

"Of course," Luca said kindly. Arin snorted again.

"Thanks," I said, glancing between the two boys.

Luca caught and held my gaze in the rearview mirror. "Try to get some sleep, Kirie. I'll wake you up when we get there." Luca's low voice sent chills up my spine, and I felt a sudden, powerful urge to reach out for him, to touch his skin with mine. I sat back and fisted my hands in my lap, stunned by the intensity of such an irrational impulse.

Up front, Luca and Arin whispered to one another again, heaven knew about what. Logically, I knew I should've demanded they pull the car over until they told me *exactly* where we were going. I should've forced them to explain where the light they'd created before—the same light that was within me—came from. But my eyes weighed a thousand pounds and holding my head up had become impossible. I just needed . . . one . . . moment . . . of . . . rest.

Donovan 3

The assassin sneered as the flames rise higher. Once he realized his apprentice had failed his mission…the bloody prat, he knew it would once again be up to him to finish her off.

It was really too bad that the family got out in time. With all the accelerants he had used, it was a miracle they did. Things *really* hadn't been going his way lately.

With the girl now under The Society's protection, he was going to have to play this one a bit differently. It was a simple matter of systematically extinguishing her bright light and slowly isolating her.

It sounded like fun.

With his plan now set in motion, it was only a matter of time before she showed up. He couldn't wait to get his hands on her again.

A self-satisfied smirk spread across the assassin's face as he stepped out of the shadows. He tightened the belt on his terry cloth robe and joined the other idiots on the street in their sleepwear.

Now, all he had to do was wait and watch. Let the games begin.

Chapter 12

oft sunlight warmed my face, waking me from a restful sleep. I stretched my arms high above my head and let out a long, happy groan. I felt utterly relaxed, something I hadn't felt in a long time. I kept my eyes closed and let the sunlight soak into my skin, filling me up. It seemed like ages since I'd been under the sun's bright warmth. I wanted to live in that moment forever. Reluctantly, I opened my eyes to the day.

Confusion replaced joy. It was instantly clear that I wasn't in Rylie's basement, though the sunlight streaming through the windows could've told me that. I was lying in a large four-poster bed, covered in a plush, white, down comforter. Opposite the bed, a set of tall French doors covered in white gossamer drapes glowed golden in the morning light.

There was little else in the room by way of furniture, save a small antique desk with a laptop lying on top. Nineteenth-century crown moldings and decorative wainscoting adorned the white walls. Light seemed to radiate from every surface.

I ran my hands along the soft fabric of the down comforter, startled to see that my hands and arms were filthy. Putting them out in front of me, I gasped out loud. Dried blood-coated shallow cuts ran across the surface of my palms. They throbbed slightly. I looked closer; tiny pieces of glass were embedded inside.

My eyebrows rose in concern shooting pain across the left side of my forehead. I gingerly touched my fingers to a gash that ran along my hairline. It, too, was encrusted in dried blood. I tried to remember what had happened, but my memories felt fuzzy.

I sat up, shook my head to clear my mind and replayed the last 24 hours over. It had been Friday. I clearly remembered going to the library to study the War Scroll after a normal day at school. I'd driven back to Rylie's house. Only . . .I couldn't remember making it there.

Then it hit me . . .

I squeezed my eyes shut and blood-red images of terror ran through me, leaching away any feelings of peace and happiness I had felt before. The sounds of crushing metal and breaking glass filled my ears.

My body shook as cold and acidic dread pulsed through my veins.

I was stalked.

AGAIN.

The memory of the deranged murderer made of shadows flashed, like snapshots of dread.

My mouth filled with bile at the thought of Cole's body lying at the bottom of that ravine, and I could hardly believe I had just left him there! Who does that? Someone who lights up like a Christmas tree and stabs people, that's who.

Rylie.

Rylie's home.

I held a hand to my heart. I couldn't believe the whole thing had really happened.

How had Luca and Arin played into the whole thing? It was completely suspicious that they knew just when and where to look for me. As far as I knew, Rylie was the only one I'd told I was staying late at the library. Clearly, they'd been following me. But why, and for how long? My head began to throb anew.

An alarm clock sat next to the laptop on the desk across the room. 10:30 AM. I must've fallen into a deep sleep in the backseat of Luca's car after saying goodbye to the Andersons because I had no memory of the ride over to this hotel or even checking in. I did, however, have a vague memory of being carried by strong arms, followed by the sound and rumble of a loud engine before falling back into a coma-like sleep. Not sure whether that was a dream or not, I mentally filed that piece of information away for later.

I glanced around the room again with fresh eyes. It wasn't like any hotel I'd been to. When I asked them to take me somewhere, I'd been thinking of something more along the lines of Holiday Inn. By the looks of this room, they'd more expensive taste than I.

Every muscle in my body screamed in pain as I slid out of bed and walked to what I'd hoped was the bathroom. My skin itched badly from the filth covering me, and I was desperate to get clean.

I opened an ornate door into a small on-suite bathroom with floor to ceiling white marble. There was a double vanity and open rain shower on one side, and a toilet and bidet on the other. Maybe it was a European-themed room . . .

When I moved to the vanity mirror and saw my reflection, I jumped back in fright at the wild, wide-eyed girl staring back at me. Dead leaves and sticks entangled in my long hair, and a mixture of dried blood and dirt was caked down the left side of my face and neck. Every other inch of my body was covered in dirt. I leaned closer to the mirror to inspect the gash on my forehead that was deep and irritated by dirt and grime.

I carefully peeled off my ruined clothes, put them in a pile by the door, and turned on the shower. I eased myself under the steaming spray. My head fell forward, and I closed my eyes as my tense shoulders began to loosen, the hot water easing my aching muscles.

I searched for the complimentary soap and shampoo hotels usually provide but found a bottle of body wash instead. The labeling was in French, and the contents were half-full. My chest tightened.

Strange.

I poured some of the masculine and slightly familiar-smelling body wash onto my hands, and quickly scrubbed myself down, trying to avoid reopening the cuts that seemed to be everywhere. I rubbed the body wash into my hair, as well. Tiny twigs and brown water swirled down the drain at my feet like a dirty river in spring.

By the time I reluctantly turned off the water, thick steam filled the air. I found a stack of plush, white towels in the antique cabinet under the double sinks, and I wrapped one around myself, securing it under my arms.

I wiped the fog from the mirror and leaned over the counter to inspect my injuries. Though I no longer looked like a dirty corpse, I wouldn't be winning any beauty contests any time soon. The puckered gash on my forehead was clean and pink, but there were still pieces of glass embedded into the cuts in my palms. I tilted to the side and winced as I inspected my wet hair that hung heavily down my back like tangled seaweed. It would be a nightmare to comb out . . . especially considering I no longer owned a brush.

I made a mental shopping list of things I would need to buy, including a brush, tweezers, bandages, and a change of clothes. I'd most likely have to go out wearing my ruined clothes. Shopping in a towel wasn't an option for obvious reasons. Thankfully, I still had my wallet.

A stab of panic suddenly punctured my chest. My bag! I hadn't seen it in the room when I woke up and it was clearly not in the bathroom. I rushed back into the bedroom to search for it, praying it wasn't lost or taken. I rounded the bed and nearly dropped to the floor in relief when I found my dirt-covered backpack lying on the far side of the room, just out of sight. I lifted it onto the rumpled comforter, feeling a little guilty for soiling the beautiful white fabric.

I began unloading my bag onto the bed. I immediately tossed aside the few textbooks I'd left in there the day before. Inside one of the inner pockets was a small makeup bag filled with emergency essentials. I placed it on the bedspread.

I found my wallet next. Thankfully, nothing was missing inside, including the $120 in cash I had pulled out of an ATM just days before. I placed my wallet next to my makeup bag. Reaching back into my backpack, I found mom's letter.

I traced a finger across my name, scrawled in Mom's elegant handwriting, letting the paper's smooth texture calm me. I held my breath as I stared down at the innocent-looking paper. Not for the first time, I was tempted to open the damned thing once and for all. Over the past few weeks, I'd run my finger beneath the envelope's sealed opening countless times, but I could never bring myself to tear it open.

With a sigh, I held the letter to my chest and closed my eyes as if in prayer. I wasn't ready to read her last words to me. Not yet.

I carefully laid the letter on the bed and reached up to twist the diamond stud in my ear. Mom's cardigan was gone forever, but I at least I still had these few pieces of her with me. I focused again on the last of my earthly possessions laid out on the bed. It wasn't much, but I supposed it could be worse. I could be dead.

I was missing one last thing. *Where was my phone?* I searched for it in the pockets and corners of my bag but came up empty. I looked under the bed, in the sheets, and on the small desk. Nothing. I let out a frustrated sigh. It must've fallen out of my bag the night before. I made a mental note to get a new one as soon as possible.

I surveyed the room again, searching for new clues as to where the boys had dropped me off the night before. Nothing about this space read hotel room. I was going to be seriously pissed if they took me to Alena's apartment after all. I walked over to a narrow door on the far side of the room and found a small closet. Any hope that I'd had about being in a hotel room disappeared the moment I let my hands trail along the dark men's clothing hanging on the rack.

Eyes wide and pulse thumping, I turned and looked up again at the ornate crown moldings lining the room. European architecture always fascinated me, and I recognized the nineteenth-century Victorian Era style. The chips in the original wood floors at my feet told a story of their own in their chips and scuffs. Time was everywhere.

I pulled open the French doors and hesitantly stepped through the billowing white drapes onto a small balcony surrounded by a Victorian-style rod-iron railing. The cool fall air caressed my bare skin, causing me to shiver. City sounds engulfed me along with the scent of baked bread mixed with a hint of sewage. I put a shaky hand to my mouth as I looked down at the narrow, tidy street below. My balcony was four stories up from the ground floor. The building directly in front of me was a white stone five-story, Haussman-style building with dormer windows stretched across the front. My eyes filled with tears, blurring the gorgeous scene before me. I'd always wanted to travel abroad, though I could've never imagined it would happen like this.

I wiped my wet eyes with the backs of my hands and looked out over the Mansard-style rooftops at the Eiffel Tower in the distance. My skin grew hot as my inner spark came to life, a response to the warring emotions that swirled inside me. Joy. Anger. Sheer terror.

I was in Paris, France! *Paris*, with nothing to my name but a wallet full of American dollars, an unopened letter, and a borrowed towel for clothing. When Rylie joked about Arin and Luca kidnapping me, I wouldn't have guessed she'd hit the nail on the head.

With my towel tightly pulled around me, I rushed back inside and out the bedroom door. The room beyond was bright and open. On one side was a simple, small but organized kitchen, and on the other side was a living room with overstuffed couches. The original wood floors continued throughout. The simple elegance felt expensive.

Some of the adrenalin drained from me realizing neither Arin nor Luca were there. I turned to a second bedroom on the left of my door. I leaned my ear against the closed door and heard soft snores from within.

I stepped away, unsure if busting in on a sleeping kidnapper was a good idea and walked to the living room, instead. A giant flat-screen T.V. was mounted on the wall above a stone fireplace, and the entertainment stand below was crammed full of various electronics and gaming systems. It looked like a bunch of teenage boys lived there.

I moved around the sofa and heard something rustle behind me. I screamed and spun around, nearly losing my towel. Luca lay half-naked and half-awake in a pile of blankets on the couch. I grabbed my towel tighter to my chest and stepped back, the heat in my cheeks burning my own skin.

Luca stretched his arms above his head and yawned. "Good morning," he said without meeting my eyes.

I tried to respond, but my tongue was a hunk of lead in my mouth. I attempted not to stare at his perfectly sculpted chest, but it wasn't easy. *Holy crap, he was gorgeous.* The heat traveled from my burning cheeks into my shoulders and chest, likely giving me the appearance of a semi-burnt chicken. For several long seconds, I stood mutely in the center of the room, staring up at the ceiling, then the floor, and back to the ceiling again. Arin exploded through the closed bedroom door, saving me from bursting into literal flames. He, too, was half-naked, wearing nothing but a pair of basketball shorts.

"What's wrong? Who's screaming?" he boomed, wild-eyed and hair tasseled. His eyes landed on me, a wide grin spread across his face, and he gave a loud wolf whistle. "Damn Kirie, you make that towel look *good.*" He laughed out loud like he was the funniest guy on the planet. That was enough to snap me out of my Luca-induced stupor.

"Okay, what the hell is going on? You guys kidnapped me and brought me to *Paris*?" I self-consciously pulled my towel closer. "This isn't one of those human trafficking operations where you find a girl with no attachments, offer to help her out, and then force her into prostitution is it? Because that would seriously piss me off and you don't want to mess with me. I've killed a man," I said with all the fake bravado I could muster.

Luca sat up and raised his palms out in surrender. "It's okay, Kirie. You're safe with us," he said calmly.

"Safe?" I laughed out loud. "First of all, *you*," I pointed to Arin, "randomly show up at my science fair just hours before my parents are murdered. And *you*," I pointed to Luca, "snuck into my hospital room. Then you both appear out of the blue just minutes after someone tries to murder me, *again*, claiming you want to help just to turn around and kidnap me and take me to France while I'm sleeping. And you expect me to feel safe with you?" I shrieked. "And why doesn't anyone wear a shirt around here?"

"This is coming from the girl wearing nothing but a towel in the middle of our living room." Arin chuckled and pumped his giant pectoral muscles up and down. "And we brought you to Paris because we *live* here." He rolled his eyes as if it were an obvious fact.

Anger and embarrassment burned through me so hot that the room felt like it would catch on fire.

"Look, let's find you some clean clothes, and then we can sit down and talk this through," Luca said. It may have been my imagination, but it looked as though there was a slight blush on his cheeks as well. "There's much you still don't understand." He shifted uncomfortably on the couch and kept his green eyes focused somewhere to the left of me.

"Sorry, guys, but I don't think anything you own is going to fit me," I replied sarcastically.

"I'm sure Alena has plenty of spare clothing she could lend you."

Luca turned away and leaned down to pick up a shirt from the floor and put it on. All thought left my head as I watched his back muscles move in symphony with his abdominals as he moved the shirt up and over his head. He was mesmerizing. Arin cleared his throat loudly, startling me from my trance. I shifted my body to hide my face.

"I'll just run next door and ask Lena for some extra clothes," Arin said. "I love waking her up. She gets all feisty." He slapped Luca on the arm as he walked out of the door still half-dressed.

"Good luck, mate," Luca yelled after him.

The front door slammed shut, leaving Luca and me alone again. The loaded silence that filled the air was so thick it was nearly suffocating. We awkwardly gazed off in different directions for several uncomfortable minutes before I attempted to break the silence.

"Um, so . . . Alena. Isn't that the girl you both mentioned earlier? She lives in Paris, too?" Though I'd never met this Alena girl, I was willing to bet she was the breathtaking girl who accompanied Luca to my parents' funeral. This day was getting worse by the second.

"Uh, yeah. She's an old friend. The three of us have known each other for a long time." Silence filled the space again for a long beat before Luca cleared his throat and continued. "You may find her a bit . . . difficult. I thought it fair to warn you."

The apartment door blew open as if on cue, and a whirlwind with honey-blonde hair and long legs stormed in. Arin followed eagerly as if he were anticipating a great show. Alena barreled down on Luca, putting her fists on her hips.

"Luca, what were you thinking bringing her here? Does Abbott know what you did?" She yelled with a thick Italian accent.

Arin must indeed have woken her because she was wearing nothing but a tiny pajama set, and judging by her mood, she was not a morning person. I took a hesitant step back, careful not to catch her attention.

"It was Abbott's idea, actually," Luca replied in a patient tone, lifting a hand in my direction. Alena turned to look at me with raised brows as if she just realized I was in the room. Her eyes narrowed dangerously.

"Fine. But why is she *here*, in *your* apartment, wearing *that?*" She pointed at me in accusation. I shrank back and pulled my long, tangled hair forward in an unsuccessful effort to cover myself. Arin laughed loudly from the doorway as if the situation was hilarious. "Shut up, you *idiota*," Alena snapped and proceeded to call him every dirty name in the Italian language. Some of her words made me wish I wasn't already fluent in Italian.

"Lena . . ." Luca said as if talking to a misbehaving toddler. "First, I can have whomever I please in my apartment, as you well know. Second, Kirie was attacked last night and is unable to wear the blood-stained clothes she came here in." Alena rolled her eyes and folded her arms over her full chest. "She needs to borrow some clothes for just a little while. Please."

"Whatever," she huffed and stalked back out the door, slamming into Arin's shoulder on her way out.

"Well, brother. I'd say you got off pretty easy," Arin chuckled.

"I won't hold my breath," Luca replied with a sigh.

"She seems . . . nice," I lied.

Luca gave a small laugh. "Nice, she's not, but don't let her appearance fool you. She's bloody brilliant."

"I'll keep that in mind." I made a mental note never to underestimate Alena.

In a matter of moments, Alena burst back into the room carrying a handful of clothing. "Look, none of this is going to fit you. I'm so much taller than you." She looked me up and down again with a disapproving glare. "But I suppose it's better than *nothing*." She walked over, thrust the bundle into my arms, and then threw herself down on the couch next to Luca. And

I thought *Rylie* was a drama queen.

"Um, thank you. I'll . . . be right back." I walked toward the room I had slept in the night before. Just before I went in, I realized this might be Luca's room, seeing that he'd slept on the couch. I turned back to him. "Is it ok if I use this room again?" I asked, suddenly shy.

"Yes, of course. Take all the time you need," Luca said politely.

"She was in your bedroom?" Alena growled as I shut the bedroom door behind me.

I could hear Arin laugh again in the background. I couldn't quite figure out what type of relationship Luca and Alena had. Her obvious jealousy suggested they were in some kind of relationship, though Luca didn't seem very happy about it.

I set the bundle of clothes on Luca's bed and took a deep breath. I was in Paris, France! It was almost too much to comprehend. I'd never been outside of the United States before. Mom liked to stay close to home, and other than a few trips to neighboring states, I'd never been anywhere. I was beginning to realize just how sheltered she kept me all my life. Everything was changing so quickly that I didn't recognize myself anymore.

I had to admit, even though Arin and Luca had basically kidnapped me and taken me across international waters, probably illegally, given my lack of proper documentation, my gut instinct was to trust them. I had gotten to know evil fairly well in the last month and a half, and they didn't have the same darkness as Cole and Donovan. In fact, they were the exact opposite. Even Alena seemed to radiate light . . . if not kindness.

As I began to lay out the clothes she'd brought over, it dawned on me that I had slept in Luca's bed the night before. Just thinking of it caused my chest to glow with some emotion I wasn't quite able to name yet. A soft flame bloomed in my chest, and I tamped it down quickly before it had the chance to grow.

I had to focus on the task in front of me. The pile of clothes included a pair of dove-gray linen pants, a neutral-colored long-sleeved shirt, and a dark gray cable-knit sweatshirt. Each item was simple in design, yet obviously expensive. I glanced at the tags which confirmed my suspicion—high-end designers.

I put the pants and shirt on, and sure enough, Alena was right; they were all too long. I rolled the waist of the pants twice so that I wouldn't trip. I then pulled a sweatshirt over the t-shirt and rolled the sleeves up. I went back into the bathroom to look in the mirror. My hair was still a wet mess, but the clothes would do.

I quickly grabbed my emergency makeup kit and returned to the bathroom mirror. I put on a thick coat of mascara in an effort to draw attention away from the dark circles under my eyes and put a blush over my pale cheeks. Then, I combed through my long hair with my fingers and pulled it back into the best braid I could manage. I might not have been at my best, but at least I no longer resembled the walking dead.

I stuffed my makeup bag and ruined clothes into my backpack and headed toward the door. I was determined to get some answers, like who the hell these people were and if they were truly like me. I hesitated with my hand on the doorknob for a moment. I was overcome by an ominous feeling like whatever waited for me on the other side of that door would change everything I knew about my world.

I took a deep breath and walked through the door.

Chapter 13

I **sat uncomfortably at** the far end of the couch while the boys changed. Alena sat at the other end, inspecting her nails and ignoring my presence. I didn't really mind since she was unpleasant to speak to anyway. Arin reentered the living room first, breaking some of the tension. He wore jeans and a hoody, his sandy-colored hair standing on end as if he'd thrown on the sweater in a hurry. He must have been worried about leaving me alone with Alena too long.

"Guys, I'm starving," he said, leaning back and stretching out his abs. His stomach gave a loud growl, emphasizing his point.

Luca soon joined us.

"We'll have to go out. There isn't a speck of food in the entire flat." Luca grabbed his wallet from the end table and slipped it into the back of his worn jeans that sat low on his hips.

"You'll have to wait for me to get dressed because bonehead over here dragged me out of bed." Alena gave Arin a death glare. "*And* I get to pick where we eat." No one argued.

I ran and grabbed my dirty backpack from Luca's room and followed the boys to the hallway to wait for Alena. Standing against the wall next to Luca, I quietly inspected the cuts on my hands. The sores became more irritated the longer I left the glass inside them. I really needed to ask the boys to take me to a drug store to get a first aid kit or even go to the local Instacare, if Paris had such a thing. The idea of shopping or going to a doctor in a foreign country made me sick with nerves.

Several minutes later, Alena flounced out of her apartment, looking effortlessly beautiful in dark-washed jeans, a loose-fitting sweater that fell over one shoulder, and an infinity scarf. I peeked over at Luca and saw him staring at her with an unreadable expression.

A sharp stab of jealousy stung me like a wasp. For the first time in maybe forever, I'd wanted to get a guy's attention. Not just any guy, a guy that could understand me, one that wouldn't be afraid of the *real* me. But, with a girl like Alena around, I might as well have been invisible.

She boldly led the way down the grand foyer and onto the Paris streets. As we walked along the sidewalk, I soaked in all the sights and sounds. Red and orange leaves hung from the trees lining the road, and a crisp chill hung in the air. Music played in the distance, mingling with blaring horns and revving motors. My eyes darted everywhere, soaking it all in. History and artistry were everywhere I looked—in the buildings, the streets, the people. It was hard to imagine just hours before I was in a small town in Colorado surrounded by flames and sorrow.

After walking several blocks, we stopped at a corner café with red awnings and small round tables beneath striped umbrellas. It was everything I would imagine a French café would look like. I followed our small group inside the warm, fragrant shop, and breathed in the smell of fresh-baked bread and cooked meat. My empty stomach was cramping in hunger, and I couldn't remember the last time I ate.

Standing in line, I stared at the large chalkboard above the counter. Colorful chalk listed what, I assumed, were various breakfast items. Over the years, I'd learned Italian and Spanish, but I'd never gotten around to French. There was no need, really, since I'd never thought I'd *actually* get to visit France in my lifetime. Not with a mother like mine. I would've said it's funny how things change, but it really wasn't.

Alena stood confidently at the front of the line, chatting in fluid French with the young girl behind the counter. I felt smaller just standing next to her, literally and figuratively. All too soon, she moved away, and it was my turn to order. I glanced back at the boys for help, but Arin and Luca were busy whispering about some guy named Abbott, utterly oblivious to my distress. I took a deep breath and started picking out words I could easily identify.

"Jus D'Orange and Croisssant . . . s'il vous plait," I said in my best interpretation of a French accent. I must've pronounced something wrong because Alena gave a rude snort behind me. When I turned around, she was already sashaying off toward a table near the back corner of the café.

"Ce sera huit euros," the girl behind the counter said as she went to fill my order. My stomach dropped to the floor. I was so busy worrying about the language that I hadn't thought about how I would pay. I began frantically fishing through my bag for my wallet, wincing as the cuts on my hands brushed along the rough surfaces of my bag. When I pulled out my American bills, the cashier shook her head and gave me a dirty look.

"I got it," Luca said from behind me. He reached over my shoulder and handed the girl several euros. His chest brushed against my shoulder, and my face heated in embarrassment.

"Thank you," I said with my eyes focused on the counter in front of me.

"No big deal," he said with a shrug.

The rude barista handed me my order, and I quickly moved

away from the counter. I held the croissant and juice close to my chest, the cool condensation of the frosty cup soothing my throbbing palm.

My face grew hotter as I searched the small space for a place to sit. The café was crowded with late-rising Parisians, and unfortunately for me, the only chairs available were at Alena's table. I considered just standing to eat, but I was still exhausted from the night before, and my sore legs begged for rest. I gathered my courage and walked over to her table. Her food sat untouched as she quietly stared down at her smartphone.

"Do you mind if I sit here?" I asked politely. Nothing. Not even a flinch. "Ok . . . I'll take that as a yes," I said more to myself.

I carefully pulled the chair back and sat down with as much dignity as I could muster— a moment worse than entering the high school cafeteria, and that was saying something. I kept my eyes down, focusing on not puking all over my first real-life French croissant. It didn't help that hot waves of dislike practically radiated from Alena.

I sighed in relief when Luca and Arin joined us at the table and sat across from each other between Alena and me. Arin's arms were filled with various pastries, a large hot chocolate, and a cup of orange juice. I guessed it took a lot to maintain his mountainous size. Once Arin placed his food on the table, he leaned back and pulled up a newly vacant chair from the table behind him, placing it beside his own.

"Are you expecting someone," I asked, pointing to the chair.

"Sure am. Abbott's meeting us here for breakfast," Arin replied.

"He's back in town?" Alena forcefully set her phone on the table and folded her arms. "Why didn't you boys tell me?"

"Nobody wants to talk to you this early in the morning. You're scary," Arin said.

"You haven't begun to see scary, cretino!" she growled.

Luca and I silently watched Arin and Alena argue. I was almost impressed. They'd obviously done this before like a brother and sister who'd practiced annoying one another for years. Under any other circumstance, I might've laughed.

My tired mind wandered as the volleying insults became more creative. Who could this Abbott guy be? The way that the others spoke about him made him sound like he was the leader of the group. I assumed he lived in Paris, too, since he was already on his way to the cafe.

Wait?

"If you all live here in Paris, what were you doing in Colorado? I know none of you went to school with me," I blurted out, interrupting Arin's and Alena's squabble. "I really appreciate your help last night, but I still don't understand how I ended up in France or who you people are."

"I think I can help you there," a familiar voice said behind me. I spun around in my seat and saw my high school A.P. History teacher, Dr. Johnson, standing in the crowded café wearing his signature penny loafers, sweater vest, and half-moon glasses on the tip of his nose. Even half a world away, he still managed to look the part of the nerdy professor.

My world tilted a little as if it had been nudged off its axis. "Dr. Johnson? What are you doing here?"

"Well, Kirie, I'm here for you," he said kindly. "May I?" he asked, indicating the empty seat between Arin and me.

"S-sure," I replied.

Dr. Johnson sat down and took a pastry from Arin's pile. "You don't mind sharing, do you?" He clapped his hand over Arin's shoulder in a friendly gesture.

"I guess I have a few to spare," Arin said with a smile. "How was your flight?"

"Long. I'll never get used to traveling in a steel prison thousands of feet above the earth." He shook his head. "I see you've all made it here safely."

"We had to pull a few strings to get Kirie into France, given her lack of passport. Otherwise, it was no big deal," Luca said, joining the conversation. Alena had gone back to silently staring at her phone, which Dr. Johnson ignored. He would never allow *that* in class . . .

"I don't mean to be rude, but could you all cut the small

talk and tell me what's going on?" I asked.

"Yes, of course. I apologize." Dr. Johnson set his chocolate croissant down and brushed off his fingers. His face took on a sober expression as he leaned over the table toward me. "Kirie, many terrible things have happened to you lately, seemingly without any real explanation. These brutal attacks on your loved ones and yourself, however, are anything but random. You were brought to Paris by Luca and Arin for your protection . . . and for the protection of those you love," he said, peering at me over the rims of those ridiculous glasses.

My eyes dropped to the table. So it was true, then. My parents' deaths, the Anderson's home, Cole's death . . . *it was all my fault.* Logically, I already knew I'd been the common denominator, but hearing it aloud made it painfully real. Shame washed over me.

I swallowed the lump forming in my throat. "I don't understand. Who are these people, and what do they want with me?"

"You've become the target of a dangerous ancient organization called, The Order," Dr. Johnson said.

I quirked an eyebrow. "The Order?" Was this guy serious?

He nodded. "The men who tried to kill you were their henchmen. We call them Shadowmen for obvious reasons."

"No offense, but this is starting to sound like a movie script," I said with a disbelieving laugh.

One side of his mouth lifted as if he were fighting a smile. "No offense taken. I realize this all sounds unrealistic but given what you've seen and experienced this last month, I think you'd agree that there are things in this world that defy your previous assumptions."

I thought of the living shadows, Cole's and Donovan's black eyes, and my light. I had to admit he had a point "Ok. Assuming what you're saying is true, what do these Shadowmen want from me?"

Dr. Johnson leveled me with a knowing look. "They hunt you for what you are. They wish to eliminate your inner light."

My face began to burn anew, and I cursed my fair skin. I'd never spoken of the light I hid inside me, and never showed anyone beyond Mom what I could do. I felt suddenly naked and exposed and even more aware of Luca's quiet presence beside me. I hid my hands beneath the table and hunched my shoulders.

"I don't know what you're talking about," I mumbled.

"Kirie," Dr. Johnson said, dipping his head to peer at my downturned face. "It's nothing to be ashamed of."

I tucked my chin in, refusing to meet his gaze.

"It's a great honor, in fact. You are what the War Scroll refers to as a Child of Light, though we go by a different name these days."

Alena let out a loud yawn and stood, her chair scraping

along the floor with a screech. "I'm going to go back to my apartment. I don't feel like sitting through another one of your little talks. No offense, Abbott. You know I love you." Alena leaned over and kissed the top of his head just before sauntering out of the café.

The mood at the table lightened considerably with her exit, though Luca and Arin remained silent, seemingly content to let Dr. Johnson take the lead.

"Sorry about that. Alena can be a bit prickly at times," Dr. Johnson sighed.

"I noticed," I whispered under my breath. I wanted to ask why everyone kept calling him Abbott, but ever since he'd given our class the assignment to study the scroll, I'd felt this nagging sense that there was something there, some clue as to what was happening to me. I had to know what it was. "I don't understand. How could The Dead Sea Scrolls possibly have anything to do with my . . . ability?"

Dr. Johnson put a finger up. "We'll get to that, but before you can understand the significance of the War Scroll, you must first understand the basics. Consider the scientific Law of Conservation.

"Energy is neither created nor destroyed; it simply transforms from one form to another," I said, holding back a sigh. Everyone knew this.

Dr. Johnson nodded. "Correct. The essence or energy of all

living things has no beginning or end."

"What does my *energy* have to do with my parents' deaths?" I asked.

Dr. Johnson leaned forward in earnest. "It has everything to do with who you are and what you mean to this world. Each of us is made up of different degrees of energy based on varying factors. You, we," He swept a hand around the table to include the boys, "are simply made up of more light and energy than most. A lot more. That's why you have the gift of light. It's also why learning comes so easily to you. You are *literally* enlightened."

I nodded my head slowly, acknowledging the semi-solid logic in his claims. "Okay, but what does that have to do with the War Scroll?"

"Tenacious as always," he chuckled. "The War Scroll foretells an apocalyptic war between two groups of people: the Children of Light and The Children of Darkness."

"Yeah, I read the scroll. Homework, remember? But an apocalypse? Really? I didn't take *you* for the kind of person who believed in fairytales." I folded my arms tightly over my chest.

"Hey," Arin leaned forward, seeming put out at my tone.

Dr. Johnson raised his hand, and Arin obediently sat back in his chair, properly cowed. "No, no. That's fair. I know this must sound bizarre to you, Kirie. But think about it. Almost every society and religious organization on Earth teaches or has taught that the world as we know it will eventually end. The Islamic religion preaches an eventual end to all life. Christians and Buddhists teach that the denigration of society will one day lead to widespread war and utter destruction. The War Scroll, a Jewish text, simply is another end-of-days account. We often use it as a reference because it contains more specific information about the war."

I quickly put it all together. "Okay. So, I assume The Order is The Children of Darkness." Dr. Johnosn nodded encouragingly. "That must mean you all are The Children of Light? Am I right?"

"The Society of Light, to be specific," he said with a straight face. I tried not to roll my eyes, but it was a losing battle.

"The Society and The Order, or Shadowmen, as we call them, have been locked in battle for centuries."

"What are you all fighting for?" I almost couldn't believe I was even having this conversation. Though, to be honest, since my parents died, nothing in my world made sense.

"That's a big question and not easily answered. Essentially, it's a war between light and dark, freedom and bondage. For as long as humans have walked this planet, there have been those who've wanted to control others for power and dominion. We—The Society of Light—fight for mankind's right to live and think freely. It's been a long and constant battle," he said wearily.

I pinched the bridge of my nose and scrunched my eyes shut as I tried to connect the dots. "Okay. That still doesn't explain why these shadow jerks want *me* dead. What threat do I pose? I'm just a dorky science nerd from the states. Do they just really hate smart kids?" I let out a humorless laugh.

Dr. Johnson gazed at me with a steady eye. "You know there's more to you than that."

I snapped my mouth shut, still unable to talk about my ability.

Dr. Johnson continued. "Just as you're made of pure energy, they're made of pure darkness. You bring light to the world, something The Order hates. Recently, The Order identified you, and Donovan was assigned to your case—a serious misfortune. He's known for his cruelty and lack of respect for life."

Dr. Johnson's eyes momentarily traveled to Luca, staring fixedly at the table, his food untouched. "Where one Shadowman might be content to take out their target alone, Donovan will eliminate an entire family simply for fun, as he did in your case."

"Lucky me," I deadpanned.

"I'm truly sorry for your loss." Dr. Johnson looked at me as though he shouldered some of the pain and guilt I did . . . as if that were possible.

"Thank you." I cleared my throat and changed the subject.

"If The Order is simply an organization, why can't The Society of Light, or whatever, destroy them at the source?"

Dr. Johnson sighed and shrugged his shoulders helplessly. "That's the goal, of course. However, rooting out the source of darkness has proven difficult at best. They operate in secret and darkness, never really coming together in any real way. Over the ages, their organization has taken different forms in corrupt governments, slavery, genocide—every hateful practice that brings darkness back into the world. They're all driven by a hatred for light and freedom. Yet, after all these centuries of war, no one knows who leads the Shadowmen or from where."

We sat in silence, letting the heavy words percolate. "I have to ask. Why do they keep calling you Abbott? Is that your first name or something?"

"Well, no," he said, shifting in his seat. He slipped his half-moon glasses off the tip of his nose and set them on the table. "I'm afraid I haven't been entirely forthcoming with you or Rock Canyon High School about my identity. My real name is Uriah Abbott. Dr. Johnson is just my high school substitute persona."

He gave such a guilty expression that I almost laughed. The truth was his admission didn't shock me in the least. It made perfect sense, really. He never fit the role of the average high school sub.

"Why would you go to all the trouble of creating a fake identity just to get a job as a high school substitute? Don't you have better things to do?" I asked.

"This *is* what I do. My life's work with The Society of Light is to identify Sons and Daughters of Light across the globe, hopefully before the Shadowmen thugs do. Unlike most cases, you were especially hard to find. Your mother hid you so well that it took us seventeen years to find you. And a bit too late, it would seem." He gave me a sad smile.

I pushed that last comment to the side. "What do you mean, hid me well?"' Sure, Mom was overprotective, but it wasn't like I was locked in a tower like some fairy tale princess. I led a fairly normal life, just like Mom wanted.

"Children of Light typically stand out. They achieve great things early in life, which usually gains attention from others either through the media, I.Q. tests, and so on. You, on the other hand, flew under the radar, so to speak, your entire youth. Your mother created a sort of bubble around you, shielding you from any national or regional attention. That is, until recently."

"What changed? What could I have possibly done to bring those deranged murderers into my life?"

"It was your interest in biophotonics, actually," Abbott explained. "We actively monitor all online academic chat boards and found you asking incredibly advanced questions for your age."

"My science fair project," I whispered. My stomach dropped. *Parisxxxi8.* Someone must've monitored our conversations. I wrapped my arms around myself and shivered, feeling violated.

Abbott nodded. "Yes. That and the recent tragic deaths of your parents. So, I placed myself as a teacher at your school in order to ascertain whether you were a Daughter of Light, as we suspected. Once I realized you were what we'd hoped for and more, I called in the reinforcements." He spread his hands wide, indicating both Arin and Luca.

"Arin to the rescue," he said, puffing out his chest. I ignored him.

"Unfortunately, the Shadows use similar tactics to identify young Bright Ones," Abbott said.

Luca shifted uncomfortably in the seat next to me and cleared his throat. I turned away from Abbott, shocked at Luca's tortured expression. He looked like he was about to be sick. "I'm really sorry about your family, Kirie. Donovan got the jump on us." His hands were in tight fists on top of the table as he continued to stare down at the tabletop. "And then last night . . ." he swallowed hard. "We were keeping tabs on Donovan alone. He's never called in reinforcements before. He's too prideful about his work. We weren't expecting Cole."

My eyes filled with tears. "It was you in the hospital that

night, wasn't it?" Luca raised his jewel-green eyes to mine. "You healed me, didn't you?" Again, I had this overwhelming urge to reach out to him, pull him into me. I nearly had to hold myself to my seat.

"I did. I just wish I hadn't had to," he said as if he were in pain. The scars etched into my bones ached in response.

"Luca, what that man did to me and my family wasn't your fault."

I felt sorrow and understanding flow through the space between us, connecting us like an energy current. I could swear for a moment Luca felt it, too, before his eyes hooded over again.

"Hmm." Abbott thoughtfully hummed as he looked between Luca and me. "Well, I think we've given you enough to think about for one day, Kirie. There's still much to teach you, but perhaps now's not the time."

I glanced around me, surprised we were still in the small café. The morning crowd had died down, and only a few patrons remained. Those who were left ate, talked, and peered at their cellphones as if the world hadn't just rolled off its axis into another galaxy. Everything I knew about the world had changed in just a matter of minutes, and nothing would ever look the same for me.

"I have so many more questions, though. Like, how do you measure a person's light and energy levels? How did Luca heal me earlier? Can I use my light to do that? And if so, what else can we do? And why are we in Paris of all places?" I looked at each of them in turn. "None of you seem to be *French*."

"Kirie, slow down," Abbott laughed, putting his hands on mine. I winced in pain as the glass shards pressed deeper into the gashes. Abbott's brow furrowed, and he turned my palms face up. He made small tsking noises as he looked over my cuts.

"I see you've not fully recovered from your ordeal last night. Arin, Luca, why haven't you taken care of this?

"Sorry," they said in unison.

Abbott sighed heavily. "Ok. Take Kirie back to the apartment and attend to these wounds. I'm going to go pick up a few necessities for her."

I turned back to Abbott. "What kinds of things are you shopping for?"

"From what I understand, you lost all your personal belongings in the Anderson's house fire." I nodded in the affirmative. "I'm going to find some clothes and other necessities for you, so you won't have to borrow things from Alena anymore," he said, pointing at my rolled-up sleeves.

"*You're* going to go clothes shopping for me?" I lifted my brows, eyeing his sweater vests. I cringed thinking about the items he might pick for me.

He laughed at my skeptical look. "Don't worry, I have the

best personal shopper in Paris to help me.”

“You may want to rethink that, Abbott,” Arin said. “Alena may not be much help this time. She doesn’t seem to have a great love for Kirie at the moment. She’s been a she-devil all morning.”

“I did pick up on that, Arin. Thank you.” Abbott stood up from the table, taking his half-eaten pastry with him. “I’m sure I can still convince her to be helpful. She owes me quite a few favors, after all.”

“When can we talk again?” I stood, reluctant to let him go. I had more questions than answers at this point.

Abbott put a hand over my shoulder, and a sense of warmth and well-being flowed through me. “Soon. I know you’re scared and confused right now, but you can trust Arin, Luca, and Alena. You’ll find that they can be great resources for you. After all, they’ve all been in your shoes once.” He gave me a reassuring smile before turning to leave. I watched as the only person I knew in thousands of miles walked out the café door.

“Well, I’m totally full!” Arin said, stretching his arms high above his head.

Luca signed. “Let’s get back and fix this,” he said, pointing to my hands.

Ever since the subject of Donovan came up, Luca’s mood had become dark and moody. I wanted to reassure him again that he wasn’t responsible for Donovan’s actions, but instinct told me not to bring it up.

"I'm ready, too," I said.

I carefully picked up my untouched breakfast and backpack with my fingertips and followed the boys out.

Outside, the sun peeked through fluffy white clouds, and the cool morning air had warmed slightly. As we walked back to the apartment, I tilted my face upward and closed my eyes, soaking in the solar energy and filling the empty places within me. When I opened my eyes, I noticed Arin and Luca had rolled their long sleeves up to the elbows. They held their arms out slightly, exposing their skin to the sun like I had. And it finally occurred to me.

I wasn't alone.

The meadow and the mountain with desire

Gazed on each other, till a fierce unrest

Surged 'neath the meadow's seaming calm breasts,

And the mountain's fissures ran with fire.

"Attraction"

By Ella Wheeler Wilcox

Chapter 14

ack at the apartment, Arin headed straight to his on-suite bathroom for a shower. I stood awkwardly in the entryway next to Luca who hid his hands in his pockets, looking as uneasy as I felt.

"Um, I'm just going grab a few things and then we'll get started," he said to the floor. I nodded in response, my mouth suddenly dry.

Luca disappeared into the small corner pantry in the kitchen, and I sat down at the oak kitchen table, surveying the apartment again. Other than the giant flat-screen TV and the mess of electronics stuffed into an ornate cabinet, the apartment looked nothing like the bachelor pad it was being used as. Each piece of furniture and décor element matched the age and style of the building perfectly, down to carved wooden dining chairs. I doubted the boys had a hand in picking any of it out.

Luca emerged from the pantry carrying a small first aid kit

and sat in the chair next to mine. He shifted in his seat until he faced me, and our knees nearly touched. His energy pressed in on me, causing me to shiver.

He lifted one of my trembling hands and held it aloft. The contact sent electricity down my arm and straight into my heart, which began to race. Touching Luca was like sticking my finger into a light sock—electrifying.

"I'll need to remove the shards of glass before I can heal these cuts. This may hurt," he said in warning.

"Heal them?" I said stupidly. "Do you mean how you healed my neck in the hospital?"

"Yeah, like that," he said with a half-smile. His green eyes met mine briefly before focusing on my cuts again.

Luca's lean shoulders were hunched over my open hand as he removed the pieces of glass one by one with a pair of tweezers. I jumped slightly each time another piece was removed. It too was like being electrocuted by tiny wires. The combination of the pain in my hands and excitement from being so close to Luca was almost too much to bear. I tried focusing on breathing slowly, only to be surrounded by Luca's scent. It was an intoxicating combination of liquid sunshine and sandalwood body wash. I wanted to lean into him . . .

"Next," he said, snapping me out of my trance.

"What?" I asked, blinking.

"Other hand, please." Luca reached for my right hand and

took it in his.

"Oh, right. Sorry," I mumbled. My face heated.

I studied Luca's face as he worked methodically over my cuts. It was as if a great artist like Michelangelo carved his perfectly chiseled features. I'd seen cute boys before, but Luca was something else, something more. Realizing I was staring like a perv, I glanced away.

"So, um, how long have you known Dr. Johnson, I mean, Abbott?"

"I've known him since I was nine years old," he said without looking up. "He rescued me from a rather difficult situation. He's the closest thing I have to a father."

I remembered Abbott had mentioned that Luca and the others could empathize with my situation. Did he lose his family, too?

"What happened?" I asked. Luca paused with the tweezers just above my skin. "I'm sorry. You don't have to tell me if you don't want to," I said, embarrassed by my thoughtlessness. I, of all people, knew better than to open old wounds.

"No, it's alright." He went back to work on my hands while he spoke. "My situation is not much different from yours, actually. I'm originally from a small town in Italy. The people Abbott told you about earlier, the Shadowmen, they found me when I was only three years old." He paused and took a shaky breath. "They sent Donovan for me, as well. He killed my parents and my older sister first. When he finally got to me, he took me with him instead." He shrugged as if it were no big deal. "He was obsessed with the idea that he could train me to be a shadow. It was like some sick experiment to him." Luca cleared his throat. "Thankfully, Abbott and The Society found me on the London streets and took me in. Abbott has raised me like a son ever since."

I gazed at his perfection, his pure light, and was amazed at how seemingly unaffected he was by his horrific upbringing. I could see none of Donovan's darkness in him. I couldn't *imagine* being raised by that twisted maniac. It was a miracle he was still half a human, let alone this amazing creature.

"I'm so sorry you had to spend any amount of time with that creep. He's the worst kind of monster." I shuddered at the thought of those soulless black eyes.

"Yes, well, that was long ago," Luca said, setting the tweezers down. I inspected my cuts as he cleaned my palms with sanitation wipes from the first aid kit. They were a shredded mess.

"Okay, what now?" I asked nervously. The last time he healed me, I was barely conscious, and I didn't know what to expect.

"Just relax," he said, his low voice hypnotic.

Luca carefully took my hands and closed his eyes, bowing his head as if he were praying. For a prolonged moment, nothing happened. In anticipation, I shifted uncomfortably in my seat and stared down at our joined hands. Luca's palms began to warm around mine. My eyes shot to his face, and I was shocked to see that light had begun to radiate off every inch of his skin. It shone brightly and steadily grew in intensity. I stared at him in complete awe. He was the most beautiful thing I'd ever seen.

Light poured through his hands into mine, filling my entire being with peace and warmth, and my shredded skin began to stitch back together right before my eyes. I thought of my research on biophotonics. Here was *visual* proof that light can heal. Tears rolled down my cheeks. I hoped one day I'd have the chance to tell Parisxxxi8 about this.

When my wounds were fully closed, Luca set my hands on the table and held his right palm to my forehead. The ache that had been there since the attack disappeared completely. All too soon, the light began to fade, and the warmth along with it. The room felt suddenly colder, and I shivered.

Luca opened his eyes and stared into mine. They were a bright jewel green, sparkling with some inner light. He reached up and wiped the tears from my cheeks with his thumbs.

"There, all better," he whispered.

My body instinctively leaned into him as if some unseen magnetic pull was moving me forward. He was the sun, and I was his planet. I stared into his eyes, our faces inches apart. I could feel his warm breath on my skin. From the first moment I saw his jade eyes in the hospital room, I felt undeniably attracted to him. In that moment, I was sure he felt it too. I closed my eyes and moved slightly forward.

Luca jerked away from me, the legs of his chair scraping along the wooden floor. My eyes flew open in surprise. The light in his eyes faded quickly, and his expressionless face shut as abruptly as if he'd slammed a door in my face. Luca stood up from the table and walked back into the kitchen without a word, taking the first aid kit and his warmth. It was like being dropped into a pool of ice.

Hot shame and embarrassment washed over me. I'd never experienced the sharp sting of rejection so strongly. I pulled my hair over my shoulders to hide my burning face. Stupid, stupid, stupid.

"I should probably check my emails and get caught up on work," he called from the kitchen, obviously grasping for an exit strategy. By work, I assumed he meant Society business, though, despite my curiosity, I was too mortified to ask.

"Oh, okay, sure. Thanks for . . . you know . . . fixing my hands," I said with a strangled voice.

Luca walked past me into the living room to a small bookshelf stuffed with books of varying shapes and sizes. He grabbed a well-used paperback and placed it on the table in front of me. It was a French phrasebook.

"You might want to learn French. It will make your life a lot easier, trust me," he said before walking to his room, locking the door behind him.

I put my newly healed hands over my eyes and groaned. I couldn't believe I tried to *kiss* him. What was I thinking? *Obviously*, he wasn't into me. Guys like Luca don't go for girls like me, especially with a full-grown temptress like Alena flouncing around. Luca was out of my league.

I studied my palms in awe. Even the little scars from my childhood had disappeared. My body was full of conflicting emotions. Moments before, I witnessed the raw power of light at work, like witnessing a miracle. At the same time, I had just been rejected by the boy of my dreams. Embarrassment, amazement, confusion, excitement . . . it was completely overwhelming. So much had changed in the last 48 hours, and I didn't know what to think or how to act.

I took a deep, cleansing breath and turned my attention to the one thing in my life that wasn't complicated. I picked up the French phrasebook Luca had given me and walked over to the couch to study. Settling into the corner of the couch, I tucked my feet underneath me and began reading.

When I was about one hundred pages in, Arin emerged from his room dressed in a high-collar sweater and dark-washed jeans. His hair was still wet, making it a shade darker. Though he didn't make my heart skip a beat like Luca did, I had to admit he was stupidly good-looking.

"Feeling better?" he asked with a heart-stopping grin. My lips turned up in response.

"Yes. Look." I put my hands out for him to see.

Arin walked around the couch and sat down next to me. The springs groaned in protest. A cloud of musky cologne rolled off his skin. It smelled of bergamot and tangerines. It smelled of wealth.

He held my hands for inspection. I could feel a current of energy flowing beneath the surface of his skin, though I didn't feel the same intense energy as when Luca and I touched. Being in Arin's presence was more comforting than electrifying. It wasn't a bad thing, considering.

"They look like new," he said. "Luca always had the magic touch."

You could say that again.

"Mes mains sont beaucoup mieux," *My hands are much better,* I said in French.

"Ah, très bon! Brushing up on your Frenchy skills, I see." Arin pointed to the book in my lap. "Not bad for one morning. You might actually pick it up faster than Alena did. I can't wait to be the one to tell her." His deep laugh vibrated through my chest.

"For being a Son of *Light*, you don't act very bright," I joked.

"Ouch, that hurt." He threw his hands over his heart as though I'd shot him in the chest. "I'll have you know I'm no dummy. I recently graduated from Ecole Normale Supérieure at the top of my class."

"You went to ENS Paris? I thought it was impossible to get in there," I said in disbelief.

ENS Paris was arguably the top University in all of Europe and one of the top-ranking universities in the world. The student body was incredibly small, and the admission process was rigorous. Only the elite were accepted. The coursework was also known for being especially difficult, and ENS Paris had always been notorious for its high-achieving graduates.

"Kirie, nothing is impossible, especially for us." He reached up and patted the top of my head. I swatted his hand away.

"Seriously, though, how'd you get in? And why ENS and not Harvard or some other American school?"

"After we graduated high school, Luca, Alena, and I were stationed at the Paris Center of Light which was built in the late 1700s during the Enlightenment Age. The High-ranking Society members who built the center also established ENS, so it makes sense that many of us study there. Plus, admission is guaranteed once you join our ranks."

"So, The Society of Light is based in different locations worldwide?"

Arin nodded in affirmative. "Of course. It's a big world out there, and The Society has existed in one form or another since the beginning of human existence. Its roots run deep," he explained.

"Uh, huh. What do you all do for The Society?" I said, thinking of Luca's earlier comment about having to go to work.

"It's simple. We bring light and knowledge to the world," Arin recited as if it were his mantra. "We also prevent The Order from taking over and destroying mankind."

"Ok . . ." I processed that for a moment. "Then what is it that you do to stop them?"

"Our most important job is to educate people," Arin said with a shrug.

"Really? I thought you said you were at war."

"We also fight Shadowmen, but it isn't the most important thing we do. Consider all the nations today and throughout history that held absolute power over their people. What's one of the first things they take away from the public?" He said with raised eyebrows.

I mentally ran through all the totalitarian regimes in the world and searched for a common theme. North Korea immediately came to mind. Their government was known for controlling all information going in and coming out of their borders. Other governments in history also limited the public's access to books and discouraged literacy.

"They limit information?" I guessed.

"More specifically, knowledge and truth. The more ignorant their people are, the easier they are to control." Arin threw his arm over the top of the couch behind my head and angled his body toward mine, obviously excited by the subject. "That's why The Order wants to eradicate the Children of Light from the Earth. We encourage and empower people to think for themselves, which takes away from the absolute power they crave."

"Huh. That actually makes a lot of sense," I said, nodding.

We sat in silence for a moment as the information sank in. It was clear that I could no longer see things in the small and narrow way I had before my parents' deaths. I was beginning to realize that my views on history and the world around me had been incredibly simple. I was going to have to rethink *everything*.

I looked forward to the challenge.

"How old are you, Arin," I asked, craning my neck back to look up at his face.

"Twenty. Why?"

"You're a bit young to graduate from a prestigious four-year college. How did you manage that?"

"I had a bit of a head start. I lost my family when I was pretty young, so The Society took me in and put me on a fast track through my education," Arin said.

"I'm sorry for your loss. Are all three of you orphans,

then?" I asked. Based on what I had seen and heard, I assumed The Society adopted Alena like they had the boys.

"All *four* of us are, Kirie," Arin said, placing his outstretched arm across my shoulders and squeezing me in a comforting embrace.

My heart sank when I realized he meant me. "Oh, right."

I knew I was an orphan, but having someone else put it into words was shocking and painful. I put my hand over my mouth, trying to choke back the tears. Arin, noticing my distress, pulled me closer to his side. His warm torso wrapped around me like a cocoon.

"Sorry. I didn't mean for that to sound so harsh," he whispered in my ear.

Luca walked out of his room, holding a cellphone. He immediately zeroed in on Arin's arm on my shoulders, and his face hardened to stone. Arin must've noticed, too, because he slowly pulled his arm away and shifted a few inches over on the couch.

"Hey, brother. Kirie here was showing me her new skills with the French language," he said with an easy smile.

"Looks that way," Luca said in a dangerous tone.

"Right, well, I think I'm going to go grocery shopping. We desperately need food in here," Arin said, maintaining a cheerful demeanor under Luca's glare. He turned to me and asked "voulez-vous aller à l'épicerie avec moi?" *Do you want to go to the grocery store with me?*

"Je vais rester et étudier," *I going to stay and study*, I replied in French.

"See, Luca. She's a natural!" He beamed at him.

"I know," Luca deadpanned. "Let me grab my wallet, and I'll go with you."

Luca briefly disappeared back into his room and came back out wearing shoes and an expensive-looking jacket. For orphans, they sure dressed well. I decided to find out how they made a living while also earning degrees at prestigious universities. The thought of money suddenly reminded me of my own monetary issues.

"Hey, do you guys know how I can exchange my cash for Euros?" I asked as they headed out.

"I can do that for you . . . if you want." Luca offered his eyes not quite meeting mine.

"That would be great." I opened my backpack and pulled out my wallet. "I don't have much on me, but it's better than nothing," I said as I handed him the bills. He carefully took it from me so that our fingers didn't touch.

"We can also take you to an ATM later if you want," Luca said, looking at the dollar bills in his hand.

"Thanks. I'd appreciate that," I said, forcing a smile.

It appeared as though my misjudgment in the kitchen earlier had changed things between us. Luca could barely look at me, let alone touch me. He probably didn't want me to get any more ideas about the two of us. I wanted to find and hide in a deep hole for the rest of the century.

"Let's head out, then," Arin said. He walked to the door and held it open for Luca. "Are you sure you don't want to come with us, Kirie?" he said hopefully.

"I'm still pretty tired from last night. Plus, I should probably study some more before I venture out and make a fool of myself again."

"Okay, we'll be back soon," he said with a wave.

Luca silently followed his friend and roommate out the door, shutting it behind him. I welcomed the silence. With my book propped up on a throw pillow and my head lying down on the armrest of the couch, I continued to memorize the French language. One hour and a hundred pages later, my eyes began to grow heavy.

It felt like it was only hours before that I was being hunted by a deranged murderer in Colorado. Along with the drama of losing everything I owned in the fire and suddenly being in Paris, France taking a crash course in French—I was exhausted.

The words before me became a blur, and exhaustion took over. I closed my eyes to rest them for a moment and fell into a deep sleep.

Chapter 15

woke to the sound of shuffling feet and slamming cabinet doors. Male voices floated from the kitchen, and I sunk deeper into the couch and closed my eyes, listening.

"Do you think he followed our false trail?" Arin whispered.

"Hard to say. There hasn't been any chatter in the last 24 hours. He could be anywhere," Luca whispered back.

"I'd feel a lot better if I knew where he was. I hate being in the *dark* like this." Arin chuckled at his own joke.

"Haha, funny," Luca said humorlessly. "She's taking it pretty well . . . considering."

Arin grunted in agreement. "They've done an initial autopsy on Cole's body, confirming a single stab wound to the chest. It was a lucky shot," he said.

"He's *lucky* I didn't get to him first. I wouldn't have made it so quick and tidy," Luca's voice was low and rumbling like a gathering storm.

"Chill, man. He didn't cause any permanent damage," Arin said with a quiet chuckle. "What I don't understand is how she did it. Few untrained agents have survived a direct attack like that, and she's done it twice now. There's something special about your girl, Luca."

"She's not *my* girl." Luca heavily slammed something down onto the counter, making me flinch.

His harsh words felt like physical blows. I wrapped my arms around my middle, trying to hold the gaping hole in my chest together.

"Hey," Arin hissed, "keep it down. You'll wake her."

"Sorry." Luca sighed. "Look, Donovan is likely furious right now. He's not going to just let this go. It won't be long before he shows up in Paris."

A knock at the door halted their conversation, and heavy footsteps moved across the room toward the foyer.

"Arin, check first," Luca warned.

"I know, I know," Arin murmured. I opened my eyes to slits and watched as Arin peered through the old-fashioned peephole in the wooden door. "We're good. It's just Abbott."

He unlocked the deadbolt and opened the door to a harassed-looking man carrying several large shopping bags. Arin stepped forward and took the overstuffed bags from Abbott's hands with ease, placing them in the entryway.

"Thank you," Abbott replied, his shoulders falling in relief.

His eyes fell on me. I sat up on the couch, stretching my arms out with a yawn, trying not to wince at my own poor acting.

"It looks like I may have woken you from a nap," Abbott said, looking me over with concern. "I apologize."

"No, it's alright. I'm feeling much better." I gave him a polite smile.

"I'm glad to hear it." He motioned to the bags at his feet. "Alena and I purchased a few necessities for you. I think you'll find she has good taste if not good manners," he said with a laugh.

I stood and walked around the couch to see what he'd brought. There were various bottles and jars of high-brand cosmetics in the smaller bags and rich-colored fabrics and shoeboxes in the others. Expensive designer's names were etched into the side of each bag in silver and gold lettering.

"That's very nice of you both. I can reimburse you as soon as I get to an ATM." I didn't want to feel like a charity case, and thanks to my parents' life insurance policies, I could afford Alena's 'good taste.' Maybe.

"Oh, no! This one's on me. Consider it a welcoming gift from The Society of Light," he beamed.

I took a step back, my brows knit. "Oh. Thank you, but I'm still not sure about the Society stuff."

Abbott smiled. "I guess I *am* jumping the gun a bit. You

probably want to know more before you commit to anything. How about we take you over to The Center tomorrow morning, and we can discuss your future and any questions you may have?" He seemed so hopeful I couldn't turn him down.

"Um, sure," I said, shrugging one shoulder. "It would be nice to get settled in first."

I stared back at the bags Abbott had brought in, and a startling realization hit me. I had nowhere to put these new clothes. No bedroom. No drawers. Not even a corner to stuff them in.

I was officially homeless.

My stomach soured. I was adrift. Now, more than ever, I had no ties or attachments to this world or place in it. My parents, home, friends, and now even my country were all lost to me. All I had left was my fake AP History teacher and a small group of ridiculously good-looking strangers.

Abbott seemed convinced that my future lay with The Society of Light. Maybe he was right. Maybe he wasn't. I had a sudden, overwhelming urge to message Parisxxxi8 to ask him for his advice. But he'd been taken from me too, in a way. Our conversations about the science of light had been monitored, and continual contact might only put him in danger.

"Abbott, may I ask you a question?" I asked hesitantly.

"Anything, anytime," he said kindly.

"What happens to me now? Where will I live? I assume I

can't just go back home." The word "home" stuck like paste to the back of my mouth, making breathing difficult.

"That would be unwise," Abbott said, nodding. "There's a spare room for you in Alena's flat. These apartments are owned by The Society and are used to house its older students that are here for school and training."

Oh, no. "I'm not so sure that's a good idea. Alena doesn't seem to like me very much."

Arin barked a laugh, and I cast him a glare.

"She can stay here for a while, Abbott. I'll take the couch," Luca said from the kitchen. I looked over at him in surprise. After what happened, or didn't happen, that morning, I assumed he'd be happy to be as far away from me as possible. Luca locked eyes with me, his expression unreadable. I dropped my gaze first.

"I wouldn't want to put anyone out. Perhaps I should find my own place in the States." I played nervously with the hem of Alena's sweater.

"It isn't safe for you there anymore," Luca said, pulling my eyes to him once more. "Donovan will do everything in his power to complete his mission. You'll be surrounded by Society members here in Paris."

I turned to Abbott. "But, what about school? All my classes."

"With all of the AP classes and online college courses

you've taken throughout the years, you have more than enough credits to graduate," Abbott said. "There's no need to finish your senior year."

I knew he was right. I could've graduated a year—maybe two—early, but Mom had insisted I continue to go. She wanted me to have a 'normal' life as if normal was ever an option for someone like me.

Again, I felt the loss of what could've been. I would miss senior skip day, dances with my friends, my own *graduation*— all the ceremonies unique to senior year slipped through my fingers like smoke. If I was to be honest with myself, they'd been buried with my parents.

Pressure built up behind my eyes, and my nose began to burn. "I think I need some time to process all of this," I said thickly.

"That's quite understandable," Abbott said. "Take all the time you need. Let the boys know if any of these items don't fit, and they'll exchange them for you." He glanced over at the boys in the kitchen with an expectant expression.

"We're here to serve," Arin said with a salute.

I looked down at the rolled pants and slightly oversized sweater, suddenly anxious to change into something of my own.

"Could I use your room to change, Luca?" I said, peeking over at him tentatively.

"Of course. Arin and I need to head out in a minute anyway. Take all the time you need," he said with a polite smile. My heart gave a twist.

"Thank you." I began gathering the heavy, oversized bags into Luca's room.

"Here, let me help with that," Abbott said, reaching for the bag nearest him.

Together, Abbott and I dragged the heavy bags to the center of Luca's room, and I followed him back out to get my backpack. Arin and Luca were finished in the kitchen and were standing in the small foyer, buttoning up their black jackets.

"These kids and I have a full day," Abbott said with his hand on the doorknob. "But I'll be back first thing tomorrow morning to pick you up."

"Wait, where are you taking me? Is this place in the city?" I asked.

"Don't worry about that now. Take some time to relax, and I'll explain it all in the morning," he said with a reassuring smile.

I nibbled on my bottom lip as Abbott slapped Arin and Luca on their shoulders on his way out, promising to meet up with them later that day.

I bent down to pick my backpack off the floor, remembering my cellphone was still missing.

"Has either of you seen my phone? I think I dropped it

somewhere."

"Sorry, babe," Arin said as he approached the door. "We disposed of it before we got on the plane."

Disposed of it? My bag slipped from my fingers and hit the floor with a thud. "I'm sorry, what?"

"We couldn't risk Donovan tracing you," Arin said with a shrug.

"How am I supposed to call Rylie and let her know I'm ok?" I asked him.

"We also can't have you calling your friends and telling them where you are." Arin rolled his eyes at me as if my question was beyond stupid.

"I can't call *anyone*?" I protested.

"I'm sorry. It isn't safe," Luca said, stepping toward the open door.

"For how long?" My heart began to pump wildly. I'd never been without my phone.

"Just until The Society issues you one that can't be traced," Luca said, facing me from the doorway. "Even then, you can't tell anyone where you are. It would put all of us at risk."

Alena appeared in the hallway, her perfect mouth turned down in annoyance.

"Are you guys ready to go yet?" she asked with one hand on her hip.

"Hey, sunshine! We just finished up here," Arin said, joining her in the hallway.

"Let's go already," Alena snapped. She turned on her heel and stomped down the richly carpeted hallway.

"We'll be back later tonight," Luca said, his voice softening. "There's plenty of food in the kitchen now, so feel free to eat whatever you like. Keep the door locked, and don't open it for anyone. And *stay inside*." Worry lines formed around his eyes, making him appear older than his twenty years.

"Ok, got it," I said, nearly rolling my eyes. Where would I go?

I waved goodbye and locked the deadbolt behind them.

In Luca's room, I riffled through my new clothes and settled on a pair of black skinny jeans and an oversized grey sweater. I had to admit, they were a perfect fit. I guess Alena wasn't *entirely* horrible.

In one of the smaller bags, I found a brush and hairdryer, which I used to straighten the rat's nest that was my hair. I stood in front of the bathroom mirror, looking at my reflection. The girl staring back appeared older and maybe a bit more experienced. I suppose murder and near-death experiences did that to a person. I was never going to be the same girl I was before. A light lit my eyes. Maybe I could be something better.

Feeling more myself than I had in days, I took out Mom's letter and sat in the middle of Luca's bed, folding my legs beneath me. I stared down at my handwritten name, running a finger across the ink. I'd done this so many times it had become a kind of ritual. Like so many times before, I tried to imagine her writing it. The ghost of an image floated up in my mind of her sitting in bed, a notepad propped on her up-tucked knees, and a pen tapping the lined paper.

I twisted one of Mom's diamond earrings in my ear and closed my eyes, playing the sound of her voice over in my mind like a recording, letting the tenor and the warmth of her envelope me like a hug. Since her death, I'd been holding on to those memories and almost memories, fearing that bit by bit, I would forget the little things until, one day, she'd be entirely lost to me.

My thumb traced the edge of the envelope's sealed flap, and it lifted slightly. My heart kicked up a beat. I'd delayed opening the letter for weeks, half fearing it would reveal something big, half fearing it wouldn't. The alienness of my surroundings made me crave something from home more than ever, though, and I found myself peeling back the flap and opening the envelope. I pulled out a lined sheet of paper, folded in thirds. It was a letter, written in mom's elegant script. The page trembled in my hands as I read.

Kirie,

I've written this letter in my head over and over for years. There's so much I want to tell you, but I've struggled to put it into words, until now.

First, I want you to know that you're the light of my life. Every day I have with you is a gift. I'm sure every parent thinks that, but I'd like to believe it's even truer for me because of who you are. Your brilliance and light make the world a better place. You amaze me every day; sometimes, I can't believe that I get to be your mom.

I want you to know that it pains me to hold you back the way I do. You naturally want to get out there and do big things. I want that for you, too, but there are some things you just don't understand yet.

I know I've prevented you from being your true self, held you back. The truth is, I'm afraid, terrified really, that one day *they*'ll find you the way they found your birth father.

Kirie, your father didn't die of cancer the way I led you to believe.

From the moment I met your father, I was drawn to him, not just because he was so handsome, although that was definitely part of it. He was brighter than the California sun, and I felt happier being around him. He seemed to make the space around him brighter. We fell in love very quickly. Those were some of the best days of my life.

A few weeks after we met, your father came to me and told me there was something different about him. To me, that was obvious, and at first, I didn't understand what he was trying to tell me.

He told me he could create and control light and was part of some great movement to save humanity from darkness. I was already so in love that I just pretended to believe him and understand. But I didn't . . . not really.

Then, one day, strange men with black eyes began to show up. We would see them at the store, at the beach . . . everywhere we went. They would stand off to the side and just watch us. During those days, your father grew uneasy, and he rarely left my side as if he thought I was in danger from these strangers. I was young and silly, so I didn't mind. I enjoyed the extra attention he was giving me.

One night, as we left a movie theater, one of those men followed us to our car. Your father took me by the shoulders and said he was going to talk to the man and ask him why he was following us. He told me to go back to my apartment, where he'd meet me later. I didn't want to leave him alone with the black-eyed stalker, but he insisted.

He didn't come back that night. I waited months for him to return, but he never did. I never heard from him again.

I didn't want to accept that he was really gone, and sometimes I find myself looking for him in the crowds, even now.

When I first saw your face, I knew you were just like him. You're the embodiment of pure light, even more so than your father was. It both delighted and terrified me. I knew I had to protect you from his fate, so I hid you away. I know this has been frustrating for you, but I did what I thought was best.

I love you more than you can imagine. I see how you are maturing into a beautiful woman, and I know I can't keep you safely tucked away forever. I just hope I have done enough to keep the monsters at bay. I hope you can understand and forgive me in time.

I know you're going to do great things in this world. I can't wait to see you one day realize your true potential. I'm so proud of my shining star.

Love,

Mom

A tear fell on the paper and smeared the ink. I carefully used the hem of my sweater to pat it dry but let the following tears run down my face. I was numb and lost as I stared blurry eyed at the page. All these years . . .

Every feeling, from depression and amazement to sorrow and resignation, hit me like a firehose. Mom's words gave me both comfort and anguish. Initially, I was just happy to hear her "voice" again, but that feeling quickly soured, and anger set in.

She knew *all along* what was different about me, that I wasn't the only one like me in the world, and yet she kept it a secret. Maybe things could've turned out differently if she confided in me, and we could've somehow protected ourselves. I hated that she wasn't even around for me to yell at her for it.

My cheeks burned as my anger turned to the monsters that took her from me . . . the real reason my life was in shambles. Those bastards killed all *three* of my parents. I tried to imagine what my life would've been like with my father in it. Would he have stuck around and married my mom? Would he have gone on and done amazing things in his life with me and Mom by his side? I guess I'd never know.

So much of my life had been decided for me. I never asked for any of this. I didn't ask for the gifts I was given, nor the consequences that followed. It wasn't right that I had to be held back from my passions just so I could live an invisible life. It wasn't fair that my parents had to lose their lives because of who I was and what I could do, or that I had to live without them.

I couldn't sit any longer. I jumped off my bed and paced back and forth, seething over the injustices. My fists tightened into balls. I wanted to throat-punch someone—anyone. I could've killed Cole all over again, this time on purpose. I threw myself face-first onto the bed and screamed into the pillow. Tears clogged my throat as I punched the bed repeatedly. I raged until I had nothing left inside me.

I flipped onto my back and stared up at the ceiling. My puffy, tear-soaked cheeks stung from the salty tears. I took a deep breath and let it out slowly.

I miss you, Mom.

I missed the security I felt in her care and having someone to go to when I was scared or upset. I even missed Barry's calm presence and benign personality. I'd taken them both for granted, and now they were gone forever.

I crawled under Luca's covers and wrapped my arms around myself. I silently laid there, trying to remember the sound of Mom's voice again, the smell of her perfume, and her barking laugh when I said something stupid. Slowly, as I drifted to sleep, Mom's face was replaced by darkness, and I let it pull me into its numbing embrace. The darkness morphed into something else. A dream perhaps, though it held more weight.

I became aware that I was no longer in Luca's room. The sand beneath my feet was rough and wet, and the moon brightly shone down on the ocean stretched out before me, casting a golden trail along its surface. I soaked in what little light it offered and felt at peace.

On either side of me, an expansive beach stretched out with no beginning or end. It was beautiful in a lonely kind of way. I moved to my right and walked along the silky white sand for what seemed like days. I was dressed in a light summer dress that flowed around my legs in the warm breeze.

A movement behind me caught my attention. Turning to look, I saw only darkness. I shook off my unease and continued walking along the edge of the world as the salty waves sprayed up against my legs.

Once again, I was aware of a nagging presence behind me. It felt menacing.

This time, instead of turning, I stood still, staring out at the golden sea, and waited. At first, there was only silence. Then, a cold breeze blew past my shoulders, blowing my long hair forward. I wasn't alone. A presence stood beside me, though I saw nothing but a shadowy figure. It was an empty space, absent of any light, amidst the dimly lit night.

"Who are you?" I asked the shadow.

"I am The Void," a low and hollow voice replied. Its words echoed as if spoken in an endlessly deep tunnel.

"What do you want from me?" My tremulous voice seemed small and feeble in comparison.

Being in its presence felt like standing in a dark, empty room with no doors or walls. The sensation was larger than anything I had ever felt, yet completely lacked substance. The hope and peace I felt beneath the moon's rays were replaced with a sense of nothingness so vast it nearly choked me.

"I want what was mine in the beginning," the shadow said. His words flowed over me like an ocean wave, cold and powerful.

"I don't know what you mean," I said, stepping back.

"All that was mine, will be once more. Your light cannot stand in my way, Bright One."

In one swift movement, the shadow rushed toward me, swallowing me whole.

All light . . . gone.

All feeling . . . gone.

All meaning . . . gone.

Darkness surrounded me, stealing the energy from my being, and everything that made me who I was drifted away into oblivion. I floated in The Void for centuries and became one with its nothingness . . .

"This is your fate, Bright One," The Void said. His endless voice traveled through and over me, disappearing across the vast space. "You cannot escape it."

I gasped, waking to a darkened room. I couldn't remember where or even who I was for several long minutes. My insides were hollowed out, and I felt as though I was choking on loss and despair. The absolute hopelessness was heavy on my body like a crushing weight.

I covered my face and sobbed as if grieving a major loss, but this time, I'd lost myself. I curled into the fetal position, wrapped my arms tightly around my torso, and tried to hold myself together.

The bedroom door opened, and soft footsteps crossed the

room. The bed dipped to one side as someone slid into the sheets beside me. Strong arms wrapped around me from behind, and warmth enveloped me, chasing away the shadows.

"Shhh, it's okay, Kirie," the low voice whispered in a way that grounded to the earth.

I held on to the name he spoke, repeating it in my mind as if a single word could give me back to myself.

A soft glow filled the room and energy flowed into me, quieting my sobs and thawing my ice-covered insides.

Luca.

I recognized his unique energy. My muscles loosened, my swollen eyes drooped closed, and his light seeped into my body, fully restoring my sense of self. I leaned into his firm chest, soaking his energy like a cactus in the desert rain. Slowly, hope and light replaced the emptiness, and calm settled over me like a warm blanket.

Chapter 16

Soft sunlight filtered through white gossamer drapes, slowly waking me from my sleep. I reached out for Luca but found his side of the bed cold to the touch.

I stretched my arms and legs wide and reluctantly climbed out of bed. My feet landed in a pile of something coarse and granular. I leaned down to inspect it, noticing tiny sparkling stones shimmering amid pure white sand. A shiver of dread ran through my body.

Impossible.

I quickly ran to the shower to wash the evidence of the disturbing dream off my skin. Was it possible that the beach in my dream had been real in some way? I shook my head, convinced I was losing my mind. Perhaps the sand had been there before, brought in after a trip to some tropical location. With a private jet on hand, who knew where Luca and the others had been?

I pushed the thought from my mind and stood under the hot water for several long minutes, letting its warmth loosen my aching muscles. Although Luca's light had comforted me in the dark, I still felt physically and emotionally exhausted. The words in Mom's letter continually played through my mind like a broken record, and I struggled to shake the cold dread that lingered from the surreal dream.

All too soon, the water began to run cold. I reluctantly climbed out of the shower to get ready for the day. I rifled through the shopping bags on the floor and decided to wear a pair of heather gray slacks and a snug-fitting black sweater. They were the most mature items in the bag, and I wanted to make a good first impression at the Center of Light.

Back in the bathroom, I put on a tasteful amount of makeup and styled my hair long and loose. Carefully, I placed my pajamas back in the shopping bags along with the rest of my meager earthly possessions and left them by the bedroom door. I paused to look around the tidy yet simple room. As much as I wanted to stay, I really couldn't take over Luca's space any longer. Unfortunately, that meant embracing the idea of being roomies with Alena, the she-devil. Lord, help me.

With a heavy sigh, I exited Luca's room and was immediately surrounded by the heavenly smell of bacon. My empty stomach cramped in response. Arin stood with his back to me in the kitchen, cooking at the small stove. Luca sat on the couch watching the Paris Morning News in yesterday's clothes. My face flushed at the thought of him holding me close the night before. The innocent moment had felt incredibly intimate, and I suddenly felt shy being in the same room with him.

"Good morning, beautiful!" Arin called over his shoulder. "How'd you sleep?"

"A little rough, actually," I croaked. My voice sounded like sandpaper.

I gazed at Luca for some reaction, but he continued looking forward without acknowledging my presence. His careless rejection felt like a punch to my stomach.

"Breakfast is almost ready," Arin said. "You'll feel better once you've eaten. Food fixes everything."

"Do you need any help?" I asked.

"No, ma'am," he said in a faux Southern accent.

"Ok, if you're sure," I said with a shrug.

As I walked toward the kitchen, something flashed across the TV, catching my attention. I stood behind the couch and watched as breaking news unfolded. According to the reporter, several monuments across Paris had been vandalized overnight.

A series of small explosives had been set at the foundations of the Notre Dame, Sacre-Coeur, and Fontaine des Quatre Saisons, causing limited structural damage. No one was hurt, and so far, it was still unclear as to whether they were terrorist attacks or pranks. I peeked over at Luca again to see his reaction. His brow furrowed, and his mouth turned down in a frown as he watched the TV with intensity and focus. He looked . . . worried.

"Yo, brother! Food's ready," Arin called to Luca, pulling his attention away from the report.

"Right. I'll get the plates." Luca turned off the TV and got up from the couch.

He stretched his arms above his head with a yawn and a sliver of skin peeked out from under his raised shirt. I was instantly, stupidly distracted. Luca caught my stare as he turned to walk toward the kitchen, and I quickly dropped my eyes to the floor, caught. I awkwardly tried to think of something to say to cover up my embarrassment.

"So, Arin, do you always do the cooking?" I asked.

"If I want to live. Luca can't even toast bread. Burns it every time," he said with a laugh.

"Hey! I'll have you know I haven't burned toast in years. It's just that you're just so much better at cooking than I am. There's simply no reason for me to get in your way," Luca said in a haughty British accent.

I stood back and watched their brotherly banter. Arin seemed to bring out a lighter side of Luca. Whether it was the many years they'd known each other or the fact that Arin made everyone smile, Luca seemed to relax around him, like the world wasn't resting on his shoulders, if only for a moment.

Arin placed a large platter of meat and croissants in the middle of the table, along with a fruit and cheese tray. It looked and smelled like heaven. We all sat down to eat with Arin in the chair next to me and Luca on the other side of the table, as far away from me as possible.

"Alright, dig in guys!" Arin said in his cheerful, booming voice.

We each filled our plates high and began eating. The food was every bit as good as Mom's, and that said a lot. And, it turned out, Arin was right; the more I ate, the better I felt.

"You seriously should be a chef," I praised him.

"I know, right?" he said around a mouth full of sausage.

"You'll have to excuse his poor manners," Luca said, rolling his eyes. "He's part caveman."

Arin burped loudly. "And proud of it!"

I laughed out loud. Arin might be gross and annoying, but he was really starting to grow on me.

Luca cleared his throat and reluctantly looked at me for the first time that morning. "So, there's been a change in plans. Abbott won't be picking you up this morning. He's asked that I take you over to The Center instead."

I quickly swallowed the chunk of fruit that suddenly lodged in my throat. "Oh . . . cool. Is Abbott usually pretty busy?"

Arin nodded. "He holds an important role in the Society of Light. He's the Director of Children of Light Identification for all of Europe and North America," he said with pride.

"Once we get there, he'll introduce you to the other high-ranking Society members," Luca said.

"I have to admit, I'm a bit nervous," I said sheepishly. "I'm not sure what to expect."

"You'll be fine," Arin said with a dismissive wave. "Abbott will stay by your side the entire time."

"I guess that's okay then," I said.

"Arin's right; there's nothing to worry about," Luca assured me. "After I drop you off, I'll retrieve your new phone so you can call your friends tonight and reassure them that you're safe."

"Thank you."

Moments later, Luca got up from the table and disappeared into his room to take a shower and get ready. I stayed and helped Arin clean the dishes. I washed; he dried.

"So, do you wanna tell me *where* The Center is?" I asked Arin as I handed him a clean, wet plate.

"Not really," he said. I gave him my nastiest glare, making him laugh. "Hey! I just want you to be surprised."

"Ugh, you suck," I grumbled.

"Ready to go?" Luca asked from his bedroom door.

"Arin and I were just finishing up." I dried my wet hands

on a dishtowel and threw it at Arin's face for good measure. "I just need to grab a few things first." Luca watched us as he walked past the kitchen, a frown tugging at the corners of his mouth.

I quickly grabbed my wallet and a jacket from Luca's room and met him at the front door. Arin waved goodbye from the couch where he was putting his shoes on. An unnamed tension hung in the air as Luca and I strolled side by side down the empty hallway.

"Sorry I've taken over your room for so long," I said, peeking sideways at him.

"It's quite alright. I wasn't at all uncomfortable." He said, his mouth turning up in an endearing half-smile.

My heart gave a happy sigh, and a tingly feeling spread across my entire body. Nearly every girl I knew that was my age had crushes and even fallen in love a time or two, but I'd never understood what all the fuss was about . . . until now. I could easily fall for a boy like Luca.

"That's very generous, but I think I'd better move into the apartment next door tonight so that you can have your room back," I said as we walked onto the sidewalk out front. We faced the street and watched cars and bicyclists zip by.

Luca's smile dropped slightly. "Yeah, that's probably for the best."

"But, hey, if you hear screaming coming through the walls,

please come and stop Alena from killing me," I joked, trying to lighten the mood. Luca's returned smile felt like sunshine on my skin.

A black Renault Grand Coupe pulled up to the cub, and an official-looking man in a black, tailored suit and dark sunglasses stepped out of the driver's seat.

"This is us," Luca said, putting his hand on the small of my back and nudging me forward. My breath hitched at his casual touch.

The chauffeur nodded respectfully to Luca as we approached and opened the back door for us to climb in. Luca let me slide in first and then situated himself as far away from me in the back seat as the space allowed. I swallowed hard and turned to stare out the window, ignoring the burn behind my eyes.

Neither of us spoke as the driver navigated the car through the busy Paris streets. I watched as it flew past my window. Paris was a perfect mixture of rich history and modern living. It was beautiful and so different than anywhere I'd been before, which wasn't saying much since I'd never really been anywhere. Before long, the car stopped in front of a large stone building.

"Je vous remercie, Hugo," Luca said to the driver. He climbed out of the car and held the door open for me.

"Merci," I called forward as I followed Luca out.

I joined him on the sidewalk, and the driver sped away. We stood side by side at the edge of an expansive plaza that stretched out in front of an imposing building, the front of which was lined by Roman columns topped by a majestic dome that rose high above the surrounding buildings. My heart sped up. I recognized this historic landmark from my AP History class. Incredibly, the Panthéon was even more impressive in person. As excited as I was to see it, however, I couldn't quite understand why we were there.

I turned in a circle, trying to pinpoint which of the surrounding buildings The Center of Light might be located in. Just as I was about to ask that question, Luca began walking toward the Panthéon's stately entrance.

"Where are we going? I hurried to keep up with his long strides. "I thought we were going to The Center. Isn't the Panthéon just a mausoleum?"

"As far as the general public is concerned, that is its main function. This building, however, has been connected to the Society of Light in some way or another since the Enlightenment Period," Luca said. "It's been a meeting place for Society members for over 250 years. More recently, it has become the location of the French Center of Light."

I followed Luca through the plaza toward the rod iron gate surrounding the front entrance. I tried to figure out *where* the Society could *possibly* hide its Center inside one of Paris' most famous and visited monuments. The Panthéon wasn't exactly "low profile."

Luca confidently walked up the stone steps under the tall, white pillars to a dark, two-story panel door. Inside the foyer, he strolled up to a female attendee and held out a badge he'd taken from his pants pocket. The blushing young woman stupidly stared at Luca with her mouth slightly ajar. She wordlessly waved us forward as if in a trance without even glancing at his badge. I couldn't help but laugh a little. I knew how she felt, poor girl.

The interior walls were lined with columns that mirrored the outer ones and were covered by colorful works of art dating back hundreds of years. The Panthéon was built in the shape of a cross with three short arms and one long. Directly beneath the done was a giant mosaic clock. A metal pendulum hung by a long cord swung back and forth along the clock's surface. The slow, swinging motion was both peaceful and hypnotic.

I let my eyes travel up the stone walls to the magnificent inner dome several stories above us. Light shone through the high windows, giving the space a celestial glow. The ceiling was like a honeycomb of smaller domes surrounding the larger one in the middle. Bright, expressive art depicting stories of Frenchmen and Saints filled the empty spaces between. In all my seventeen years, I'd never seen anything so magnificent.

I wandered aimlessly through the crowds of tourists as I

marveled at the statues and stunning architecture surrounding me. Even the floor at my feet was a work of art with its black and white mosaic tile work.

"Beautiful, isn't it?" Luca asked from behind me.

"Incredible!" I spun around and saw him staring at me with a strange, unreadable expression. Unsure if I'd done something wrong, the smile slipped from my lips.

After an uncomfortable moment, Luca cleared his throat and said, "Come, I want to show you something."

He led me to a set of twin staircases that led down to a subterranean level. As I followed Luca down the wide, stone steps, his strong, broad shoulders distracted, and I nearly missed a step. I quickly grabbed the railing and concentrated on putting one foot in front of the other.

At the bottom, was a large room with rounded ceilings supported by more stone columns. Wall lamps hung along the perimeter, illuminating the darkened space, and informational plaques and posters were displayed along the walls. On either side of the room were alcoves housing various sarcophaguses containing the remains of the Panthéon's infamous patrons.

Luca stepped back, letting me lead the way as I explored the underground crypt. I lost myself in the honeycomb of hallways and tombs. Despite the many tourists filling the space, a certain hush was in the air. Something about the setting inspired reverence. It was like standing on holy ground.

I turned and gazed at Luca, who patiently followed me. "This place feels ancient. How old *is* this building?" I asked quietly. Truthfully, I knew everything about the Panthéon's history; I just wanted an excuse to hear Luca speak.

"Originally, this was the location of an old decrepit abbey dedicated to St. Genevieve. In 1744, Louis XV commissioned Jacques-Germain Soufflot to restore it. Soufflot's inspiration for his design was light, actually. He wanted to infuse it into every corner of this building. Sadly, he died before he could complete his work, and much of his vision wasn't realized. Now, this building is used as a burial place for France's exceptional men and women." Luca ran his hand along the stone wall as we continued to walk. "Soufflot was a member of the Society of Light. You'd be surprised by how many of the men and women buried here were."

We stopped at a statue of a man wearing a long cloak and carrying a book in one hand. At its base, etched into stone, was the name VOLTAIRE. Behind it was an alcove that housed his stone coffin.

"Let me guess, Voltaire was also a member of the Society," I joked.

"Of course," Luca said seriously. "Voltaire fought against oppression and tyranny and brought light and knowledge to his country. He's exactly what an Agent of Light *should* be."

"Oh. Well, that makes sense," I said, suddenly feeling two

feet tall. "Did he have . . . special powers like you?"

"Like *us*, Kirie. And no. Although they were quite brilliant, Children of Light haven't had the *unique* ability to harness the power of light until the last one hundred years or so."

"I'm still having a hard time thinking of myself as a 'Child of Light'," I said, making quotation marks with my hands.

"It really isn't anything new. You've always been who you are. You're just able to put a name to it now."

"It isn't that simple. I still don't even understand what being a Child of Light means. How am I supposed to know if this path is right for me? I didn't even know any of this existed two days ago." Tears of frustration clouded my eyes.

"This is who you *are*, whether you accept it or not. Nothing you do can change that," he said with a sigh.

"Well, what about you? When Abbott found you as a boy, did *you* just automatically know that you wanted to fight against darkness in some crazy war?"

Luca's eyes shifted into the color of a stormy sea. "I've been fighting darkness all my life," he said darkly.

An uncomfortable silence filled the suddenly vast space between us. Clearly, I'd touched on a sensitive subject. My heart hurt for this beautiful, damaged boy. The scars Donovan left on him years ago must run deep. I wanted to close the distance and comfort him in some way.

Luca cleared his throat. "We should probably get going.

Abbott's waiting."

He abruptly turned and strode back toward the staircases that led to the main floor, the tension in his shoulders visible. I hurried after him, nearly running to keep up with his angry pace. About halfway up the wide staircase, my foot caught along the edge of a step, pitching me forward. Strong, steady hands caught me by the shoulders just before my forehead connected with the stairs above me.

"Oh, my gosh!" I gasped, looking up at Luca. "I'm so sorry,"

His stern face and shoulders softened. "No, it's my fault. I was going too fast. I forget how short you are."

Luca carefully brought me to my feet, grabbed my hand in his, and pulled me up the rest of the stairs. I held on tightly to him and I soaked in his heady energy.

Touching Luca was like touching pure electricity. It made me feel alive in a way I had never felt before, like standing in the sunlight . . . only much, much better. I stared up at his profile to see if he could feel it, too, but Luca didn't give anything away.

Once we reached the main floor, he dropped my hand and turned toward the front doors. I glanced around, confused.

"I thought you said The Center of Light was here. Why are we leaving?" I asked.

"Are you always this impatient?" he said sarcastically, a

small smile playing at the edge of his mouth.

"More confused, really," I replied.

Luca stopped and turned to look at me. "Do you trust me, Kirie?" The force of his gem-green eyes and my name on his lips left me speechless. All I could do was nod yes.

"Good," Luca said and continued to a pair of solid doors just off the side of the main entrance. Like a gentleman, he held one of them open for me. On the other side, was an old, handleless door with a high-tech keypad next to it. Luca took the badge out of his pant pocket again and held it up to the face of the keypad, turning the light on top from red to green. The door slid soundlessly open, revealing an opulent elevator cab.

I held my breath and followed Luca inside. The elevator was made completely of glass floor to ceiling with gold hardware and trim. Stone surrounded the elevator, and light reflected down from above. Once the door shut completely, Luca placed his palm on a small scanner set within the glass wall and the elevator shot upward. I reached out and grabbed onto the gold railing to steady myself.

Within seconds, the stone walls gave way to a 360° view of the city below. In the distance, I could see the Eiffel Tower and Notre Dame.

"Soooo, the Center of Light is on the *roof*?" I asked, trying to hide my amazement behind sarcasm. "It's funny, I didn't see it from the road.”

“Not everything is as it seems, Kirie. You should know that by now,” Luca said with a smirk.

“Yes, I should,” I mumbled.

When the elevator reached the rooftop level, it slowed to a stop. As the door slid open, the world around me changed. One minute, I was looking through the glass at the green metal roof of the Panthéon; the next, I was staring at a bright, spacious reception area.

“After you,” Luca said, holding the elevator door open for me. With my mouth hanging open, I entered a light-filled room.

Donovan 4

From a distance, the assassin watched as chunks of stone from the famous Fontaine des Quatre Saisons flew through the air. Men, women, and children fled as debris shot out into the small crowd of tourists.

The exercise aimed only to inflict minimal damage. Their panicked screams were just an added bonus.

Based on the concentrated number of Society members tracked there recently, Paris had finally been identified as a probable location for one of the twelve Centers of Light. Since The Society of Light loved their symbols of enlightenment and freedom of expression, it was also highly likely they were using a historically significant establishments to hide their operation.

The plan was to set off small explosions at the city's various monuments and historical buildings. They'd know they hit the jackpot once they saw frantic Society members running around. Simple.

Luckily for the assassin, he didn't need to waste time searching for the girl after *they* took her away. He was already in Paris prepping for the planned attacks when his sources found her in a small café in the 7th Arrondissement. A surveillance team had been trailing Luca for weeks, so they immediately knew he had brought her home to the City of Lights. They'd lost them once they left the airport, but that was a small matter.

This was just the break he needed. Isolating her in such a large, unfamiliar city would make his job much easier. His luck was finally turning.

The assassin lifted his long-range binoculars and scanned the crowd. So far, no members of The Society had shown up. Another location was crossed off the list . . .

Chapter 17

he spacious rectangular room was made of floor-to-ceiling glass windows. Sunlight filled the inner space, leaving little need for artificial light.

I looked all around, trying to orient myself. From my mental calculations, I guessed the room was situated somewhere on top of the longer section of the cross in front of the dome.

Directly opposite the elevator sat a white marble reception desk framed by a cascading water feature that extended toward the glass ceiling. A stylish young man wearing black-framed glasses sat behind it.

"Bienvenue, Luca! Comment allez-vous aujourd'hui?" he asked with an easy smile.

"Je suis très bien, meci," Luca replied in French. "Aaron, I'd like you to meet Kirie. She just arrived from America."

"Ah, welcome, Kirie. I'm happy to meet you," Aaron said in heavily accented English.

"*Je suis heureux de vous rencontrer ainsi, Aaron.*" I replied shyly.

"Tres bon! Your French is exceptionnel!" He clapped his hands. "When did you learn?"

"Yesterday," I said, ducking my head.

"Bien sur!" Aaron said with a laugh.

"Will you let Abbott know we've arrived? He's expecting us." Luca said, switching back to French.

"Absolutely!" Aaron picked up a sleek, cordless phone and spoke in rapid French before hanging up again. "Monsieur Abbott is ready for you. You may go back."

I waved to Aaron and followed Luca around the reception desk into a large, spacious room. The energy hit me like a fist to the stomach. The open space was a beehive of activity. Modern white desks were set up in staggered rows in the middle of the room. Neatly dressed men and women of all ages and nationalities sat behind the desks topped by transparent computer screens. Many talked into sleek black headsets at their ears while others moved quickly around the room, consulting with one another. The air buzzed with electricity.

I followed Luca as he worked his way across the room, my eyes darting around like ping-pong balls as I tried to take it all in. The inner glass wall that curved around the Panthéon's dome was lit with what looked like giant screens. Large maps of the European nations were displayed on the wall like a high-tech war room.

A live news feed of the overnight attacks on Paris' historical monuments played on one of the screens. A severe-looking woman in a sleek black suit and heels stood before it, taking notes on a leather-bound notepad. It looked like a scene straight out of a CIA movie.

"What do all these people do here?" I whispered to Luca. Several people looked up as we passed, curiosity plain on their faces. I dropped my eyes to the ground to avoid eye contact and walked a little closer to Luca.

"This is our inside unit," he said. "They provide tech support and keep tabs on any current events that may be significant to our operation. This Center is essentially the central hub for The Society in this part of Europe. We couldn't do what we do without them."

I looked up at Luca, brows furrowed. "How many Centers of Light *are* there in the world?" I asked.

"Twelve in total. Each center is located in current or past . . . epicenters, so to speak, of enlightenment or advancement," he replied. "For instance, there's a Center in Rome, Edinburg, Seoul, and London. They act as lighthouses across the globe. That's partially why people are drawn to them."

I thought about which of the twelve centers my birth father

may have trained at. I could very well be in the same building he spent most of his youth in. The idea made the hairs on my arms stand on end.

Luca led the way out of the 'war room' and into a wide hallway that curved along the dome into one of the shorter arms of the cross. Unlike the open space behind us, this portion was sectioned into offices, several on each side with a hallway in between. Each was separated by frosted glass walls.

"Abbott's office is here on the left," Luca said, pointing to the plaque beside the door with his name on it. "I've got to run to meet Arin. Abbott will take it from here."

My stomach soured. "Oh, okay," I said with a forced smile. "Thanks for showing me around today."

"It was my pleasure," he said, smiling back.

"Um, I'll see you later?" I asked, sincerely hoping I wouldn't have to find my way back to the apartment by myself.

"Absolutely," Luca said, walking a few steps away before abruptly turning around to face me again. "Look, I know it can be a bit overwhelming at first, but don't let this pomp and pageantry intimidate you. Don't forget, you're strong."

He'd said the same thing to me back in the hospital when he healed my neck. His belief in me made me stand a little straighter.

"Thank you," I said.

Luca nodded once and continued back the way we'd come.

Once he was out of sight, I took a deep breath and turned to face Abbott's office. I let my heart rate settle before knocking on the tall glass door.

"Come in," a familiar voice called from inside.

I turned the doorknob and walked into a large, open office. A long, wide desk sat in front of a glass wall that looked out onto the busy Paris streets. The tall windows and sparse furnishings gave the space an airy, open feel.

An older man wearing a stylish three-piece suit and tie stood up from the large desk. He looked like someone you wouldn't want to mess with . . . someone with power and influence. It took me a moment to remember it was Abbott!

His new ultra-professional appearance so sharply contrasted with his typical nerdy professor look that he was nearly unrecognizable. Even the half-moon glasses he always wore at the tip of his nose were missing. His hair had been freshly cut and styled, and his posture spoke of confidence. I instantly missed the other Abbott. He was much less intimidating.

"Welcome!" Abbott boomed.

"Hi," I said, stepping further into the room. "You look . . . different this morning,"

"Yes, well, I may have overdone it with the old professor bit back in the States. The sweater vest and reading glasses were mostly for fun. Unfortunately, today it's back to the real world," he chuckled. "Luca gave you a tour of the lower level, I presume?"

"If by 'lower level' you mean the world-famous historical monument you all built your fancy fort on top of, then yes, he did," I joked, amused by his casual reference to the Panthéon. "It was amazing."

"Oh, good! Just give me a moment to finish up here and we'll begin our tour."

Abbott shut his ultra-thin, black laptop and began stacking the papers on his desk in tidy rows. While I waited, I examined his office. The décor was similar to the rest of the building with its sterile, modern appeal. The only color in Abbott's stark white office came from the two paintings that hung on the walls, one on either side of the room. I narrowed my eyes. The paintings were strangely familiar. I walked to the one on the left to take a closer look. It was an abstract painting of a romantic night scene with stars reflecting down onto the water below.

My heartbeat quickened. I knew this painting! I inspected it again to make sure I wasn't hallucinating. Then, I ran across the room to examine the other painting, another colorful abstract, this one of a man's face. My mouth hung open as I stared at it in total awe. Both paintings were incredibly beautiful and *outrageously* valuable. I swung around to face Abbott who was leaning on the edge of his desk, watching me with a fatherly smile.

"Are these real?" I squeaked. Surely these weren't genuine Picasso and Van Gogh pieces.

"Being a high-ranking member of the oldest and most powerful organization on earth allows for certain perks," he said with a shrug.

"Wait! They *are* real?" I said in disbelief.

Abbott nodded.

I gazed back at the Picasso before me and marveled at its iconic lines and colors before running back to the other side of the room to nearly drool over Van Gogh's "Starry Night Over the Rhone."

I'd never been this close to an original piece of priceless art before. The way Van Gogh painted the light reflecting on the water was magical. My chest swelled with pure joy as I studied the brush strokes made by the master's own hands. I felt as giddy inside as a preteen meeting her celebrity crush.

I looked at Abbott. "Thank you for sharing these with me." The expression on his face stopped me. He stared at me like I did at the paintings, with awe.

"What? Is something wrong?" I asked, my face heating.

"Kirie, you're *glowing*," he said, his voice thick with unshed tears. "I haven't seen a light this pure since I found Luca on the streets of London."

I looked down at my arms. Light spilled from every pour.

It was so clear and bright it made the white walls appear almost yellow in hue. The color of my light was different from when I defended myself against Cole, though I had no idea *why*. I'd hid my ability away for so long that I was completely unfamiliar with the complexities of my own body.

"Why . . . how?" I stuttered.

"You're still untrained, so your light shines through only when you're feeling extreme emotions. In this case, it seems to be brought out by pure joy," he said, wiping his wet eyes.

I peered down again at my hands, turning them over. My light was *beautiful!* After a few moments, it began to fade, and all that was left was my pale, unremarkable skin. I felt disappointed at its absence.

"How's all of this possible?"

"I'm sure you've noticed that you're not quite like your peers," Abbott said as if it were obvious.

"Well, I've always done pretty well in my classes," I said modestly. Abbott raised his eyebrows. "Okay, I have above-average intelligence," I conceded.

Abbott raised his eyebrows even higher as if waiting for something. I didn't know what he wanted from me . . . or at least, I didn't want to admit that I did.

"Kirie, there's even more to you than mere brilliance and we both know it. There've been enlightened individuals during every generation of human life. Brilliant, magnificent individuals, and while it's true that you're very *smart*, there's much more to you than just that." He paused for a moment, his expression becoming more serious. "Tell me about the other night when Cole attacked you."

My heart dropped in my stomach, and I took a couple of steps back. The guilt and sorrow at what I had done came rushing back. My shoulders hunched forward, and tears clouded my eyes. I didn't want to talk about what I'd done to Cole. Even though he'd meant to kill me, I felt ashamed.

"It's okay. You're not in trouble," Abbott said kindly.

"I didn't mean to hurt him, really," I whispered. "I just wanted to stop him. I'm not even sure how I did it. Light just . . . came out of me . . . and, and . . ." I couldn't say it.

Abbott slowly walked over to me and put a warm hand on my shoulder. "Kirie, you have no reason to feel ashamed for what happened. You're a Child of Light. That has more meaning than you can imagine right now but believe me when I say that it makes you special and wonderful," he explained. "Like the other Agents of Light here today, you're a warrior, born to battle darkness. This is what we *do*." He gave my shoulder a reassuring pat before dropping his hand.

I thought back to Mom's letter. She had mentioned that my birth father claimed to fight living shadows. Perhaps Abbott was right. I was my father's daughter. Still, it was difficult to think of myself as a soldier in any war. It wasn't in my *nature* to fight.

"I don't want to use my abilities to hurt others," I said. I never again wanted to feel like I did when Cole died at my hands.

"Difficult actions must be taken during times of war. Make no mistake, Kirie, we *are* at war. What you did to Cole wasn't only done in self-defense, but it was also your duty as a Bright One. Men like Cole hunt and murder innocents for sport. You bravely cleansed the earth of a great evil. The Agents of Light are here on this earth to protect others from the handmaids of darkness personified, and that's what you did."

Darkness personified. I was reminded of the vision I'd had the night before. The darkness spoke to me, even threatened me. Was that the Shadowmen's master? "I had a dream last night that the darkness spoke to me," I said. "It felt so real."

"Can you tell me about it?" Abbott asked, giving me his complete attention.

I described the dream in its entirety, even telling him about the sand I found on my feet. Abbott silently listened without interruption. When I finished, we stood in stillness for several moments while he processed what I'd told him.

"Kirie, before there was life, darkness reigned," he said slowly. "The darkness that makes up space has no beginning and no end. The dark nothingness you experienced will be humanity's fate if The Order successfully eradicates light from the Earth. That's why we're here, to give humankind a fighting chance."

"I still don't understand what you expect from me. I'm just an average high school girl. What could I possibly do to help?" I asked.

Abbott patted me on the shoulder. "You sell yourself short, my dear. I think we can both agree that you're anything but average. The abilities you demonstrated the other night were just the tip of the iceberg. You are capable of many more extraordinary things," Abbott said.

"Do other Children of Light have these kinds of dreams?" I asked.

"I have only known one other person to have such a visitation. He, too, has shown amazing potential," Abbott said like a proud father.

"Luca," I guessed.

"Yes, Luca. I found him in the worst circumstances, and even then, his light cut through the darkness like a knife."

"When he healed me, it was the most amazing experience. His light healed my wounds and made me feel better *inside*," I said, putting a hand on my chest.

"Yes, he is indeed a skilled healer. The Society's best, in fact." Abbott's face grew serious. "I've noticed your fondness for him."

I hid my blushing face in my hands. "Am I that obvious?"

I groaned through my fingers.

"Don't feel embarrassed, Kirie," Abbott said, pulling my hands from my face. "It's natural for you to feel that way about him. The two of you are similar in both ability and strength, which naturally draws you together. However, though Luca's difficult past may not have dimmed his inner light, it *has* scarred him in other ways that prevent him from forming intimate attachments. I hope one day that may change for him, but in the meantime, it's best not to get your hopes up," Abbott said kindly.

I dropped my eyes to the floor. "I actually don't think that is an issue. I'm pretty sure he's not into me anyway."

"Oh, the follies of youth." Abbott shook his head with a sigh. "Well, we better get moving. Things to do . . . people to see and all that."

I looked at the paintings wistfully one last time before I followed Abbott out of the office. We continued down the curved hallway toward the back end of the Panthéon. As we walked, I kept my eyes on the intricate design of the inner dome to my left and marveled at the exquisite workmanship.

Before long, we arrived at another frosted glass door. Abbott paused with his hand on the doorknob.

"Beyond this door is the training room," he explained. "Our head trainer, Bert, is currently teaching a class for the young agents living here in Paris. This will be the group you'll begin training with should you decide to stay with us. Come, I'll introduce you to them."

Abbott pushed the door open to a room that could only be described as an armory. Handguns, assault rifles, swords, knives, and every form of weapon imaginable lined the glass walls from floor to ceiling. My hands began to sweat.

In the center of the room was a group of boys and girls dressed in athletic wear. They sat cross-legged on yoga mats with their eyes closed as if they were meditating. The small group of five varied in age, size, and ethnicity. The oldest student looked to be younger than me by a few years. A man in his mid-twenties moved between them, quietly giving directions. I assumed this was Bert. Just like his students, he was dressed in lightweight clothing and bare feet. He was fit and had a long, stern face and brown hair cropped close to his head.

He walked slowly over to Abbott and quietly whispered, "We're almost done with our refocus."

"Not a problem. We'll just wait," Abbott whispered back.

Bert gave a small bow and walked back to his students. At the front of the class was a little girl who appeared to be no more than five or six years old. She was tiny with dark curly hair and warm-colored skin. A smile crept onto my face. The thought of her training with the weapons surrounding her was laughable. I just couldn't imagine it.

"Feel free to look around while we wait for them to finish up," Abbott said quietly.

I nodded in response and began to walk along the room's perimeter, letting my eyes travel across the massive collection of armaments hanging along the wall. The sheer number of weapons was alarming. Even more frightening, however, were the *types* of weapons being openly displayed. Assault rifles, bayonets, machine guns, crossbows; you name it, they had it.

A collection of jagged knives and swords in varying shapes and sizes was nestled right between the grenades and throwing stars. They were not your typical kitchen cutlery. No, they were the type of weapons one would only use to inflict maximum damage to an opponent.

The image of Donovan's knife sliding smoothly across my mother's throat suddenly filled my mind. Nausea slammed into my stomach hard. I covered my mouth with the palm of my hand and took deep breaths, trying not to puke all over the light wood floor.

"Alright class, roll up your mats and put them away. Run drills individually for a while," the instructor barked in French, pulling me from my thoughts. I took one last deep breath and turned around to face the rest of the room, trying to act unaffected. "And, Dayton, make sure you put your mat away right this time," Bert chided.

A small boy around eleven with spiky blond hair and a

freckled face bowed low in response. When Bert looked away, however, the boy rolled his eyes and mouthed *'whatever'* before sauntering to the back corner with a haphazardly thrown-together mat. I bit down on a laugh. Clearly, he was the troublemaker of the group.

Abbott and Bert walked off to the side of the room, angled their shoulders away from the rest of us, and began to speak in low tones. I had a sinking feeling I was the topic of their conversation. That made me uneasy.

I felt a light tap on my shoulder. Turning around, I saw the little girl from before standing right behind me.

"Hi! My name's Aonani, and you're pretty." She grabbed my hand in hers and swung it back and forth.

"Oh. Thank you," I said, taken back by her forwardness.

"I'm six. My mommy and I are from Hawaii. What's your name?" she loudly asked. "You sound American."

I smiled at her enthusiasm. "I am actually…"

"Why are you so old?" she said, cutting me off.

"What do you mean 'old'," I laughed. "I'm only seventeen."

"Most new kids are little like me," she stared up at me with innocent eyes. My heart melted.

"I see . . ." I said, smiling down at her.

A loud thud rang behind me, causing me to jump. I dropped Aonani's hand and spun around. A young girl with light, wavy brown hair and chubby, dimpled cheeks stood in front of a target in the back of the room holding a metal bow. The end of the metal arrow was in the middle of the bull's eye.

The girl lowered the bow and turned our way with a superior look. When she caught my eye, she flipped her hair over her shoulder and grabbed another arrow from the quiver at her side.

"That's Eden. She thinks she's the best in the class just because she's fifteen," the small girl said with an exaggerated eye roll.

"Shut up, Aonani," Eden yelled with a thick Australian accent. "I'm better than *you.*"

"Nuh, uh!" Aonani shot back, hands on hips.

"Girls, girls, you're both pretty," said a small Asian boy standing in front of the collection of long swords. He pulled the largest one down from the brackets with little difficulty. It was easily as big as he was.

"Well, at least *I'm* pretty. Pipsqueak over here is just obnoxious," Eden quipped.

"Eden," said a tall girl standing in front of the bayonets. "We don't want to scare away our new friend."

Off to the side, the young boy flipped, twirled, and parried with the giant sword he pulled from the wall. I hunched my shoulders to my ears and backed away slightly. He looked like a tiny ninja. There was no way that could be safe.

"Speak for yourself, Dawn," Eden said. "We have enough

girls in our class as it is." She re-focused and expertly shot another arrow at the target. The resounding thud echoed through the room, making me jump.

Dawn rolled her eyes and walked over to where I stood. "You will have to excuse Eden; she is not polite. My name is Dawn, and I am from Nairobi." She held out her hand for me to shake.

Dawn was nearly six feet tall and rail thin. Her head was shaved, and she had the darkest skin I had ever seen. She was stunning. She couldn't have been older than thirteen, yet she exuded confidence and kindness, a rare combination. A soft light rested on her like a cloak. I'd never met anyone like her before.

"It's nice to meet you, Dawn," I said, smiling. "My name is Kirie."

"She's old," Aonani broke in.

"Not so old, little one," Dawn said with a smile. "Besides, age does not matter. We all have our own path to walk."

"Yeah, but she doesn't even know anything yet," Aonani announced.

"I am glad you have come to be in our class," Dawn said, ignoring her.

I took another look around the metal-filled room, and anxiety began to creep into my chest. My instincts screamed for me to *run!*

"Yeah, about that. I'm not so sure about all of this. I'm all for learning to control my light, but training to fight just isn't my thing," I said hesitantly.

"What's wrong? Are you scared or something?" Aonani stared up at me with her mouth open in amazement.

"Yeah, kind of," I said, shrugging my shoulders. "I really don't like violence. I've seen enough of it to last me a lifetime."

Dawn touched my arm and peered at me with her expressive brown eyes. "I hope you change your mind."

"Class! S'alligner." Bert yelled out, breaking away from Abbott.

All five students promptly stopped what they were doing and lined up based on age, with Eden in the front. I took a deep breath and joined Abbott by the wall.

"I would love to let you stay and watch the rest of the class, but we need to move along," Abbott said.

"That's alright. I'm ready to go anyway." The weapon-studded walls were closing in on me the longer we stayed.

"Thank you for allowing us to interrupt your instruction, Bert," Abbott said.

"Bien sur," Bert said with a bow. "I hope to see you again soon, Kirie."

I gave a polite wave and followed Abbott to the door on the other side of the room. As we left the training room, I threw one last glance at the collection of knives hanging on the wall. My stomach soured. Although I had enjoyed meeting the others, I still had no interest in training for battle. I turned forward and noticed Abbott watching me.

"I'm sorry, Kirie. It must've been a shock to be around all those weapons," he said apologetically. I nodded in response. "Although you've recently been through some major traumatic experiences, I assure you, in time, your fear and sadness will fade. We can teach you to control and master these tools instead of fearing them. We can make you stronger."

"You don't understand," I said, shaking my head sharply. "I have no interest in learning to use guns and knives. I just . . . can't!" Tears clouded my vision, and I blinked them back angrily.

"I *do* understand your hesitation, but you must learn to protect yourself at the very least. The Order will not cease to hunt you. Please, do me a favor and think on it for a while, okay?"

I agreed without any real conviction and followed Abbott away from the training room of death.

Chapter 18

I **gazed out the** glass windows at the expansive view as we walked around the other side of the inner dome. From this vantage point, I could see across Paris. Beautiful turn-of-the-century buildings stretched out as far as the eye could see.

Again, I was struck by how different my life had suddenly become. Just last week I was living in a small Colorado town with coyotes and tumbleweed, and now, I was looking out at one of the world's most beautiful modern cities. It was difficult to process it all.

I slowed and placed my palm against the smooth, sun-warmed glass. Along the palm of my hand, I felt a soft vibration. I leaned even closer, putting my ear up the glass. It hummed quietly. Clearly, there was more to the Center's outer wall than just typical glass.

"How's this possible?" I asked Abbott. He patiently waited for me just a few feet down the hall.

"Mirrors, reflection, high-definition screens. What you see from the street is a trick of the eye . . . camouflage if you will," Abbott said nonchalantly as if explaining the function of a toaster.

"This has got to be the most advanced tech I have ever seen," I said in wonder.

"Many of the most brilliant minds in the world are members of The Society, Kirie. These walls are the least of their modern accomplishments," Abbott said with pride. "Come, Mr. Daiko is here for the day, and I'd like you to meet him."

I dropped my hand from the glass and followed Abbott further down the hall.

"Who's Mr. Daiko?" I asked.

"He's one of the three current leaders of The Society of Light. Part of his job is to travel to each of the different Centers worldwide to monitor operations and make connections with those on a local level. Luckily for you, he happens to be in Paris this week."

Yeah, lucky me, I thought in dread. Nothing like jumping headfirst into the deep end.

"Why are there *three* leaders of the Society?" I asked. "Doesn't it make more sense to have just one? I would think having more would be . . . complicated."

Abbott stopped to look at me. "It is important to maintain balance and distribution of power," he said. "Remember this, Kirie: absolute power corrupts. Not even the Children of Light are completely immune to its seduction."

Before I could respond, Abbott led the way into the final portion of the cross-shaped building. This wing was a mirror image of the office wing across from it, only without plaques beside the doors.

"These offices are for visiting dignitaries. Mr. Daiko uses this one when he's in town," Abbott said, indicating the first door to the right. "I have a few things to get done this morning, so I'll leave you two to talk. You know where my office is when you're ready to go."

What? He was just going to leave me there with this stranger. I suddenly felt like a dog being left on the side of some old farm road.

My shoulders tensed. I was completely ill-prepared to speak privately with one of the most powerful men in the world. What if I couldn't think of anything to say? What if I made a fool of myself? "I'm not so sure I'm ready for this," I confessed.

"You'll be just fine," he said, waving my concern away as if it were a pesky fly. He walked back down the hallway. "Come find me when you're finished," he called over his shoulder.

My body practically vibrated with nerves as I knocked on

the frosted glass door. A deep male voice called for me to enter. I turned the doorknob, pausing for a moment, terrified of what lay beyond. I held my breath and stepped into the office.

Sitting behind the long, white desk was a small-framed man in his mid-60s with white hair and wrinkles around his slanted eyes. I let out the breath I'd been holding. He appeared friendly and harmless, like somebody's grandpa.

Mr. Daiko stood and gave a small bow before moving around the desk and meeting me in the center of the room. Though he couldn't have been more than five foot, two inches tall, the energy rolling off him gave him the presence of a much larger man.

He reached out and shook my hand with a dry, firm grip. The energy between our joined hands was different from the shock I felt when I touched Luca. Instead of a jolt, a steady stream of pure, raw energy flowed into me.

"It's so nice to meet you, Kirie Sorenson," he said with a slight Mandarin accent. "Abbott has told me many good things about you." His smile brightened the room.

"Thank you. It's nice to meet you, too," I said politely.

"Wonderful!" He dropped my hand. "Please, come sit and talk with me."

Mr. Daiko approached a leather chair framed in brushed metal and pulled it out for me. When I was comfortably seated, he settled himself behind the desk in a tall wing-backed chair, his feet not quite reaching the ground.

I sat straight in my chair, trying to look attentive and smart. For reasons I couldn't explain, I wanted to impress this stranger. I felt like I was in an interview with the president. In some ways, I was.

"So, Kirie, I hear this is your first time out of the States. Are you enjoying Paris?" he asked kindly.

"I like this city very much. There's so much history and art here. I'd rather be here under better circumstances, though."

"Yes, I heard about your recent sorrows. I'm sorry for your great loss," Mr. Daiko said, bowing his head.

"Thank you," I said, fighting tears. "So much has happened in the last couple of weeks, and I'm still having difficulty sorting it all out."

"I understand. Finding that you're different in such a powerful way while dealing with profound loss must be very difficult to process. The Children of Light don't have easy fortunes. I've seen my own share of sorrow and pain," he said with a sad smile. "But you're here now, and your path to becoming an Agent of Light may finally begin."

"That's the thing," I said, fighting my frustration. "I still don't even understand what being an Agent of Light means."

"The answer to that is not so cut and dry. Just as there are all kinds of people, so are the Children of Light. Some are brilliant minds that bring light to the world through knowledge and human advancement. Others are great leaders who can use their charisma and essence to convince many to follow them. Then, there are those like us who are all those things and more. We are called amidst the final battle against The Order to use our light to tip the scales in our favor."

"So, you also have special abilities . . . like me?" I asked.

"We each have our own individual talents, but yes, you and I are similar. We're made up of more light and energy than the average human or even other Society of Light members. Although they're enlightened in their own right, we're able to access our energy on a much more advanced level. This makes us very powerful and important tools against darkness. You, Kirie, are meant to be a bright light in the darkest of times," Mr. Daiko said with a grandfatherly smile.

"Everyone keeps talking about this battle against the Shadowmen. It almost sounds like The Society of Light is some zealous religious organization preparing for the apocalypse," I said with a dry laugh. He didn't return the laugh, and I shifted in my seat uncomfortably.

"Although some of The Society's members have been great religious leaders, The Society itself isn't a religious organization," he said seriously. "The battle between light and dark is eternal in nature. It predates all periods, societies, and religious organizations. You and I are but a small part of this long-fought war."

I let that sink in for a moment. No matter what anyone said or how often they said it, the mere thought of *me* going to battle was laughable.

"I have to admit, I'm not completely comfortable with the idea of physically fighting anyone. Abbott showed me the training room. I'm grateful for the chance to learn to control my inner light, or whatever it's called, but I'm not comfortable training with weapons. I would rather use my gifts in more positive ways, like . . . I don't know . . . inventing things or becoming a professor someday," I said.

Mr. Daiko steepled his fingers and studied the desk in front of him.

"I understand. Your mother sheltered you from the world. This has allowed you to retain your innocence. You have a fresh view of humanity, and that's a beautiful and rare thing. However, you also have a false sense of security," he leaned forward. "Unfortunately, the war between light and darkness is real, and you're a part of it . . . whether you want to be or not. With that said, what you do with your life is for you to decide. We'll not force you to do anything you're unwilling to do." He looked up at me again with a reassuring smile.

"Honestly? I want to go to college and create things that improve the world. I'm not interested in being a soldier," I said.

I had so much more to give the world than violence. My

dreams for the future never included going to war. I wanted to grow, experience life, and give back all that I had learned.

"But Kirie, you may still do all those things. We strongly encourage all our members to further their education and contribute to the communities around them. I have several doctorate degrees myself and have accomplished much good in my life. Knowledge is a great tool against darkness." Mr. Daiko placed his palms flat against the desktop and stared me in the eye. "The Shadowmen have always used violence to spread fear and despair. We must also train ourselves to defend against this physical threat. Be assured, we only fight when it is required."

I shifted uncomfortably in my seat, unsure of what to say. Although he made a good point, I still couldn't imagine training to hurt another human being on purpose.

"I can see you need more time to think it through. I will not take any more of your day lecturing you," he said, ending the meeting.

Mr. Daiko stood and walked around the desk, meeting me on the other side. When I got up from my chair, he took both of my hands in his, and once again, I could feel the pure energy in his grip. Without saying a word, he examined my face for several uncomfortable moments. I shifted from foot to foot, unsure whether to thank him for his time or wait for him to speak. Sensing he was looking for something in me, I opted to stay silent and wait.

The energy that was concentrated between our joined palms began to move up my arms like a serpent. I tried to pull away, but Mr. Daiko tightened his grip on my hands to the point of pain. He was incredibly strong for a small guy.

"What…" I gasped.

My sight turned inward as his energy snaked its way up through my shoulders and into my head. His light moved with purpose as if it was sentient. . . as if it was searching for something.

Seemingly out of nowhere, images of my past filled my mind. I gasped out loud and stumbled backward, but Mr. Daiko held me close, his grip punishing.

My first day of 2nd grade.

Watching my mom exchange vows with Barry at their wedding.

Meeting Rylie for the first time.

Hugging Mom and telling her I loved her before heading out for the night with friends.

Mom gasping for breath.

Luca's angel eyes gazing down at me in the hospital room.

Staring down at Cole lying still in a pool of his own blood.

Tears rolled down my face as my life played like a movie before my eyes.

"Please. Stop!" I cried. I tried again to pull my hands away, but Mr. Daiko refused to let go.

His unblinking eyes were vacant, unseeing. The mental images disappeared without warning, and his foreign energy slithered out of my head and into my chest. When it reached my heart, I a kaleidoscope of emotions swirled in my core.

All my most private emotions were stripped bare. I was utterly exposed—naked. I attempted again to break free from his powerful grip, tried to hide somehow, but he held firm.

After what seemed like an eternity, Mr. Daiko's energy *finally* retreated from my heart and traveled back out through my arms. Clearly finished with his dirty deed, he simply dropped my hands and stepped back with a bow. I stared at him, mouth agape, feeling utterly violated.

I hugged my trembling arms to my chest as tears rolled down my face. "What did you do?" I whispered angrily.

"I'm sorry for my intrusion, but we must ensure that all new members have pure intentions. The Shadowmen are very cunning and have attempted to infiltrate our ranks for centuries. I had to be sure you weren't an Agent of Darkness." He put his hands together as if in prayer. "I sense great power in you, Kirie Sorenson, maybe even greater than my own. The journey before you is filled with perils, trials, and loss, but if you stay the course, you'll be able to effect great change and even be instrumental to our success. Don't be afraid of your power or its potential. Fear is a powerful tool the Darkness uses to stop us from realizing our true destiny."

"Don't. Ever. Do. That. Again." I said in a shaky voice.

"I'll never have to," he said with another bow. He walked around his desk and sat back down. "I see our conversation has taken its toll. Abbott will see you back to your new apartment so you can get settled in. I hope you choose to stay with us and learn to control your gift. It was lovely to meet you, Kirie Sorenson."

Unable to return the sentiment, I nearly tripped on my feet as I fled the room. I ran down the curved hallway that led straight back to the reception desk. Aaron smiled at me; his face gave no indication that he noticed my distress. Either I wasn't as big of a mess as I felt, or he was gracious enough not to comment.

"Hello again, Kirie. How was your tour?" he asked.

"Could you let Abbott know I'm ready to go?" My voice warbled.

"Bien sur," he said, still unfazed. Perhaps he saw this kind of thing all the time. My stomach clenched at the thought. Aaron picked up the phone and dialed Abbott's office.

Behind me were two white benches on either side of the elevator door. I picked one and waited for Abbott. I couldn't believe he'd left me with that man. Had he known what would happen? I hugged my arms over my torso as if I could cover the parts Mr. Daiko had laid bare. I squeezed my eyes shut, rocking back and forth as I forced down the bile rising in my throat.

"Kirie?" My eyes sprang open. Abbott was rounding the corner, a look of concern on his face. "Is everything alright?" I shook my head. He sighed. "I see. Should we go?" Abbott lifted an arm to the elevator.

I stood and followed him into the glass elevator. We rode in silence to the main floor and out the Panthéon's front door. A black sedan was waiting for us along the curb in front of the plaza. A new driver stood by the back door and held it open as we approached. Abbott slid into the spacious backseat, and I silently followed.

I stared out the window sightlessly the entire trip back. The city that captivated me mere hours before no longer held my interest. Abbott must've sensed I wasn't ready to talk because he kept his eyes on his smartphone, making no attempt at conversation.

The driver pulled in front of the apartment building, and I nearly jumped out of the car. My limbs were numb and heavy as I stood on the unfamiliar sidewalk. I watched as passing Parisians went about their business walking dogs, pushing baby strollers, hailing cabs . . . ordinary things. They flowed around me like a river over rock.

Abbott joined me on the sidewalk and touched my elbow. "Let's go up and get you settled into your new home," he said, gently steering me toward the lobby.

Again, neither of us said a word as I followed him up the elevator and down the hall past Luca's and Arin's apartment. At Alena's front door, Abbott took a key out of his pocket and unlocked it, leaving it ajar for me to walk through.

Alena's apartment wasn't what I expected. Though it was identical to the boys' in layout and size, Alena's apartment was a dump. Clothes and shoes covered nearly every surface of the small space. The phrases *hot mess* and *dumpster fire* ran through my mind. My skin itched from just being in the chaotic space.

Abbott stepped into the living room. "I had Arin and Luca bring your things over for you. Your room is on the left and you'll find everything you need inside." That meant I would be sharing a wall with Luca. That was the one bright side of this impossible situation.

"Your new cellphone is in your room," Abbott continued. "My number has been added to your contacts, so feel free to call anytime. If you must call a friend in the States, please keep it short and remember not to let anyone know where you are. Although it's a secure line, you can never be too careful."

I nodded, still unwilling to speak. Abbott put his hands in his pants pockets and breathed a patient sigh.

"I can see your meeting with Mr. Daiko was difficult. I hope you know that no harm was meant. The screening is standard practice and a necessary step when admitting new members into The Society of Light. I hope you'll not hold it against us," he said.

So, he *did* know what Mr. Daiko was planning. And still, he'd left me alone with him? "He had no right to my memories and feelings," I whispered fiercely.

"When it comes to war, Kirie, we must make hard decisions for the good of the whole. You'll learn this in time," he said simply.

I folded my arms over my chest and turned my head away. "I strongly disagree."

"As is your right. If you're still willing to learn to control your energy tomorrow, text me, and I'll send a car for you. Your funds have all been transferred to a new account here in France, and your new bank card is in your room. The Society of Light believes in personal freedom. What you do from here on out is up to you. With that said, I must remind you that Donovan and others like him are still actively hunting you. I truly believe that your best chance of survival is with The Society." Abbott paused for a moment before continuing. "We just want what's best for you."

I turned to face Abbott. "So, it's stay or die? That doesn't really sound like a choice, now does it?"

"Kirie, I've been doing this a long time now, and there's always an adjustment period," he said in a parental tone. "Trust me, you're taking this much better than some. You should've seen Alena when we brought her in. We had to sedate her."

The image of a miniature Alena taking on a bunch of adults made me smile, and I felt the tension in my shoulders relax a little. Despite my anger over Daiko, Abbott still had the ability to set my fears at ease. I couldn't help but feel safe around him. And, although I hated to admit it, he made some good points. I had a lot to consider.

"Well, I need to get back to work. If you need anything at any time, feel free to call me. The others will be back tonight. Stay inside until then. It isn't safe for you to be wandering on your own."

"Okay," I shrugged. Where would I go?

At the door, Abbott turned and said, "I sincerely hope you decide to stay with us, Kirie."

I stood in the center of the sloppy, silent apartment for several long minutes after he left and considered my choices. For the first time, I was in control of what happened next. A world of possibilities lay before me. Nothing was stopping me from getting on a plane and leaving all this craziness behind. I thought about going back to Colorado but immediately threw the thought aside. There was nothing there for me anymore.

All my life, I secretly dreamt of going to a tropical beach. I yearned to feel the sun on my face and the sand on my feet. Obviously, Mom preferred to keep me close to home. But nothing prevented me now from picking an island on a map and living on the beach for the rest of my life. Maybe if I kept a low profile by living in a grass hut somewhere, Donovan would never find me.

Although that plan was enticing, my heart wasn't in it. I couldn't hide for the rest of my life. I wanted to be a part of something bigger than myself. I wanted to *finally* spread my mental wings and see what I was capable of.

Then there was Luca. Even though he didn't seem to like me romantically, the thought of never seeing him again was depressing. I just wanted to be where he was. I knew it was pathetic, but I couldn't help feeling drawn to his energy. I'd never met anyone like him before. I feared I never would again. And maybe—just maybe—something could develop between us down the line. After all, miraculous things happen every day.

I didn't know if I wanted to stay and join the Society of Light long-term, but maybe I should at least stick around for a while. Maybe I didn't *have* to train to be a killer. Perhaps they had a desk job I could do instead while I attended university.

I looked around the messy apartment again and let out a loud sigh. On the other hand, staying also meant rooming with Alena, a thought I dreaded almost as much as training with knives. It was almost enough to force me into hiding.

No closer to deciding, I gave up and checked out my new bedroom. Inside was a large, four-poster bed opposite a pair of French doors, framed by white drapes. Other than the addition of an antique chest of drawers, the room was identical to Luca's. I had to admit, I liked sharing a wall with him. It was shameless and pathetic, but I didn't care.

On top of the white comforter, my new clothes were folded in tidy rows. One of the boys must have laid them out because Alena didn't seem like the type to fold anything . . . especially for me. I put them away in the drawers.

A cellphone and a white envelope lay on the small desk. I opened the envelope and found a new bank card, with my PIN and bank information, all in French. I set it aside, picked up my new phone, and turned it on. It was unlike any device I'd ever seen. It was about the same size as the typical smartphone; only it was as thin and as flexible as a credit card. There was nothing like it on the market.

On the home screen, there were few apps besides the call function, maps, contacts, and an icon that looked like a sun. I pulled up my contacts and found Abbott, Arin, Luca, Alena, Bert, and The French Center of Light listed there.

My social circle had just gotten a lot smaller.

I missed Rylie.

It was two o'clock in Paris, so she would just be getting up for the day in Colorado. Desperate to hear a familiar voice, I dialed her number, hoping she wouldn't screen my call—no such luck. It rang a couple of times before her voicemail picked up.

"You've reached Rylie. Leave a message. Or don't . . .

whatever!" *Beep.*

I pressed the end button and sat down hard on the side of the bed. An overwhelming feeling of loneliness came over me. I curled up on my side, hugged a pillow to my chest, and let myself cry.

I wake and feel the fell of dark, not day.
What hours, O what black hours we have spent
This night! What sights you, heart saw: way you
went!
And more must, in yet longer light's delay.

"I Wake and Feel the Fell of Dark, Not Day"
By Gerard Manley Hopkins

Chapter 19

**ang!**

Clank!

Thump!

I groaned and sat up in bed. It took a few minutes to orient myself. It seemed like I was always waking up in a new bed these days. Nothing about my new room felt like home, including the loud, obnoxious noises just outside my bedroom door.

Another loud bang came from the direction of the kitchen. I covered my head with my blanket and groaned again. I didn't know what was worse, being stalked by deranged killers made of shadow or living with Alena. Clearly, Alena was incapable of subtly . . . and consideration for sleeping roommates.

I reluctantly got out of bed and stretched my arms and legs.

I'd fallen asleep in an awkward position the night before, and my back and neck muscles ached. I would've loved to put off speaking with Alena indefinitely, but I'd have to see her sooner or later. Plus, I was starving. So, I gathered my courage and walked out of my bedroom and into the dangerous unknown.

Alena stood in the middle of the small kitchen making breakfast with the grace of a Tasmanian devil. Dirty pots and pans covered the limited counter space, and the eggs and milk sat out on the counter. My left eye twitched as I looked over the utter chaos surrounding me.

I stepped over a pair of shoes on my way to the kitchen. Clearing my throat, I said, "Good morning, Alena."

"Oh, good. You're up," she said, flipping her messy hair over her shoulder and glaring at me. "Look, we need to go over some ground rules."

"Yeah. Sure," I said.

She held up a finger. "Rule number one: if you plan on getting up early, keep it down. If I don't get enough sleep, I get cranky. Do not wake me up. Ever."

I bit my tongue to hold back a sarcastic response. Hadn't she just woken me?

She held up another finger. "Rule number two: leave my stuff alone. I have everything where I want it, so just . . . don't."

I raised my hand, feeling like a student. "Actually, wouldn't it make sense if we kept our stuff in our rooms? That way no one will mess with it."

"Look," she said, putting a hand on her hip. "This is my apartment. Mine. You're just a guest here. I expect you to keep your things in your room, but I can leave whatever I want wherever I want. Understood?"

"I thought The Society owned the apartment . . ." my words trailed off as the heat of her glare intensified. I gulped.

She put up a third and final finger. "And rule number three: we're not friends. I only agreed to let you stay here because Abbott asked me to. If it were up to me, you'd go back to the States where you belong."

"Oookay . . ."

"Oh, and Arin sent over a muffin." She rolled her eyes and pointed to a large blueberry muffin on a paper plate.

"That was nice of him," I said.

Alena scoffed. "It's disgusting how they baby you." She took her plate of French toast and eggs to the dining room table and set it on a stack of papers. Then, she turned her back to me, clearly done with our "conversation."

I picked up the muffin and returned to my room to eat in peace, neither Alena nor I speaking to each other as I passed. I had no idea why she hated me; although, instinct told me it had something to do with Luca. Not that she had anything to worry about there. Again, I wondered what kind of history lay between them.

Alone in my room, I stood in front of my balcony doors and pulled back the drapes. Mid-morning sunlight shot rays across the sky just over the Victorian-era rooftops. Bits of light filtered through the glass panes, creating rainbows across my chest and arms. I closed my eyes and soaked up the energy from the sun's rays. I smiled as my core warmed, and a feeling of wellness spread through me, head to foot.

I opened the French doors, and stepped onto the balcony, breathing in the crisp air. Paris was stunning in the fall, with its changing leaves and sparkling amber sunlight. I watched the hustle and bustle of the city streets below while I ate the blueberry muffin Arin made for me. I bit into a large blueberry, and sweet and tangy juice exploded across my tongue.

I smiled. Arin could seriously bake.

Alena audibly stomped out of the apartment about half an hour later, presumably on her way to do official agent business. She slammed the door as she left, vibrating the walls around me. I breathed a sigh of relief and waited a few more minutes to ensure she was truly gone before going back out to the kitchen to throw away the paper plate.

Standing in the middle of the living room, I looked over the dumpster fire that was my new home. It was what I imagined a frat house full of smelly college boys would look like, only instead of jockstraps and basketballs, stiletto shoes, and designer jeans littered the floor. I didn't know if I wanted to cry or scream. Instead, I hid myself in the only place in the world I had control over—my room.

Sitting in the center of my sun-warmed bed, I pulled out my new cellphone and opened my last conversation thread with Parisxxxi8.

Brightgirl101: You there?

I held my breath while I waited for a response. It felt like an eternity since we last talked. So much had changed since the school science fair. My world had exploded and reformed itself into something unrecognizable. Paris belonged to another time, one where my parents, hopes, and innocence still lived, and I almost couldn't believe he still existed in this new world.

Still, I missed him. Paris had been the only one to express interest in my biophotonic studies. He was the only one who understood my obsession with finding ways to use light to treat sick patients. I smiled, thinking of how close my hypotheses had been to the truth. Light *could* heal. I'd seen it with my own eyes, though I had no idea how anyone could transfer Luca's incredible ability into clinical use. Still, it gave me hope for the future.

Luca.

I thought of him putting his warm hands over mine and using his energy to piece me back together. His light had soothed more than just my torn hands. Perhaps light could heal emotional wounds, too. I imagined what it would be like to master that kind of ability, to simply put my hands on a patient and make them whole. Was it possible? I was a Child of Light, too, was I not?

My breath caught in my throat when three little dots appeared on the screen, chasing all other thoughts from my mind. Paris was writing.

Parisxxxi8: I'm here. How've you been?

I didn't know how to answer that question, so I lied.

Brightgirl101: Fine. You?

Parisxxxi8: Better now that I'm here with you.

Heat spread up my cheeks and I reminded myself once again that Paris could be a forty-year-old weirdo living in his mother's basement.

Parisxxxi8: Have you made any new progress on your device?

Brightgirl101: No, sadly. Life's been a bit crazy lately.

Parisxxxi8: Sorry to hear that, luv. Anything I can do to help?

Brightgirl101: Cheer me up? Tell me something normal.

Parisxxxi8: You assume I'm acquainted with normality. Thankfully, this is not the case. Normal is overrated.

Brightgirl101: Lol. Tell me something happy, then.

Prarisxxxi8: A new tenant just moved into my building, and she's created quite a stir. I think you would like her.

Brightgirl101: Me? Why?

Prarisxxxi8: Because she's a lot like you.

Brightgirl101: How would you know? We've never met.

Prarisxxxi8: True. Well, then. She matches the version of you I have in my mind. Does that make you happy?

The question caught me up short, and the smile that had formed on my lips slipped. Happy? Me? It was a question I hadn't considered for myself, at least not for a long time. Happiness was for normal people who knew who they were and where they fit in the world. I shook my head and focused once more on my screen.

Brightgirl101: She must be amazing, then.

Prarisxxxi8: That she is. Look, I've got to run. Can we chat later?

Brightgirl101: Sure. Thanks for cheering me up.

Prarisxxxi8: At your service. *Tips hat

I spent the rest of the day on my bed using my smartphone to polish up my French and learn more about the country's rich history. I got lost in my head, and soon shadows in my room grew long across the hardwood floor. I hadn't eaten since breakfast and my empty stomach growled at me in protest.

I weighed my options for dinner. There was no way I was going to help myself to anything in "Alena's kitchen," and I wasn't comfortable enough to go to the grocery store on my own. Mom always took care of the groceries; I wouldn't even know where to start. So, I decided it was time to explore the city on foot a little.

Abbott had warned me to stay inside, but I'd never been out of the Western United States before, and the temptation to explore Paris was impossible to ignore. I was in the City of Lights, after all. How could I not do a little sightseeing? Plus, there were something like seven billion people in the world. The chances of running into Donovan or any other shadow this far from home were statistically impossible. And I had to get out.

Earlier that day, I'd run across an article online about a café in Paris named Le Procope. Historical giants like Voltaire, Napoleon, Benjamin Franklin, and Thomas Jefferson were known to have dined there regularly. It'd even been used as a meeting place for the Liberty Seekers during the French Revolution. The idea of standing where those amazing men stood was too tempting to turn down. Mind made up, I grabbed my jacket, wallet, and cellphone and headed out the door.

The street out front was busy with locals rushing home from work and school wearing backpacks and carrying suitcases. I stood outside the apartment entrance and watched them with envy. It was weird not having to go to classes or be somewhere at a specific time, and for the first time in my life, no one would be waiting for me. I literally had nothing to do, nowhere to go, and no one to do it with. Who knew such freedom could feel so lonely?

I heaved a heavy sigh and plugged in the address for Le Procope in my phone's map app. It was further away than I thought, several kilometers, but I'd been stuck inside without any real exercise for too long, and my legs itched to move.

With my hands in my jacket pockets, I walked eastward, taking in every detail and committing them to memory. In the dimming daylight, strings of twinkle lights blinked on. They were wrapped around balcony banisters and limbs of trees lining the streets. Bundled fir trees sat in front of a quaint neighborhood store, and the scent of pine hung in the chilly air. Paris, it seemed, was getting ready for Christmas.

I inhaled deeply and smiled to myself. This was my favorite time of year. Mom's too. She used to get overly excited and decorated for Christmas well before Thanksgiving. She couldn't help herself.

Mom had a way of making the season magical. Every inch of our home was covered with glitter, lights, and fresh pine garlands. I could almost smell her gingerbread cookies baking in the oven and feel the warmth of the fireplace on my skin. I pressed my palm against my aching chest. This would be my first Christmas without her. The thought made me feel hollow inside.

By the time I reached Boulevard Saint-Germaine, walking had officially lost its appeal. I was out of breath, and my feet were aching. The only thing I'd eaten the entire day was the muffin Arin sent over, and I could feel my energy dipping dangerously low. I reassured myself that it wasn't much further and pushed forward.

Just as I was on the verge of passing out, I reached the street on which Le Procope Café was located. My shoulders fell forward in utter relief when I saw the famous sign hanging above the restaurant door. I couldn't wait to sit down and eat something . . . anything. I would've skipped the rest of the way to the restaurant if my feet had any feeling left in them.

Like most establishments in the city, Le Procope was set within a tall seventeenth-century building surrounded by various shops and cafés. The historic restaurant's facade was painted a deep blue and lined with square windows and carved wooden plaques displaying historical information. Fresh garlands strung with lights hung from the second-floor balcony, creating a festive atmosphere. The main entrance was a set of glass doors framed by tall floral vases. An oval sign hung above them with the words "Restaurant Le Procope Fonde en 1686."

To the right of the entrance was an open display of pastries and baked goods. Sweet and savory smells drifted from the open window, causing my mouth to water, and my stomach to cramp in anticipation. I hobbled toward the restaurant and all but ripped the handle off the front door.

Walking into Le Procope was like walking into the past. Inside the small entryway was a sweeping marble staircase that led to the second floor. The deep red walls were accented by regal gold trim and crown moldings. Black framed pictures of the many famous patrons throughout history covered every inch of the space.

Le Procope was not only a restaurant; it was a gallery of antiques, marble busts, and portraits. Everywhere I looked there was something new and amazing to see. The space was so full of history that I could almost feel the ghosts of the scholars, politicians, and activists from the history books floating nearby.

"Bonjior. Combien Seront diñer avec vous cesoir?" a pretty blonde hostess asked.

"Un juste," I replied.

"Bien. Suivez-moi," she said.

The hostess led me through a set of French doors to a small table just to the left of the lobby. I removed my jacket and sat down at the cloth-covered table. She handed me the menu and wished me a good meal before walking away.

I shifted in my chair. I'd never gone to a restaurant on my own before, and it was strangely embarrassing—shameful even. I pulled my long hair forward and tucked my chin self-consciously, fearing the other patrons' pitying stares.

A female server came to my table and asked for my order. I quickly browsed the options and settled on the Revolutionaries' beef tenderloin with Dauphinois gratin. I absentmindedly played with the edge of the tablecloth, my mind wandering as I waited for my food to arrive.

So much had happened in the last month and a half and there hadn't been time to process it all. My parents' deaths forced me to grow up all at once and I didn't know how to live in this new adult world. I was standing at a crossroads, paralyzed by anxiety and grief.

I thought about my discussion with Abbott earlier. He promised that joining The Society of Light would keep me safe from the Shadowmen. But when was fighting on the front line of any war *safe*? My empty stomach twisted. Perhaps safety was never truly an option for me to begin with.

Then there was Luca. I was tempted to join The Society just to stay close to him, yet I knew that could also end in tragedy. The energy between us was strong, and I could easily see myself falling head over heels for him . . . maybe I already was. But Luca clearly wasn't interested in me in a romantic way. Getting closer to him would only end in more heartbreak. I didn't know how much more my battered heart could take.

The server arrived with my food, pulling me from my

thoughts, and I wasted no time cutting into the tender beef. The tension melted from my shoulders as the salty juices filled my mouth with a rich smoky flavor. The Bordelaise sauce and cream-drenched potatoes were equally good, making me question if I'd ever really lived before that moment. The long, punishing walk to the restaurant had been worth it.

When I nearly finished my dinner, the restaurant door opened, and cold air blew into the café, causing the hairs on my arms to stand up. I turned to see a small group of twenty-year-olds entering the lobby. There were three of them: two average-looking boys and one girl with bright red hair.

I straightened in my chair, instantly recognizing her from somewhere. I flipped through my photographic memories, trying to place her.

*My X-ray machine falling to the ground, dark eyes filled with hatred, black emotions taking over. . .*the science fair! That was *her.*

The meal in my stomach turned to stone.

This was bad.

Chapter 20

7 billion to one.

And they'd found me.

I should've listened to Abbott. I should have stayed inside.

I slid my arms through my jacket sleeves and zipped it to my neck as calmly as possible. I peeked over at the group again. They stood in front of the hostess's desk, seemingly waiting to be seated. Darkness poured off them, a black hole within an otherwise vibrant nebula. One of the boys, short and stalky, turned his gaze toward me. His eyes were dim and lifeless, confirming what I already knew. *Shadowmen.* I tore my eyes from his and pretended to study my plate, my heart pounding loudly in my ears.

Through the fabric of my jacket, I felt the temperature drop. A shiver rippled through me as I held onto the edge of the table with a white-knuckle grip, fighting the urge to run.

How could I be so stupid? After everything I'd gone

through, I should've *known* I'd never be safe no matter where I went.

Dammit!

I quickly formulated a plan. I'd taken a virtual tour of the restaurant that morning, so I knew there was another door in back that led out onto a small, cobblestone street. If I could just get through that door undetected, I may have a chance at evading them.

I pulled a stack of Euros out of my wallet and, without counting the bills, threw them onto the table. With forced calm, I stood from my chair and casually walked toward the back of the restaurant, hoping they hadn't seen me leave. I weaved through tables and rushing servers holding trays full of food, fighting the urge to run the whole way. Pushing through the heavy wooden back door, I stepped onto a narrow, centuries-old cobblestone street lined by a row of shops. Tourists and shoppers strolled about the charming courtyard, unaware and unconcerned.

I glanced back to make sure they hadn't followed me and saw the trio pushing their way through the restaurant door. They moved in my direction with a singular focus, one of the boys in the lead. He was tall and lean with black, beady eyes that locked on me like a cat with its prey. His brazenness was shocking. Unlike Cole, this one wasn't even *trying* to be covert. Terrified, I stumbled backward into a portly, middle-aged woman.

"Aie," the woman yelled.

"Excusez-moi," I said, red-faced.

"Amèricains!" She shook her head in disgust and walked off.

I spun around and ran down the cobblestone street, my feet slipping on the slick, uneven surface. Angry yells followed me as I wove through the heavy foot traffic, bumping into random people. I threw another backward glance. The Shadowmen were still there. My heart pounded harder, and my breathing accelerated as I picked up my pace. My already aching feet burned from the abuse.

The street ended at Boulevard Saint-Germzin, the road I'd walked down on the way to the restaurant. On instinct, I headed in the direction of my apartment. Without breaking stride, I pulled my cellphone out of my jacket pocket and tried to call Abbott, but despite my efforts, the screen remained black.

"Dimmit!" I cursed again, tapping the screen again and again. I could've sworn I had plenty of battery life left. I slid my useless phone into my back pocket and ran as fast as I could down the boulevard, throwing panicked glances behind me every minute or two. My stalkers kept a steady distance behind me, never getting too close to really do any harm. It was as if they were taunting me, trying to wear me out. It was working.

Before long, my energy waned, and my legs began to slow. I couldn't keep going for long. I needed to find a way to shake them.

I ran through my options in my head. Obviously, I couldn't lead them back to the apartment and give its location away, nor could I call for help. All that was left to do was to hide. But where?

An idea formed when I spotted a group of teenagers standing in front of a small coffee shop. I rushed forward and elbowed my way into the center of the rowdy group. Shielded from sight by the teens' bodies, I ducked inside the coffee shop. The small space was full of loud customers, sitting at tables or standing in line. Unlike le Procope, this establishment was old in a *bad* way. Paint was peeling from the walls and the tilted tables were covered with stains and crumbs.

I flattened my back against the wall next to the front window and counted the seconds as I waited and prayed for the shadows to pass. My body tensed, ready to run each time the door squeaked open, but only strangers entered. After several torturous minutes, I snuck a glance out the front window. The group of teens had moved on and the sidewalk was nearly bare of pedestrians. The Shadowmen were nowhere in sight.

I let out a short sigh of relief. I'd lost them—for now. Still, I couldn't stay there forever. I needed to find a better hiding place. I looked around the cramped space without any real hope. I could try hiding behind the counter, but the employees would likely kick me out. Perhaps I could hide beneath a table at the feet of the other patrons. I almost laughed at the ridiculous idea. Just then, a server holding a tray walked through a swinging door carrying food and drinks, and a better plan formed in my mind.

Unlike in America, there were very few alleyways in Paris. Instead, most buildings had closed courtyards in their centers. Based on this building's age and shape, this one was likely the same. When no one was looking, I quietly slipped through the swinging door into a brightly lit kitchen beyond. Cooks in white aprons sat around a metal prep table, chatting in French. When the door swung shut behind me, the men looked up.

"Hey, vous n'êtes pas censé être ici," one called to me.

"*Please, where's the back door,*" I pleaded in French.

"Tout droit vers la droite," he answered, pointing to the back corner, clearly annoyed.

"Merci!" I yelled over my shoulder as I ran past them.

"Amèricains!" another cook spat.

I careened around the back corner of the kitchen into a short hallway that led to an old metal door. I used my body weight to shoulder my way through the surprisingly heavy door and force it shut behind me.

I sagged against the cold metal and took several steadying

breaths. The courtyard before me was surrounded by high walls that blocked out nearly all sound, providing an unnerving reprieve from the city noise. The late afternoon sun dipped below the building's edge, casting shadows and creating dark corners across the courtyard.

Twinkle lights were draped haphazardly on the few barren trees around the perimeter, providing the only light in the space. There were three weathered benches in the center separated by planter boxes filled with dead bushes. Brown and red leaves covered the seats of the benches as if no one had sat there in months.

Behind me, the door to the café opened briefly before falling shut again. The scent of fresh coffee momentarily filled the air. I spun around to see who was there but found myself alone. I turned back toward the center of the courtyard and a shadow flitted across my peripheral vision. I spun around and saw no one.

My impromptu escape plan suddenly didn't seem so brilliant. I was trapped like a fish in a barrel. Standing alone in the middle of the courtyard, I heard crunching leaves under heavy feet. Feeling like an insane person, I spun in circles, searching for invisible ghosts. I slapped my hands over my mouth to hold in the screams trying to claw their way up my throat.

The footsteps were getting closer; time was running out.

If I could just get through one of the doors lining the courtyard before they got to me, I might have a chance. Dropping my hands from my face, I ran to the nearest door to my right and pulled the handle. It didn't budge. I ran to the next two doors, only to find them locked. Another cold wind blew through the courtyard, stirring the dead leaves.

"No, no, no." Pure panic threatened to paralyze me as I ran from locked door to locked door.

Just as I reached the final door, all the light in the courtyard disappeared–not only the lights on the trees but the fading sunset, too. It was as though someone put a black tarp over the sky. My pupils dilated as I searched for any sign of light, but the darkness was complete.

Soft footsteps approached me from all sides. My body broke out in a cold sweat, and I began to shake violently from head to toe. My time was out.

I backed up slowly, not knowing where the attack would come from. The temperature dropped sharply, and the air around me became thinner and harder to breathe. I balled my shaky fists and raised them in a defensive position.

Like a soft wind, whispers floated across the courtyard, bouncing off the walls. Their echoes pierced my chest, and hopelessness washed over me like a tsunami. I was drowning in dark thoughts as the sinister whispers hijacked my mind.

I'm weak.

I'm nothing but a shattered little girl.

Who cares anyway? There's no one left alive who truly loves me.

I'm nothing but a waste of space and oxygen.

Cold despair seeped through my veins, leaching every ounce of light from my pores, and I began to sway back and forth as if my body no longer had the will to stand. I fell forward onto my knees.

Somewhere to my left came a high, shrill laugh, and light footsteps danced toward me. Cold breath stung my cheek. I flinched.

"I can't imagine why you worry them so much. Look at you . . . so small . . . so weak," a girl said close to my ear. I flinched from her sudden nearness.

My long, heavy hair was suddenly lifted off my shoulders and twirled painfully around a tight fist. I was too lost to cry out.

"You're nothing but a pretty little doll," she purred in my ear. "With Bright Ones like you, winning the war will be almost *too easy.*" The girl leaned over my hunched shoulders and jerked my head backward. I gasped in pain. "What a pity."

"Ciara! Get it done," a deep male voice snapped.

"Ahhhh. You're no fun, Adrian," she whined like a petulant child.

"Dimitri will not tolerate another failed attempt, Ciara. Be done with it already."

"Fine, but I still don't know what all the fuss was about. Look how weak she is. I hardly had to try with this one," she said in genuine disappointment.

"It's not your place to question our directive. If The Order says she's a threat, then she is," said another boy with a heavy Spanish accent.

"Yeah, yeah. I know," she sighed.

Ciara wrapped my hair around my throat like a noose. Pulling tightly from behind, she lifted me off the ground. Darkness spread through my mind like a thick mist, chasing away the last bits of lingering light. I felt formless, nameless—everything that made me who I was, no longer existed.

"Well, at least all this beautiful hair won't go to waste. I have to say, death by hair is rather unique." She giggled and pulled tighter.

I welcomed death.

I longed for it.

I embraced the darkness as consciousness began to slowly slip away.

Suddenly, a bright light filled the courtyard. Ciara released my hair and I fell to the ground, my heavy hair falling forward and covering my face. I gasped for breath as a cacophony of noise filled the courtyard. Grunts, curses, and heavy thuds surrounded me. My slow mind tried to make sense of it all, but it was as though my thoughts were trapped at the bottom of the ocean.

I pulled my hair back with numb fingers and peered out at the courtyard beyond. The intense light blinded me. I immediately shut my eyes before carefully cracking them back open into slits. Shadows and streaks of light moved in and out of my focus faster than my eyes could follow. It was pure mayhem.

I shook my head and slowly pushed onto my hands and knees. A large object flew past me and landed a mere foot away with a loud "oomph." I looked over and saw the face of one of the shadows lying on the ground. Blood poured from his nose and left eye. And then he was gone, evaporating like smoke.

I screamed and crawled away, falling over myself in an effort to escape. I backed up until I ran into the cold brick wall. I huddled against it and blinked frantically, willing myself to snap out of my drugged state. The courtyard was filled with the brightest light I'd ever seen, even brighter than the light Luca had used to heal me.

It was a familiar light and it called to me in an almost intimate way. On instinct, I opened myself to it, letting it soak into my skin. Like a desert rain, it brought me back to life, chasing away the hopelessness and sorrow that had filled my body. Within moments, my mind was clear.

I watched the scene in front of me again with clarity. Luca

was in the center of the open space; a radiant light pulsed off him, illuminating the courtyard with a power stronger than the sun. He was stunning and terrifying in his brilliance.

He sat atop Ciara, pinning her to the ground. She struggled viciously to fight him off without success. The short, stocky shadow lay on the ground behind them, groaning, and the other boy lay a few feet from me, holding his bloody face. Each of their eyes was squeezed shut against the pulsing light.

Suddenly, Ciara stopped struggling. She slowly looked up at Luca. Like spilled ink, Ciara's pupils began to spread across the whites of her eyes until they were nothing more than two black orbs.

Luca stilled, his grip on Ciara loosening. His face slackened, and his eyes glassed over as if he were stunned. Like a setting sun, the light in the courtyard began to dim by degrees. The other two shadows hung back, breathing heavily as they pressed their hands to their wounds. They watched Luca and Ciara with a look of anticipation on their twisted features.

"Luca," I yelled. It was as if I hadn't spoken. His face remained unfocused as Ciara's black stare held him captive.

I struggled to my feet, using the wall as leverage. "Luca, snap out of it," I pleaded. Hot tears ran down my face. "Please!"

A smile, sharp and wide, spread across Ciara's pale lips. Luca's proud shoulders suddenly hunched forward, and his face twisted into a grimace. He let out a sudden, tortured cry that seemed to be ripped from his core.

I stumbled forward. "Stop it! You're hurting him," I screamed at the redheaded witch.

Without breaking eye contact with Luca, Ciara laughed. "That's the point, stupid."

I rushed toward them, but the tall Spaniard grabbed hold of me, pinning me against his chest. I pleaded with Luca to look up, but he wouldn't–no couldn't–respond. I watched helplessly as Luca wilted under the girl's stare. His light diminished until the courtyard was as dim as twilight.

I struggled against the shadow's hold, but no matter how hard I tried, I couldn't break his grip on me. Ciara was killing him. Somehow, I could *feel* the life and light seeping out of him. I thought of the night my mother died. How I'd just stood there while Dimitri slit her throat. I saw the light leave her eyes knowing there was nothing I could do to save her. Like then, I felt utterly useless.

No! My breaths came in and out in shallow puffs as anger and frustration grew inside me. I couldn't let it happen again. I wouldn't let the darkness take what was mine *again*.

"Mine," I whispered fiercely. Luca was *mine*.

A deep pressure began to build within me, hot and unrelenting. I let my anguish feed the energy, and with every agonizing moment, it grew. The intensity of it was terrifying, and I thought I might crumble under its weight. My vision narrowed as the pressure began to centralize in my chest. All I could think about was my mounting need for release.

Unable to hold back any longer, I let the energy go with a cry. My arms flung wide as my veins filled with fire, and the darkened courtyard flared to life. Pure, white light pulsed off my skin in waves, chasing the shadows from every corner and crevice.

The shadow holding me let go with a cry, and the others shielded their faces with their arms. The courtyard quickly filled with their screams. They writhed against my light, angry red welts spreading rapidly across their exposed skin. Glass shattered all around us, and far-off cries rose in the distance. Yet, all of this seemed unimportant to me.

"Kirie!" I felt a warm presence in front of me. I focused my gaze.

Luca

He stood before me. His eyes, now lucid, mirrored my light like a verdant forest on a bright summer's day. As we stared at each other, a stream of energy flowed between our bodies, connecting us. It was warm, exhilarating, and intimate in a way I'd never experienced before, like a thousand first kisses. My veins sang as my light intensified, and I could see the full spectrum of colors in it, clear and bright.

As the energy continued to build, a low hum filled my ears,

drowning out all other sounds. I no longer felt connected to my surroundings. Time seemed to slow, and I glanced around me with detached awe. Each brick, stone, and bench came into clear, high-definition focus in the brilliant light. Tiny particles in the air drifted lazily like a slow ballet. I looked down at my glowing skin in amazement. It was all so beautiful. *I* was beautiful.

The earth released its hold on my body, and my feet left the ground. Alarm flashed across Luca's perfect features as the distance between us grew. Shaking his head, he yelled something at me, but words meant nothing. I was above it all, nothing but pure energy.

A glint of metal flashed across my peripheral vision, and a sudden pain shot through my shoulder—hot and stinging. Confused, I peered down and saw the hilt of a blade protruding from my skin. It was as if a wet blanket had been tossed over my fire.

My vision narrowed, and the ground rushed toward me. Luca's blazing green eyes were the last thing I saw before the world went black.

Chapter 21

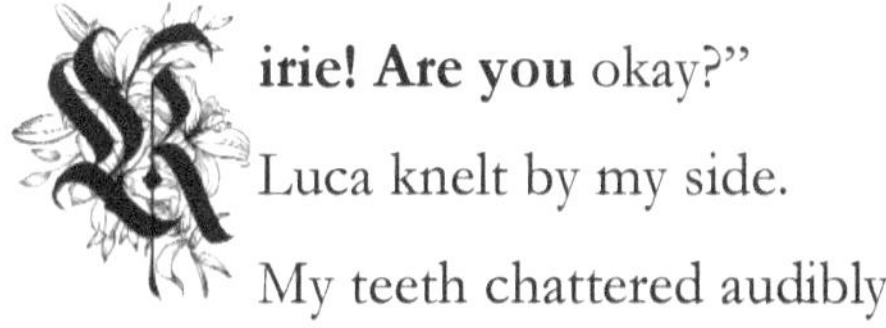

irie! Are you okay?"

Luca knelt by my side.

My teeth chattered audibly.

Luca was bent over me as he examined the blade embedded in my shoulder. I shifted under his gaze, sending a sudden searing pain through my torso. I cried out.

"It looks as though it's just a shoulder wound," he said, glaring at the protruding hilt. "I'm going to kill them for this," Luca hissed.

I lay still on my back, trying not to jostle the blade again, and glanced around for the three shadows. Nothing. Moonlight lit the courtyard once more, and tiny lights twinkled on the barren tree branches. It was as if someone had flipped on a light switch. They were gone.

My body tremored violently from shock. "W-what h-happened to me?"

He shook his head, brows tightly knit. "I'm not sure. It was like you were more light than human. I've never seen anything like it. I thought you were going to burn all of Paris to the ground."

My chest tightened. "H-has that ever h-happened to you?"

Luca looked away. "No." The single word was a closed door to further questions. "Look, I know you don't want to hear this now, but we need to get going. A disturbance like that won't go unnoticed."

Sirens wailed in the background, punctuating his point. I stared up at the shattered windows surrounding the courtyard. My stomach twisted when I realized I'd done that.

"Did anyone get hurt?"

Luca followed my gaze, concern etched in his furrowed brow. "I don't believe so. Well, other than Ciara and her crew."

The sirens grew louder. Luca tentatively touched the knife's hilt. Fire-hot pain shot through my upper body so intense it knocked the breath from me.

"Don't touch it!" I gasped.

"Kire, I have to remove the blade so we can move," Luca said.

He reached for me again, and I shrank away. "Wait! Shouldn't a doctor in a hospital do that?"

"Why would you need a hospital?" he asked, confused.

I opened my mouth to state what should've been the

obvious answer, but snapped it shut again.

I shook my head, remembering.

He can heal me.

Luca sighed. "Kirie, please. We need to hurry. There are three shadows actively hunting us, and the authorities are on their way."

"But they left . . ."

Luca shook his head. "It isn't that simple. Ciara doesn't give up. We need to get this thing out of your shoulder now so we can get to a more secure location where I can fully heal your wound."

Reluctantly, I nodded. He placed a hand around the hilt of the blade. Fresh waves of pain assaulted me, and I cried out, grabbing his hand to stop him.

"Wait. Can you just heal it now?" I whimpered, tears filling my eyes.

The wailing sirens reached a crescendo. The police were likely just on the other side of the building. "We don't have time. Kirie, please, you need to trust me."

Luca put a warm palm on my cheek, and a feeling of peace settled over me. The pain in my shoulder lessened a bit, and the suffocating anxiety in my chest subsided a fraction. I took a deep breath and nodded for him to continue.

"Right. Let's sit you up, okay?" Luca gently helped me into a sitting position, being careful not to jostle my injured arm.

He began unbuttoning off his jacket. My face heated when he set it aside and pulled his Henley shirt over his head, revealing his ridiculously sculpted chest.

My anxiety ramped right back up. "What are you doing?" I asked with wide eyes.

"I need something to stem the flow of blood with. This is all I've got." Luca leaned over me, wrapping one hand around the knife handle and placing the wadded-up t-shirt next to it.

I *tried* to look away from his naked torso. Honestly, I did. But he was so close, and my eyes had a mind of their own. The heady electricity flowing between us was intoxicating, and I momentarily forgot how to breathe. The courtyard spun around me.

"On the count of three," he whispered. His warm breath washed over me. I shivered. "One . . . two . . . three."

Luca pulled the long knife from my flesh with a wet, sucking sound. Dark spots filled my vision, and I bit down hard on my scream. Luca threw the knife to the side, pulling my jacket and shirt down over my shoulder, exposing the wound. He pressed his wadded-up shirt firmly on top of it and pulled my jacket back over my shoulder to hold it in place. Tears ran rivers down my face. I bent forward and rested my forehead on my knees. My tears pooled on the dead leaves littering the ground.

Luca put a power-filled hand on my back and let his energy seep into me. This time, instead of comfort, I felt a screaming urgency. "Kirie, I know you hurt right now, but you need to get up," Luca said.

I attempted to stand, but the pain pulled me back to a huddled position on the cold, rough ground. My stomach twisted and bile rose in my throat. "I can't," I sobbed.

There was a commotion on the other side of the café door. The police were almost there.

Luca put an arm around my back and lifted me from the ground. The world tilted sideways before I could get my feet under me, and I fell forward. Luca caught me before my face hit the ground and helped me gain my feet. He bent down to my level and locked eyes with me.

"I need you to be strong, my love," he pleaded.

I bit my bottom lip and shook my head. I wanted nothing more than to be strong for him, but I couldn't see past the pain. My stomach gave another sudden, painful twist. I pushed Luca away with my uninjured arm and heaved the contents of my stomach all over the cobblestone floor.

Letting out an obscene curse, Luca swung me up into his arms and rushed toward the exterior wall. He set me down next to one of the many doors and I leaned against the rough stone for support. Luca shot a bolt of light at the door handle, and it fell to the ground with a metallic *clank*. He wound his arm around my waist and muscled the door open.

We stumbled into a dark storeroom. Luca held up a hand

and illuminated the cramped space. It was full of haphazardly stacked boxes and must and mildew hung in the damp air. I leaned on Luca as we weaved through the mess. On the other side of the storeroom was a clothing shop, dark and closed for the night. Blue blinking lights from the police cars out front lit up the dim space.

Luca led me to an armchair along the wall and eased me into it. I sat slightly forward, trying to avoid getting blood on the upholstery, and held my injured arm close to my chest, stifling my sobs as Luca cautiously approached the front windows of the shop. The blue lights painted his skin a ghostly hue.

"There are only two police cars, and they seem to be focused on the coffee shop. We should be able to leave unnoticed." Luca turned back to me, concern etched into his beautiful face. "Will you be able to move?"

I held my breath and nodded, unable to speak through the pain.

Almost reluctantly, Luca walked over and knelt in front of me. He put an arm behind my back. I leaned into his warmth, my body cold and clammy. "I'm sorry," he said in my ear. "I would heal you here, but the light would give us away."

"I-it's okay," I said through chattering teeth. "I just want to get out of here."

Luca sighed into my hair, raising goosebumps on the back

of my neck. I shivered again, but not from the cold. Slowly, he helped me to stand, and we approached the shop door side-by-side. A few doors down, a lone police officer stood apart from the others. He leaned forward, utterly still as he watched the coffee shop entrance.

"Is he…" I whispered.

"A shadow? Likely," he replied through gritted teeth. "Just act naturally and keep your eyes forward. We don't want to draw attention."

"I'll try," I said.

Luca slowly turned the lock and eased us out onto the street. Averting our eyes from the blue flashing lights, we walked eastward on Boulevard Saint-Germain. I shot a single glance behind me. The officer continued to watch the building. I let out a shaky breath.

Walking was torture. I focused on putting one foot in front of the other as I struggled to keep up with Luca's long strides. The Paris nightlife was in full swing, the streets full of partygoers and bar hoppers in boisterous clusters. Despite the chilly fall air, a group of laughing girls passed us wearing tube tops and short skirts.

Up ahead, a group of young men took up most of the sidewalk. They held drinks in plastic cups and spoke loudly over one another in quick French. As we attempted to pass them, one stumbled into me, his sour-smelling beer splashing across the front of my jacket. I put a hand over my mouth to muffle my cries as razor-sharp pains shot through my shoulder. Tears leaked from the corners of my eyes.

"Watch it, mate," Luca yelled, pushing the man away.

He raised his fist in a crude gesture in response. "Va te faire foutre!"

Luca rolled his eyes and put his arm around my waist again, steering me away from the rowdy group. "Are you okay?" he whispered down to me.

My answering groan made him tighten his grip on my waist. Luca half carried, half led me away from the crowds as we continued down the road. I followed his lead, nearly delirious from pain. When we approached the first crossroad, Luca turned right. At the next intersection, we turned left. Luca continued to lead us on a serpentine-like route, turning right then left at each new road we came to. All the while, his eyes anxiously tracked side to side and upward in search of hidden dangers.

Every few minutes, I pulled my cellphone out of my pocket, hoping for a signal. The phone remained dead, an ominous sign.

As we stepped onto a quiet residential street, a dark shadow brushed past my shoulder, sweeping my long hair forward. I cried out and grabbed onto the sleeve of Luca's jacket. He stopped abruptly, let go of my waist, and squared his shoulders to the dark night. I held my arm close to my chest and searched the shadows for movement.

On a gust of wind, whispers filled with menacing laughter and indistinguishable words swirled around us like a twister. Luca zeroed in on a dark spot a few feet away, and shot a blinding bright light directly at it, casting the shadows into the dark night with a shriek.

"Run!" Luca yelled.

Fear sent a shot of adrenaline through my veins, and I took off at a run, following Luca as we weaved through the darkened Paris streets. I held my breath, focusing on staying upright as the up and down motions sent shock waves through my injured shoulder.

Turning onto a busy road lined with shops, Luca grabbed my good hand and pulled me inside a brightly lit convenience store. He led me down the narrow aisles, clearly searching for something. I followed him mindlessly, thinking of nothing but the pain.

"Here we go." He picked up a small first aid kit.

Without skipping a beat, he escorted me back toward the front of the store where a long line of people waited to check out.

"Here, hold this," he said, dropping my hand and passing me the first aid kit.

He walked past the people waiting in line, heading straight

for the exit. For a panicked moment, I thought he intended for me to leave without paying. I'd never stolen anything besides the cookies hidden in my mom's closet when I was a child, though I wasn't sure that really counted.

I opened my mouth to protest just as Luca pulled out a stack of Euros from his back pocket and casually threw it on the cash register as he passed. The store clerk watched with his mouth wide open as we walked straight out the front door.

"I think you overpaid," I called to him as I struggled to keep up.

"I suppose it's that man's lucky day, isn't it?" Lucas said. He turned and threw me a forced smile. "You might want to put that in your jacket so you don't have to carry it." He pointed to the small box in my hand.

"Oh, right."

I slipped the first aid kit into my jacket and continued to stumble after him. We speed-walked up and down random streets with no clear destination for what felt like miles. The pain in my shoulder only intensified with every step. Black spots crowded my vision.

We rounded the corner, and Luca abruptly steered me off the sidewalk to a dark alcove between two residential buildings. It was a small space, no wider than two feet across. Luca placed his hands on either side of my head, trapping me between the wall and his body.

"What . . ." I began.

Luca put his mouth next to my ear and whispered, "Shhh."

Just then, an icy wind blew down the street, lifting the decaying leaves from the gutters. A violent shiver ran up my spine. I looked past Luca's shoulder where a dark form moved in the night about a hundred feet up the road.

The shadow—it was alive. It moved side to side, searching predatorily. The acidic taste of fear filled my mouth, and I slid further into the alcove. Luca moved with me, our bodies sliding against one another, setting my frayed nerves alight.

"Stay still," Luca breathed into my ear. I nodded a silent response. Our cheeks brushed, the rough stubble on his face not entirely unpleasant. My skin burned hot with exertion and a kind of desperate desire. A sudden overwhelming urge to pull Luca closer, to merge his skin with mine, gripped me as our energies intertwined. I bit my lip hard and willed myself to focus.

The temperature dropped sharply again, and the streetlights went out as the shadowy wraith weaved down the road. I shrank back into the rough brick wall behind me. My wound throbbed to the beat of my pounding heart.

It was going to find us; I knew it. I held onto the front of Luca's jacket until my fingers turned white and waited for the inevitable attack.

The crackling sound of dry leaves preceded its arrival. The

shadow stopped just beyond the entrance of our hiding place. Luca pushed me further into the wall. His tall, broad frame concealed me from head to toe. His energy retracted from mine and the alcove visibly darkened around us. It was as if Luca was creating his own shadows. My brows furrowed as I stared up at him. *What was he doing?*

A quiet whispering floated down the narrow alcove, low and mournful in tone. Luca quickly put his palms over my ears to mute its deadly song, and I squeezed my eyes shut against the poisonous sound. Still, feelings of sadness and discouragement managed to slither into my chest. My body sagged forward as despair seeped through my veins like venom. Luca slid his steady arms around my waist, holding me upright.

The sorrowful song dissipated like mist, taking the worst of its poison with it. Then, the shadow sniffed the air like a hound on the hunt. Renewed fear and despair washed over me, threatening to pull me further under. Luca rested his forehead on mine. His sweat dripped off his brow and mingled with my tears.

We stood motionless in our little cocoon of darkness, waiting for the moment of discovery, our quickened breaths mingling together. The night had taken its toll, and I feared I didn't have it in me to fight a shadow off again. Long moments ticked by as the Shadowman searched the surrounding area for signs of light. Then, unbelievably, the menacing presence moved on.

The temperature rose, and the streetlights flickered back on, signaling its absence. I let go of the breath I'd been holding and steadied myself on shaky legs. I waited for Luca to let go of his grip on me, but he remained pressed to me.

I looked up at him in question, and he met my gaze. As if in a trance, I stared mutely back, lost in him. Luca reached up and brushed a strand of hair behind my ear. His hand lingered on my cheek, and I melted into the hard plains of his body, letting his warmth and strength seep into me.

Luca leaned down and pressed his full lips to my neck. Heat rushed over me like a fever. "I think they're gone," he whispered against the hollow of my throat. I nearly moaned out loud. He cleared his throat. "We should probably go."

I nodded, unable to speak. Luca slowly peeled away from me, bit by bit. Each degree of separation felt like a piece of my skin was being stripped from me.

My wobbly legs screamed in protest as I followed Luca out of the alcove and down the street in the opposite direction the shadow had gone.

Chapter 22

"Luca," I called up to him. I'd been staring at his back for the past hour, fighting through the fatigue and pain, desperately trying to keep up with his punishing pace. "Can we stop for a minute? Please. I can't feel my feet."

Luca slowed down to match my stride. "There's a place we can stop nearby. Do you need me to carry you?"

My insides screamed *yes!* "No," I said. "I can go a little bit further."

I pushed myself onward until we approached a large city park. Luca steered me straight toward the expansive manicured lawn, and I was more than happy to leave the street behind.

Mature trees and bushes lined interlocking pathways through a massive French-style garden. A thick layer of fall leaves covered the ground like a multi-colored blanket, giving the outdoor space an insulated feel. Couples holding hands strolled along the paths. An older couple sat in a pair of metal chairs with their heads together in private conversation. In the distance was the outline of a palatial building.

"This is Luxembourg Garden," I said in awe.

"Yeah, good guess," Luca said with a crooked smile.

"Not a guess, really. I studied a map of Paris this morning along with the last several hundred years of its history," I explained.

"Of course, you did," he laughed. "I wouldn't expect any less."

Luca led the way as we wove through the massive park. He stopped under a grove of trees, far from the city streets. Reaching into his back pocket, Luca pulled out his sleek, black cellphone. I nearly cheered out loud when lit up.

He swiped the screen a few times and put it to his ear. "Abbott, we have a problem," Luca said, raking his free hand through his thick, disheveled hair. "No, no. She's with me now, but they found her first." He paused to listen. "Ciara was there. It wasn't good." He pinched the bridge of his nose and sighed deeply. "I'm okay, but Kirie took a blade to the shoulder . . .no, I'll take care of her. Warn the others that we have at least three shadows in the downtown area. I'll meet up with you once I deliver Kirie back home safely." Luca ended the call.

"Why do our cellphones die when the Shadowmen are around?" I asked, pulling the fully functioning cellphone from my back pocket.

Luca typed a message to someone while he spoke, the screen illuminating the sharp angles of his face. "They absorb the energy from their surroundings. The closer you are to them, the more control they have over the energy in and around you."

"So, we finally lost them?" I asked hopefully.

"Yes. We've finally lost them." He sighed in relief. "Let's have that first aid kit," he said with an outstretched hand.

"Oh, sure." I pulled the small box out of my jacket pocket and gave it to Luca. Our hands briefly touched, sending shock waves up my arms and into my now racing heart. Luca pulled his hand back sharply and cleared his throat.

"Thank you. Now, let's take a look at that shoulder, shall we?" He looked around for a moment. "It's probably best if we sit while I do this."

He found a large tree and sat down at the base of it. I sat beside him on the cold, hard ground and angled my injured shoulder toward him, my teeth chattering against the cold seeping through my jeans.

Luca hummed low. "That won't do. Here, sit in front of me so you don't have to twist." He scooted behind me and pulled me between his bent knees as if I weighed nothing. Heat spread across my face and my heart began a tap dance.

I sat motionless as he placed the first aid kit beside us and took out several items, including a plastic bag, white gauze pads, and a small bottle of rubbing alcohol. With gentle fingers, Luca pulled the collar of my sweater over my still bleeding shoulder, revealing his makeshift bandage. Carefully, he removed his blood-soaked T-shirt and put it inside the plastic bag. The cool night air sent shivers up and down my spine as he cleaned the wound with alcohol and gauze.

"You shouldn't have done that, you know," he quietly said as he worked. "Left the apartment." He grabbed another gauze pad and threw the blood-covered one into the plastic bag.

"I know. It's just . . ." I stared out at the peaceful garden, struggling to find the words to describe my frustration earlier. "It's just that I've been in hiding my whole life, you know? I just wanted to get out and live a little for once." I shrugged my uninjured shoulder. "I honestly didn't think it was a big deal."

Luca dropped his hand and leaned back. "Not a big deal?"

He was abruptly on his feet, pacing beneath the tree's barren canopy with his hands fisted in his dark hair. I sat still in the cold grass and watched him prowl like a caged predator, stunned by his overreaction. For a moment, I thought I saw thin black wisps of smoke roll off his body, but I blinked, and they were gone.

Luca let out a growl and crouched in front of me, his brows tightly pinched. "You can't take those kinds of risks, Kirie." He pointed an accusatory finger at my shoulder. "Just a few inches down, and you would've been killed. Do you know how important you are to The Society, to me?"

"No," I said honestly, still astonished by his fierce reaction.

I understood why The Society cared about my well-being. I was a valuable weapon in their arsenal. But why would *Luca* care about what happened to me? I wasn't even sure he liked me half the time. One minute he was swooping in and saving me from the Shadowmen and the next he was ignoring me like I never existed. He was about as consistent as Dr. Jekyll and Mr. Hyde.

Luca pinched the bridge of his nose and squeezed his eyes shut. "Just . . . promise to take someone with you next time you need to get out. Okay?"

"Okay," I promised, unsure of what else to say.

He relaxed with a sigh. "Thank you. Now let's fix that shoulder of yours."

Luca settled behind me once more. With gentle fingers, he pulled the collar of my sweater further off my shoulder, fully exposing the gaping wound. He covered the cut with the palm of his warm hand and pressed. My heart sped up in anticipation. The last time he'd healed me, it felt so . . . intimate. Somehow, his energy *completed* mine like a piece of a puzzle I didn't know was missing.

Light surrounded us, and Luca's hand warmed. Once again, I felt his power seep into my skin, filling me with pure, unfiltered light. I closed my eyes and let it consume me. My severed muscles and broken skin began to knit back together at an unnatural rate. I wished the process would slow down so I could experience this feeling . . . this *connection* longer. I hadn't felt so close to another human being in, maybe ever, and I didn't want it to end.

As the last of my wound closed over, I felt a warm breath caress my neck. I turned my head and opened my eyes. Luca was leaning forward, his chest firmly pressed to my back and our faces mere inches apart. Our eyes met, and I could see the varying shades of green in his irises, like a vast forest I wanted to get lost in and never come out. His gaze briefly lowered to my lips.

"How did you know where to find me tonight?" My words were a breathless whisper.

Luca searched my face as if *he* were the one looking for an answer. "It was your energy. It calls to me. I could find you in a crowded room, a frozen wasteland . . . anywhere. There's nowhere in the world where I can't find you."

My breathing quickened as Luca pushed my hair aside and lowered his mouth to my exposed shoulder, pressing a feather-light kiss where the wound had once been. I tilted my head to give him better access, my skin flushed with pleasure. Every inch of me felt as though it was on fire.

"There. All better," Luca whispered. Our eyes met once

more. "You're so beautiful."

And then he was kissing me. *Really* kissing me. His soft, full lips moved with mine in perfect harmony as if this was our hundredth kiss, not our first. My blood sang a hallelujah chorus in my veins when he licked my bottom lip.

I spun onto my knees in front of him, our chests pressed together. Luca wove his hands in my hair and angled his head, deepening the kiss. He tasted like citrus sunshine, and I had an overwhelming desire to drink him in.

Our energies intertwined in a sensual embrace, and the hairs on my arms stood up as our combined power built. I pressed harder into him as a sense of urgency rushed through me, the light inside my chest begging to be united with his. Luca fell back onto the grass, pulling me with him. Our legs entwined, and he held me tight against his chest as if he could merge our two bodies into one through sheer will. The air around us crackled with energy.

Riiing

We jerked apart as Luca's cellphone rang. Breathing hard, Luca placed his forehead on mine and cursed.

"Sorry, Luv. I've got to take this." He released his hold on me and shifted to take his phone from his back pocket.

"Oh! Of course. Yeah. You should totally get that," I babbled like an idiot.

The cold grass crinkled beneath me as I sat up and hugged

my trembling knees to my chest. Without Luca's touch, my flushed skin quickly cooled, leaving me colder than before. I struggled to catch my breath as I came down from my Luca-induced high.

Luca just *kissed* me. Me! I couldn't believe it. Just hours before I would have sworn he wasn't interested in me like that. Hell, he'd acted like I had chicken pox since bringing me to Paris. And now he was saving me, and kissing me, and holding onto me like he wanted to sew our bodies together. My head spun from trying to understand this beautiful, complex boy.

"Hey, mate," Luca said into the phone. "Not yet. I'm taking her home now." He paused to listen. "Okay, keep me posted." Luca ended the call and stood. My heart sank in disappointment. Whatever spell we'd be under was officially broken. Back to reality.

Luca reached down and pulled me to my feet. My light immediately responded to his touch, but I firmly tamped it down, not wanting to appear too eager, though that was exactly what I was.

"Was that Arin?" I brushed the twigs and grass off my legs and straightened my jacket, trying–but failing–to seem cool and unaffected.

Luca let out a long sigh. "Yes. They're assembling a team to search for the shadows who attacked us."

By "they," I assumed he meant the other Agents of Light. I

tried to imagine receiving a late-night call to hunt Shadowmen. Was that my future? Was that my destiny? Luca took my hand in his and led the way to the garden's exit.

I cleared my throat. "Are we going back to the apartment then?"

Luca nodded. "Once I know you're home safe, I'm going to meet up with Arin and Alena to help in the search."

"Please tell me we aren't walking back." I didn't know if I could walk another ten feet, let alone several miles.

"Of course not. I've sent for a car," he said in mock offense.

"There *is* a God!" I sighed in relief.

Luca laughed out loud. The sound was low, harmonious, and utterly beautiful. I glanced down at our joined hands, and in that moment, I knew. Luca had forever ruined me from all other boys.

On the edge of park, a black sedan pulled up to the curb. It was just like the one I rode in with Abbott the day before.

"Wow, that was fast," I said.

"Abbott's good at his job." He shrugged as if that was explanation enough.

Luca opened the back door and slid in after me. Our driver was a stern-faced middle-aged man in a black suit. Luca greeted him as if they were old friends and put an arm over my shoulders as the car merged into traffic. I burrowed into his warmth. Completely content, I let my heavy eyes droop close. Maybe–just maybe–things were going to be alright.

BOOM!

My eyes flew open, and a bright light filled the car. Half a breath later, Luca and I were ripped apart and thrown in different directions. My head hit the roof of the vehicle as it bounced violently on the pavement. The driver slammed the brakes, throwing us against our seatbelts.

Stunned, I pressed my hand to the top of my head where a goose egg was already forming.

"What the . . ." I turned to Luca, but he was already out of the car.

I unfastened my seatbelt and slid out after him. We stood side-by-side on the street, chests heaving as we faced an orange sky. I couldn't comprehend what I was seeing. Somewhere in the distance, something flickered brightly, casting a hellish glow over the city.

Sirens split the air with their shrill cries.

"Shit!" Luca yelled. He turned an ashen face to me. "Get back in the car!"

My stomach dropped. "Is Paris under attack?"

"Not Paris. The Center."

I looked in the direction of the flames again. In the direction of the Panthéon.

No.

"We have to go," Luca said, pushing me toward the car.

We slid back into the backseat, and Luca slammed the door shut.

"Take us to the Center of Light," he yelled to the driver.

Chapter 23

The driver sped down the road, narrowly missing parked cars and awestruck bystanders staring slack-jawed at the sky in the middle of the street.

I reached over and took hold of Luca's hand. He held on tightly though his face remained forward. A line of police cars and fire trucks, sirens blaring, appeared behind us. Our driver slowed and changed lanes to let them pass.

"Luca, what's happening . . ."

The words died on my tongue as we crested a hill, and the answer came into view. Smoke and flames billowed from the center of the plaza where the Panthéon used to be.

"Oh my gosh," I whispered. I placed a shaky hand over my mouth.

Our driver pulled behind the procession of emergency vehicles and followed in their wake. He stopped at the curb just outside the flame's reach, and I wrenched the door open and stepped out into the street. The heavy air smelled strangely like campfire smoke. First responders and emergency vehicles surrounded the square, and men and women in uniform worked quickly to secure the plaza.

As paramedics pushed and dragged tear-stained citizens away from the collapsing building, they created a clear view of the damage. I gaped at the scene before me. A hole, several hundred feet in diameter, was nearly all that was left of the Panthéon. Most of the interior and exterior walls had already collapsed into the fiery pit, and it was clear the few remaining segments were soon to follow.

I stared numbly at the smoldering crater.

All that history.

All that art.

All those people.

Gone.

Somehow, the Shadowmen had found the Paris Center of Light and wiped it off the face of the earth. Nothing of the building's power and majesty was left to salvage. Tears streamed down my face, cutting through the ash and dust on my cheeks. No one could've survived such an attack. No one.

I thought of Aaron. Though we'd only just met, he seemed like such a nice guy. Had he been sitting at the reception desk with his friendly smile when the bomb went off? What about the war room? How many agents had been working that night?

I stood motionless at the edge of the crowd, staring numbly at the chaos surrounding the square. My mind detached from my body, unable to process any more grief and fear. Something landed on the tip of my nose. I looked up. Little white flakes floated down from the sky, softly landing on my face like a gentle winter snowfall. It was beautiful in a macabre sort of way.

The immense heat and smoke from the fire soon began to dry the tears from my eyes, making them sting painfully. I blinked away the ash and turned away from the destruction. I walked through the crowd as if in a daze, searching for Luca, but there was no sign of him in the melee.

A loud creak followed by an ear-splitting crash rent the air as the last remaining wall fell into the crater. The flames popped and surged. Bystanders fell back, crying in dismay and fear. I backed away from the crush of people and collided with a hard body. I spun around, my heart in my throat, but quickly relaxed when I saw it was Luca, back from wherever he'd disappeared to.

"Come on," he said, wrapping an arm around my shoulders. "There's nothing we can do here."

I burrowed into his warmth and let him lead me back to the car. He opened the back door, and I slid limply onto the seat.

Luca put both hands against the top of the car and leaned in. I stared up at him in confusion. Every muscle in his body was tense and I could feel his power rolling off him in angry waves.

"Take her home," Luca called up to the driver.

"Wait. Where are you going?" I reached out to him, but he leaned away from my touch.

"I need to meet up with Arin and Alena. The Society is on high alert, and all agents are on active duty."

"Take me with you," I pleaded. "I can help."

Luca shook his head. "You're not an Agent of Light, and you're not trained."

"I think I've proven tonight that I can be an asset."

"You've *proven* that you have a power you don't know how to use."

I jerked back. That stung. Luca's expression softened slightly. He leaned into the car and kissed me lightly on the forehead. "One day, Kirie, I hope to fight side by side with you," he whispered. "But not tonight."

I opened my mouth to argue again, but Luca shut the door on my reply. The driver quickly pulled away from the square and Luca melted into the night. The taste of ash was heavy on my tongue as I watched the flames rage on in the rearview mirror. The irony wasn't lost on me that these creatures made of pure darkness were always setting the world on fire.

Donovan 5

onovan sat in a dark tunnel and stared at a wall of skulls. The Paris catacombs were his favorite spot to meditate and refocus. The cruelty and insensitivity of the place had a way of centering him—something he desperately needed after the month he'd had.

The girl had gotten away. *Again.* Just like in Colorado, she was alone and vulnerable, and they'd still managed to muck it up. It was yet another negative reflection on his leadership at the most inopportune time.

Somehow, this small, insignificant girl had caught the attention of The Order's top leaders. The boss himself was breathing down his neck to complete the mission. He couldn't afford any more slip-ups.

A familiar light appeared at the end of the passageway. The assassin smiled to himself. He was a skilled hunter, and part of his craft was to scrupulously study his prey. It made him one of the most successful assassins of his time. He knew the physical and mental makeup of the Children of Light and could differentiate each COL bastard merely by the color of their light. Even if he couldn't, he'd recognize Luca's light signature from miles away. In a gust of wind, the git was standing before him.

"I thought I'd find you here, you piece of shit," Luca growled. His light and righteous anger surrounded him like a bloody halo. It sickened Donovan.

"Aw, Luc, my boy," he said with a congenial smile. "It's been a while."

"Not long enough," Luca replied through clenched teeth. The two began circling each other in the cramped space, a pair of apex predators facing off.

"Come now, is that any way to treat your old da?"

Luca's face reddened. Getting under the boy's skin always gave Donovan such sweet satisfaction.

"You are *not* my father," Luca spat. "Tell me; how did find the Paris location? Where did you get your intel?"

Ah, he must have seen their latest handiwork. *Wonderful.*

"Oh, that little trick? Nice bit of work, that." Donovan beamed with pride. It had been hundreds of years since The Order had successfully identified and disabled a Center of Light. It was a great start to the end.

"You didn't answer the question. Who was your informant?

We both know you're too dim to find it on your own."

Donovan laughed at the thought of the unexpected informant, knowing Luca would shit himself once he found out. "You wouldn't believe me if I told you."

Luca's light intensified. Donovan's shadows rose in response as they continued their deadly dance.

"Give it up, Donovan. Darkness will not prevail. These minor successes will amount to nothing in the end."

"Come on, Luc, you know me. I *never* quit. Which is why your dark-haired bird is next. She's as good as dead, mate," the assassin taunted.

Luca's light flared brighter, singeing Donovan's exposed skin. "You'll not harm a hair on Kirie's head again, Donovan. I'll not allow it," Luca said darkly.

"You sound like a man in love, Luc." Donovan shook his head in disappointment. "Tsk, tsk. You know what happens to those you love, son."

The boy knew better. The murder of his family was some of Donovan's finest work. He'd forced Luca to watch their slow and painful deaths before stealing him away to be his little experiment.

Luca stretched out his glowing hands and lifted Donovan off the ground, throwing him into the bone-covered wall with an *'umph'*. Cracked skulls and leg bones rained down on the cobblestone floor. The assassin landed lightly on the tips of his feet, uninjured.

In the blink of an eye, Luca lifted Donovan up by his shirt front and slammed him hard against the wall. Another shower of fractured bones fell onto his shoulders. The boy had grown in strength these past few years.

"I am NOT your son, and you will not touch her. If you come for Kirie again, you will not live long enough to regret it, that I promise you." Luca's light surged brighter, taking on a blue hue like the base of a flame. Donovan's skin began to blister.

"Whoa, this one's really got your knickers in a twist." The assassin managed a laugh through gritted teeth. "What happened to the stone-cold bastard I molded you into? You know better than to form emotional attachments. Look how weak The Society has made you."

Luca pushed away and raised his right hand, shooting a bolt of pure energy at Donovan's chest. In a puff of smoke, the assassin disappeared, and bolt the hit the empty wall, leaving behind a black hole and scorch marks. Several feet down the tunnel, Donovan reappeared.

"You're getting faster. You almost got me that time!"

"Come closer, coward, so I can wipe that smile off your face." Luca growled.

"As enticing as that sounds, I gotta run. My sources say it won't be long before we find your girlfriend again and I want to be there when we do.”

“You sick tosser. I’m going to enjoy killing you.” Luca stalked forward, murderous rage dripping from every pore.

The assassin backed down the dark tunnel with raised hands. “You know it won’t be long until she finds out what you really are, Luc. Let me give you a piece of advice. Stick with your typical hussies. Kirie’s too good for you.” The assassin disappeared into a cloud of smoke.

“I know,” Luca said to the empty tunnel. He turned to the wall and punched a hole in the nearest skull’s face. He disappeared the way he’d come, leaving a train of blue light in his wake.

In the deathly silence, the assassin reappeared and waited for the real reason he’d come. A gust of cold air blew past him like a winter’s wind. Out of the shadows, a red-haired young woman sauntered forward. Angry red welts marked her skin. Despite her injuries, she wore a cloak of confidence and malice.

“Ah, Ciara. So good of you to come,” Donovan said.

“Tonight didn’t go well, and the higher-ups are pissed,” she said, jumping right in. Ciara never was one for small talk.

“Yes, well, we’re all having a bit of trouble with this one, aren’t we?” Donovan sighed and shook his head. “No matter. I think we have just the angle we need.”

A loud ring echoed through the dark tunnel.

"Do me a favor, will you, love?" Donovan said, pulling Luca's sleek cellphone from his pocket. Pickpocketing him had been all too easy. "I need you to be Luca's bimbo for a moment."

Ciara smiled and took the phone from his outstretched hand.

"Hello?" she said in a sugar-sweet voice. "Sorry, Luca can't come to the phone right now. I'm keeping him *really busy*," she giggled seductively. "Can I have him call you back?" Ciara lowered the phone and stared down at the dark screen. She shrugged. "I guess that's a no."

"Well done."

Donovan plucked the phone from her hand, dropped it on the stone floor, and crushed it beneath his heel.

"Hey, we could have used that!" Ciara shrieked.

"Nah, the firewall's a bitch. No one's ever broken through. It already served its purpose anyway. We've begun to break Kirie down, and it won't be long before we find our opportunity for revenge. Trust me, emotional women are reckless and stupid. She'll expose herself again and when she does, we'll finish what we started."

Ciara looked up from the broken phone. "I hope you're right because time's running out. The seventh battle has begun and for some *crazy* reason, the boss thinks getting rid of this chick will be a game changer."

"Don't underestimate what you don't understand, Ciara. Cole made that mistake and it cost him his life," he scolded.

Cole had been one of Donovan's most promising students. His ability to infiltrate any organization gave them unlimited access to information and opportunity. He was finally coming into his own when Kirie killed him. Rage filled the assassin's chest at the thought of all that wasted talent. And all because of a pretty face.

"No worries; I won't," Ciara vowed.

Donovan slapped a hand to the nearest skull. "You better not, or it will be both our heads on a platter."

Chapter 24

The city was in chaos in the wake of the bomb. Driving back to the apartment was slow-going as my stoic driver navigated streets filled with people. He parked out front and silently escorted me through the crowd back to my door. Many of my new Parisian neighbors were on the street and in the hallways. They huddled in groups, cellphones to ears, eyes to the orange night sky, arms around each other, crying.

The apartment was dark and empty, and I headed straight for my bathroom. My shoulder and back still itched where residual dried blood remained, and I was eager to be clean. As I passed the bathroom mirror, I noticed thick, white ash covered my hair and shoulders. I stopped and stared. Those tiny white pieces were remnants of the Center of Light and those unfortunate enough to be working that night. Bile burned my throat, and I began ripping my clothes off, desperate to get the death and destruction off me.

Standing under the hot stream, I traced shapes into the foggy glass with the tip of my finger, my mind far away. A flash of Luca's soft lips on my bare skin filled my mind. Goosebumps covered my arms, and a shiver ran up my spine at the memory of his warm breath on my neck. Though that moment had been so innocent, it felt incredibly intimate. Every touch and every look felt that way with Luca.

I'd never been in love before, so I had nothing to compare my feelings to, but being with Luca was like being home, something I hadn't felt since the night my parents were murdered. With the tips of my fingers, I traced my lips, still swollen from kissing him. They were also curved upward. I brushed my wet palm across my face, wiping away the smile. I had no right to feel happy at a moment like that.

I focused on washing the dry blood and ash from my hair and body and stepped out of the shower to dry off. Standing in front of the bathroom mirror, I inspected my shoulder, running my hand across the smooth skin where the blade had entered. The skin looked perfect . . . better than new.

I dressed and fell into bed. My head spun from the night's events. It had only been about an hour since Luca and I parted, but I missed him already. I tossed and turned, imagining him surrounded by Shadowmen, fighting them off on his own. I considered calling him many times to make sure he was all right, but I knew he was busy hunting shadows. I grabbed my phone and quickly wrote him a short text, something he could read later.

Thank you for coming after me tonight. Call me when it's safe.

I set my phone on the bedside table and closed my eyes. The minutes dragged on as I drifted in and out of sleep. Alternating images of shadows, explosions, and human remains turned to ash haunted me, preventing me from finding rest.

I gave up around two AM and checked my phone. No response. With a groan, I slipped out of bed in search of water. I walked into the dark kitchen and collided with Alena. She sucked in a deep breath and jumped back as if I had bitten her.

"I'm sorry, I didn't see you there," I said, hands up in surrender.

"It's fine," she said with a sigh. Alena looked as if she'd just gotten home. She, too, was covered in ash with the addition of dark smudges beneath her almond-colored eyes.

I stepped back and cleared my throat. "Did they, um, find the Shadowmen responsible for the attack on the Panthéon?"

"No," she sighed again. "We did not." She opened the fridge and pulled out a take-out box. She brushed past me and sat down at the clutter-covered table.

"And the people inside?"

"All dead," she replied without expression.

I swallowed the lump forming in my throat. "Abbott…"

Alena sighed. "Only the night crew was there. No one *you* knew."

I pulled a cup from the cabinet and filled it with water from the sink. Even in the darkness of the kitchen, I could see the sadness clinging to Alena. Clearly, the attack on the Panthéon was personal to her. Had she lost friends? I didn't dare ask. I leaned against the counter, wanting to say something, anything, but every word that came to mind seemed trivial.

"Are you okay?" I finally said.

She poked at her food with her fork, not really eating. "Not really," she replied.

"I'm so sorry for your loss," I said quietly, trying to convey my sincerity. I might not like Alena, but that didn't mean I wished this kind of loss on her. "Is there anything I can do?"

She narrowed her eyes at me. "You can stop being a femminuccia and help us." Amidst her anger was a hint of desperation. "Why have you not agreed to join The Society? What are you waiting for?"

I peered into my cup, not knowing what to say. What was I waiting for? Committing to a life of battle, for starters. I was a science nerd, not a warrior. But, walking away from this fight was becoming more difficult every day.

We sat in silence while Alena stabbed at her food with unfocused eyes. I thought of the horrors she must've seen in her short life and empathy began to worm its way beneath my skin. Yes, she was mean, but she had a far more difficult life than mine. While I was posing as a normal child, she was likely fighting shadows and bearing witness to death. I supposed I had no right to judge her.

I tried to imagine what Luca's, Arin's, and Alena's childhood might've been like. Three orphans being raised by an organization that put them in harm's way. I supposed Abbott served as a surrogate father, in a way, but was it enough? Did anyone show them unconditional love the way my mom did? Probably not.

My thoughts turned again to the boys. I cleared my throat, breaking the silence. "Did Luca and Arin come back with you? I tried texting Luca earlier, but he hasn't responded yet."

Alena looked up from her take-out box and searched my face with bloodshot eyes. She let out a derisive laugh, startling me. "Well, that was fast."

"What was fast?" I asked, my face heating.

"Look at you. You're already half in love with the boy." There was no reason to ask which boy she meant.

I set my cup down and frowned. "I don't know what you're talking about."

"Sure, you do. I've seen that expression on many girls before." She laughed again as if it were all a big joke. "Well, since you two seem close, maybe you can tell *me* where he is tonight."

"How would I know? He told me he was going to meet up with you and Arin. Did he not?"

"No. Arin and I haven't heard from Luca all night. He isn't answering his phone."

"I don't understand . . ."

Alena rolled her eyes dramatically. "I should've guessed he'd do something like this tonight. He probably ran off with one of his many women. Typical Luca."

My stomach dropped to the floor. "What are you talking about?" I demanded, pushing away from the counter.

"Oh, you know. Luca's always blowing us off to mess around with his newest girl toy. I don't know why Abbott lets him get away with it, honestly. Especially on a night like this." She tossed her hair back in annoyance.

"You're a liar," I said, my voice suddenly thick with unshed tears.

Alena put her fork down and studied me. "Oh, you poor thing. Did you honestly think he liked you?" She gave me an exaggerated pouty face and shook her head as if I was nothing but a pathetic idiot. I wanted to punch her in her perfect face. "You're nothing but the flavor of the week. Give it another day or two, and he'll get bored with you just like the others."

Anger coursed through me.

"You sound bitter, Alena," I shot back. "It must've hurt

when he told you he didn't want *you* anymore. Honestly, I don't blame him," I said, folding my arms tightly over my aching chest.

She recoiled as if I'd struck her. She slowly stood as if she were preparing to leap. "Listen, you little il menello. Luca and I have known each other for years. We have a connection you couldn't *possibly* understand. You, on the other hand, will never be anything more to him than a passing fling. You aren't even the first one this month…or the prettiest."

"You're lying," I whispered. My whole body trembled.

Alena stepped away from the table. "Am I? Luca doesn't do relationships. Never has. Try not to get your fragile little feelings hurt. It isn't personal."

Leaving her uneaten food at the table, Alena walked to her room and slammed her door. I followed suit.

Alone in my room, I paced back and forth in front of my bed as inky-black emotions swirled inside me.

She was lying. She had to be. Alena was just jealous and hateful. There was no way that what happened earlier was a play by Luca. The connection we had was real . . . I *knew* it. There had to be another explanation why Luca wasn't where he said he was. I grabbed my phone and dialed his number, determined to prove her wrong.

After a few rings, a sultry female voice answered. "Hello."

My heart stopped beating. "I'm s-sorry. Is this Luca's

number?"

"Sorry, Luca can't come to the phone right now. I'm keeping him *really busy*," the girl giggled. "Can I have him call you back?" Seduction dripped off every word.

"No need," I said and hung up.

Rejection and sorrow punched a hole through my heart. I felt like such an idiot. Of course, Luca was with somebody else. Guys like him don't fall in love with girls like me. Why would he? I was nothing.

I rushed to the French doors leading out onto my balcony and threw them open, needing air. Stumbling out, I grabbed onto the railing, sucking in deep breaths as tears rolled down my numb face.

"Rough night?" A deep male voice said.

My heart rate doubled, and I spun around. My fists instinctively rose in defense as I braced for the next attack. Arin leaned against the railing on his balcony two doors down, smirking at me in the moonlight.

I dropped my fists and let out a chest full of air. "What are you doing out here?"

Arin's trademark smile faded into a sorrowful expression as he turned to look out over the city. His brows drew together as he focused on where the Panthéon's bright dome used to be. "Just contemplating life's choices, I guess."

Before I could offer my condolences, he turned and

slipped his smile back into place. For the first time, I saw it for what it was. A mask. "How about you? What are you doing out here in the cold?"

I turned away from him. "I don't want to talk about it."

Arin chuckled. "That bad, huh? Want me to come over?"

"No," I began, but then let my shoulders drop. "Maybe."

The truth was, I was feeling completely alone. I had lost everyone important to me and was aching to confide in someone. I made a bad judgment call with Luca, and though it would likely be a long time before I trusted anyone with my heart again, I could really use a friend. Alena made it very clear that we'd never be 'besties' and, honestly, Arin was my only choice.

Just as I was about to invite him over, Arin disappeared through his balcony doors.

"Whatever," I said to the night and returned to my room. Fresh air was overrated anyway. The city had calmed through the night, and the streets were nearly empty, but the smell of smoke still hung in the air.

There was a soft knock at my bedroom door, and my mood dropped even lower. I wasn't ready for round two with my surly roommate. The door swung open, and instead of Alena, Arin appeared in the doorway, his large body filling the entire frame.

Chapter 25

I **let out a** sigh of relief. "I thought you were Alena."

"It was my impressive rack that tricked you, wasn't it," Arin said, pumping his giant pectorals up and down.

"Everything is a joke to you, isn't it," I said, rolling my eyes.

"Pretty much, yeah. It's better than the alternative." His happy mask slipped a little, momentarily revealing the sadness hidden beneath.

I perched on the edge of my bed, and Arin sat beside me. "Which is . . ." I fished.

"It isn't easy, what we do. Some days can really bring you down. Tonight especially. That was some heavy shit. One of the Shadow's most effective tools is despair, so I do what I can to keep things light . . . if you know what I mean." He elbowed me in the rib cage.

"You're such a dork," I said, unable to hold back a smile.

"I've been called worse," he replied. "Soooo, do you want

to tell me why you're feeling so down?" He raised his eyebrows. "I pinky promise to keep it a secret."

He put his pinky finger out in front of me and waited. I glanced between it and his face a few times before sealing the deal with the ever-sacred pinky promise.

"It's a really stupid thing to be upset about with all that's happened tonight."

"Maybe you'll feel better if you get it off your chest. Besides, I could use the distraction. You know, with all that's happened tonight," he said, parroting my words.

I took a deep breath and let it out. "Luca kissed me." My face burned a thousand degrees.

"Wow, he must be a really bad kisser if it brought you to tears!"

"Ugh! You're so frustrating!" I picked up my pillow and threw it at his head. He caught it mid-air with his giant hand.

"No, really, why's that a bad thing? No offense, but I kinda got the impression you were into him."

I put my hands over my face and groaned. "Am I really that transparent?" I said between my fingers.

"Yes and no. It's not really anything you said or did. There's just this connection between you two. Anyone can see it," he said.

I let my hands drop to my lap. "Great. Well, it doesn't matter anymore because that will never happen again."

Arin's brows rose. "Oh, yeah?"

"Luca told me he was meeting up with you and Alena tonight to search for the bombers. But Alena told me he never met up with you. So, I called his phone and a *girl* answered." Hearing the words out loud brought fresh tears to my eyes.

Arin gave a low whistle. "Oh, damn."

"Exactly." My shoulders fell forward in defeat.

"Are you sure it's what you think it is?" Arin asked.

"Absolutely. First of all, Alena told me he always ditched you guys to meet up with women. And second, the girl on the phone all but told me they were hooking up."

"You talked to *Alena* about it?" Arin said incredulously.

"Not on purpose. We just happen to be in the kitchen at the same time and she somehow guessed something happened between Luca and me. She was all too happy to put me in my place."

"I wouldn't believe everything Alena says, especially when it concerns Luca," Arin warned.

"Why does she care about what Luca does? Were they, like, a thing once?"

"Alena has loved Luca for years. My boy is just not into her like that. The three of us are like siblings, you know? The two of them dating would be weird."

My eyebrows knit together. "Okay, I get that. But then that girl answered his phone and—how do I explain that away?"

Arin shrugged. "I don't know."

"I know I don't have a reason to feel cheated on. He never gave me any indication that he wanted to be my boyfriend. There were no promises of forever. But I *do* feel betrayed."

"I'm sorry . . ." Arin began.

"Seriously. How can he be with me one minute, sharing this incredible, life-shattering first kiss, and then be with someone else the next? What kind of person does that?" Anger burned in my chest, giving me renewed energy. "Come to think of it, Luca probably only kissed me because he realized I was an easy mark."

"Look, Kirie," Arin said with a sigh, "this world isn't going to go easy on you. You no longer live in your happy little bubble. You're going to have to start standing up for yourself."

I sat up straighter. "You're right! I'm tired of being an easy mark. Luca, Alena, the Shadowmen, they all saw me as weak, and I'm sick of it! I don't want to be a scared little girl anymore."

"Now you're getting it. We'll make a warrior out of you yet!" He held his hand out to me, and I gave him a high five. My hand stung afterward.

Although Arin somehow got me smiling, my mood quickly soured, and sadness crept back in. I peered through my open French doors to the dark night beyond and felt my oldest companion, loneliness, return.

"Arin, can I ask you a favor?" I said, somewhat timidly.

"Anything," Arin said.

"Will you stay with me tonight?" I laughed at his scandalized expression. "I mean, will you hang out with me tonight and sleep on the couch? I just don't want to be alone . . . if that's ok."

"You got it, babe. I'm here to serve." He puffed his chest out like Superman.

We lay side by side on my king-sized bed. Arin distracted me with stories about the many missions they'd gone on. No matter how dangerous the mission had been, each tale had an element of fun and hilarity to it. I found myself laughing more than I had in months, maybe years. Being around Arin was good for my soul.

"I never asked you about your childhood. Where did you grow up?" I asked with a yawn.

He pumped his pecks up and down dramatically, his signature move. "Jersey Shores, obviously," he said, slipping into a poor Jersey accent.

I laughed out loud. "Stop. Where are you really from?"

"Kansas, actually. Born and raised on a farm, ma'am." He reached up and tipped an imaginary cowboy hat at me.

"And your family?"

Arin's smile slipped from his face, and his gaze turned to the ceiling, serious for once. I slid my tired eyes over at him, worried I'd crossed a line.

"Gone."

I reached over and grabbed a hold of his hand. "I'm sorry. Will you tell me about them?"

He suddenly seemed a million miles away. "My dad was the strongest man I ever knew. Larger than life, basically Superman in the flesh. He taught me to fish, hunt, drive a tractor. Nothing scared my dad." His mouth quirked up on one side. "Except for my mom, that is. She was five foot two and scary as hell," he laughed, and the low vibration shook the bed.

In my mind, I envisioned an older, larger version of Arin running in fear from his tiny wife, and I couldn't help but laugh with him.

Our laughter slowly turned to melancholy, as it was bound to do. "Any siblings?"

"A sister," he whispered, his voice suddenly reverent. "Her name is Arabella."

"What happened?" I asked. Nothing good, I knew. Arin was one of Abbott's orphans, after all.

Arin squeezed his eyes shut as if he were speaking through the pain. "I was ten years old and already training with The Society in D.C. when it happened. As far as anyone knew, The Order didn't know who I was or where I lived. We thought they were safe out on our farm in nowhere Kansas." Arin's eyes dropped to mine.

"But they were wrong," I finished for him.

Arin nodded. "Arabella was nine years younger than me, so she was just a baby. They found my parents' bodies in our barn, but they never found Arabella's remains."

My eyes filled with burning tears. Just a baby. "I'm so sorry," I whispered, my voice thick with empathy. He squeezed my hand in response. We sat like that for several minutes, hurting and healing a little—together.

Finally, Arin sat up and slid off the bed. "It's late. I should let you sleep."

"Arin," I called. He glanced back at me with red-rimmed eyes. "Thank you."

"Sure thing, babe," he said with a wink and slipped out of my room.

I got up early the next day, and tip-toed out into the living room. Arin lay shirtless on the couch with his ankles hanging about a foot over the end. He looked absolutely ridiculous, and I couldn't help but laugh out loud.

Arin woke up with a start and looked around the room in high alert. He relaxed his posture when he saw me sitting in the chair next to him.

"What are you laughing at?" he asked through a yawn, stretching his arms above his head.

"You trying to fit on this couch, that's what," I said with a grin. "Sorry, I didn't mean to wake you."

"That's okay, I need to get up. I have things to get done today," he said, shrugging his enormous shoulders. "The Society is officially on high alert. They're probably going to move all the agents to new locations. It wouldn't be a bad idea to pack a bag."

I chewed on my bottom lip, the idea of moving for the second time in my life stroking the anxiety burning low in my stomach. "I guess that makes sense."

There was a soft knock at the door, drawing our attention.

"I'll get it," Arin said.

I followed him to the front door.

Probably Abbott trying to convince me to join The Society of Light again. Arin peered through the peephole and swore out loud.

"What? Who is it? I asked.

"Trouble," Arin said gravely. "I should've kept my damn shirt on."

He swore again before unlatching the deadbolt and swinging the door open. Luca stood in the hallway looking as gorgeous as ever. All the feelings from last night came flooding back.

Immediately, Luca's eyes went from happy to stormy when he saw Arin standing in the doorway.

"What the hell is this?" Luca said, staring between Arin and me.

"Kirie needed someone to talk to last, so I was there for

her," Arin casually said as if it were no big deal.

"By sleeping with her?" Luca yelled.

"Dude, I slept on the couch. Shit, calm down."

"Excuse me. Over here," I said, raising my hand. Both boys looked at me with twin stormy expressions. "Arin and I just talked last night. And even if we did more, why do you care?" I asked.

"Why do I care?" Luca stepped back as if I had struck him.

"I'm not stupid, Luca. When Alena told me you never met them last night, I called your phone, and your 'girlfriend' answered." Traitorous tears filled my eyes.

"My girlfriend . . ."

"Look," I said, cutting him off. "I appreciate all you've done for me, I really do, but I'm not just another one of your playthings." I swallowed hard. "*I deserve better.*" The words tasted bitter in my mouth.

I stared at his beautiful, emerald eyes and I willed him to tell me I was wrong, that the girl on the phone was no one . . . that he cared for only me.

Instead, his shoulders hunched forward, and his eyes turned downward.

"I know you do." Without another word, he turned around and walked back down the hallway, not even pausing at his apartment door.

"Brother…" Arin called after him, but he didn't turn

around.

My splintered heart fell out of my chest and shattered at my feet as he disappeared. Tears freely fell down my face. I wanted to run after him, tell him how I felt, and beg him to explain. After everything, I still wanted him. At that moment, there was no doubt in my mind that I was in love with Luca. I wouldn't be so hurt and conflicted if I wasn't.

Arin turned to me and sighed. "Shit. I'm sorry, Kirie. I'll go talk to him if you want."

"Don't bother," I murmured. "You were right. I need to start sticking up for myself." The words felt like acid on my tongue.

Arin nodded and disappeared into his apartment, leaving me alone with my turbulent thoughts. I stood in the empty hallway, anger turning to sadness, and sadness turning to resolve. I swung around and marched back to my room. With a stiff back, I picked up my phone and texted Abbott.

Can we meet?

Whose fatal scroll is that? Methinks 'tis mine!

Why sinks my heart, why faltereth my tongue?

Had I three lives, I'd die in such a cause,

And rise, with ghosts, over the well-fought field.

Prepare, prepare!

"A War Song to Englishmen"

By William Blake

Chapter 26

We met at the base of the Eiffel Tower. Abbott must've called for a driver because a no-nonsense woman wearing a black suit knocked on my door and escorted me to yet another black sedan only minutes after I texted him.

We sat side-by-side on a green bench staring out on the manicured lawn, the world-famous tower looming above us. The air was surprisingly warm for late November, and the sun shone brightly. I glared up at it, hating the sun for the first time in my life. Its energizing presence was a mockery of all the lives lost in the attack. It was a mockery, too, of my broken heart.

Though Abbott appeared put together in a suit and tie, his mood was somber, his posture crest fallen. Neither of us spoke for several long minutes. It was a sad kind of silence, one shared and understood only by those grieving. I wanted to ask if he had lost friends in the attack, but it felt too raw, too soon to put words to it.

The cold metal of the bench bit into my skin as we watched police officers and men in full tactical gear patrol the monument grounds. Clearly, the French officials were worried the terrorists, as the news was calling them, were still an active threat. They weren't wrong.

"Thank you for meeting with me," I finally said. "I know you all must be very busy."

"Not a problem. I don't go on missions anymore anyway. They're for the young," he said, trying but failing to produce a smile. "What did you want to talk about?"

I took a deep breath, preparing to take the plunge. "I've decided to join The Society of Light."

Abbott perked up. "That's wonderful news . . ."

"With one condition," I said, cutting in.

Abbott's grey brows drew together. "Okay, I'm listening."

"I'll agree to train as an Agent of Light as long as I may continue my studies in biophotonics."

Abbott relaxed against the bench, clearly relieved by my request. "Of course, you can. We value light and knowledge above all else. As I said before, no university or institution is off-limits to you, Kirie. The society will pay for your tuition, housing…everything. You'll have to wait to enroll next fall since it's so late in the year."

"Thank you," I said, feeling relieved. Perhaps I didn't have to choose between joining The Society and following my dreams after all.

"Anything else? After your incredible display of power last night, I'm sure The Society of Light would be more than happy to give you whatever your heart desires."

My face heated. "You heard about that?"

"Kirie, my dear, your light was seen from miles away," he said without a hint of censure in his voice. His kindness did little to ease my embarrassment. So much had happened in such a short time I hadn't even considered how many people had seen my public lack of control.

"Did I cause The Society a lot of trouble by exposing my power so openly?" I asked in a small voice.

Abbott patted my hand reassuringly. "Don't you worry about that. We have people embedded in every public office in every country in the world who take care of things like this. The official report will state that an electrical surge caused the light and resulting damage. Trust me, no one will question it."

"Okay," I said, still unsure.

Abbott shifted in his seat, suddenly uncomfortable. "I must tell you, Kirie. There are whispers within The Society that you are some kind of chosen one."

I turned to him. "What do you mean, chosen one?"

"Well, as you know, The Society puts a lot of stock in the War Scroll and its predictions."

"I do. But I don't understand. Aren't all agents chosen to fight against darkness."

Abbott looked out across the lawn. "You *could* read it that way. Many do. However, some believe the scroll prophesies that Children of Light with abilities far beyond those already seen on Earth will emerge during the final battle. These chosen few are thought to be the key to our victory over Darkness. Some in The Society believe *you're* one of them."

I studied his face. "What do you believe, Abbott?"

He held a serious expression when he faced me. "I believe you have a power inside of you that's far greater than we can possibly understand. There's no doubt in my mind that you'll do great things for this world."

My eyes stung, and I quickly blinked my tears away. "Wow, no pressure, then, huh?" I said with a forced laugh.

"You'll do fine," he said, patting my hand again. "So, I ask again. Any other requests before I call The Society and give them the good news?"

I chewed on the tip of my thumb, considering. There was really only one other thing I could think of that might be a deal-breaker for me.

I dropped my hand. "I want a different roommate. Living with Alena is like living with a viper."

He laughed out loud. "That bad, huh?"

"You have no idea," I said, leveling him with a somber

expression, which only made him laugh harder. I couldn't help but join in. It was good to see him smile, if only for a moment.

He put his hands up in surrender. "Fair enough. That will be easy enough since you'll be transferred to another Center of Light in the next few days anyway."

I nodded. Arin had predicted as much. The Paris Center of Light was nothing but a crater in the Earth, and the city wasn't safe for anyone anymore. I briefly wondered if Luca would be assigned to the same city as me, but I quickly shut that train of thought down. As long as he stayed away from me, I didn't care where he went.

Abbott stood and buttoned his suit jacket. "We should probably get you back to the apartment so you can begin packing."

I gazed up at the Eiffel Tower once more, suddenly reluctant to go. I wasn't quite ready to put Paris—and, if I were to be honest, Luca—behind me. Not quite yet. "Actually, would it be alright if I stay here for a while?" I asked.

"Sure." Abbott turned to one of the trees and nodded. My female driver stepped out of the shadows and into the sun. She stood at attention, hands behind her back. "Gabriele will act as your guard until you're ready to go back."

"Thank you," I said, nodding once to Gabriele. She nodded back, her expression severe.

"I'm very glad you've decided to join our team, Kirie. I

believe you've made the right decision." Abbott bowed slightly and turned to leave.

I watched him walk down the long cement path with a heavy heart. Despite his deceit early on, I considered Abbott a friend, and his sorrow weighed on me. When he was fully out of sight, I pulled my cellphone from my back pocket and dialed a number I'd known since childhood. It rang several times before the voicemail picked up.

"You've reached Rylie. Leave a message. Or don't . . . whatever!" *Beep.*

"Hey, Rylie, it's me. I just wanted to let you know that I'm safe and well. I decided not to come back to school next semester. I've had enough credits to graduate for a while now, and after everything that's happened, I think it's time to move on. Tell your mom and dad they can stay at my house as long as they need." I paused, tears suddenly clogging my throat. "I just . . ." my voice broke. "Thank you for being a great friend. I don't know what I would've done without you and your family after my parents died. I . . . I hope you have a great life. I love you . . . bye." I pressed the end button and let the phone drop into my lap.

Both sorrow and relief swirled inside me. My old life was over. The old Kyrie was dead. No amount of grieving would bring Mom back to life or Luca back into my arms. Nothing ever would. But standing by while the Shadowmen burned the world to the ground wasn't an option either. I had to do something.

I didn't know if The Society of Light would become my new home, but I was willing to take that chance in the hopes I would finally find my place in the world.

J.B. Tucker is a novelist and short-story writer living in the Rocky Mountains with her bearded husband, three game-loving teenagers, and a small pack of doxies that follow her every move. She earned a master's degree from Weber State University in English (cohort in creative writing). By day, J.B. Tucker teaches high school creative writing, and by night, she crafts complex worlds and characters in both long and short forms.

Please visit her author page, @J.B.TuckerAuthor